IARLIE M. MATTHEWS

D1824390

I

Scott Jenkins' Road to Wonderland

A novel by
Charlie. M. Matthews

A note to the reader:

Scott Jenkins' story is the fifth installment in a series of releases, all written by different authors who came together with one idea in mind: to be part of a team that could create a world away from reality, where struggles are dealt with today in order to find a better tomorrow.

This is their journey to Wonderland.

For more information on upcoming releases, please visit Twitter @ RTWSeries or like our Facebook page at www.facebook.com/RTWSeries.

Book one – Izzy Moffit's Road to Wonderland – Victoria L. James

Book two – Paris Hemsworth's Road to Wonderland – Francesca Marlow

Book three – Ethan Walker's Road to Wonderland – L.J. Stock

Book four – Max Colton's Road to Wonderland – H.A. Robinson

Book five – Scott Jenkins' Road to Wonderland – Charlie M. Matthews

Scott Jenkins' Road to Wonderland ©2015

Charlie M. Matthews

This is a work of fiction. The names, characters, places and incidents are products of the author's imagination only. Any resemblance to actual persons, living or deceased, events or any other incident is entirely coincidental.

Front cover image: L.J. Stock.

Edited: *Content/Development Edit* by Victoria L. James

Line Edit by Heather Ross

Victoria L. James is in partnership with Francesca Marlow as co-creator of MP~Wonderland©, an independent twitter RP group that was created in January 2012 and still runs to date. All stories played out there are from the future of these character's lives and DO contain spoilers. Please be aware of this when choosing to follow.

Acknowledgments

They say that everything in life happens for a reason. That every moment in time defines the next. I stick by this, even to this day, because nothing in life is easy. We have to work for what we want and challenge ourselves daily to achieve those goals. Writing Scott's novel has by far been my toughest challenge to date. There were times when I laughed, times when I cried and swore I would give up, but I didn't. Luckily for me, I had five little ladies that fought my corner from the get-go. I can honestly say that I wouldn't be here today, publishing my first novel, if I didn't have them in my life.

Vic. What can I say that I haven't already? You believed in me when I struggled to believe in myself and my abilities. You virtually slapped me, on numerous occasions, when I said I couldn't do it. But through all the craziness and teenage tantrums, you made me laugh and you taught me how to be strong. Not only are you uber talented and gorgeous, you are also a bloody good friend, too. You took time away from your own projects to edit my words and your input into Scott's story will forever be appreciated. I love you crazy amounts.

Weezy. I will always be grateful to you for bringing Scott into my life. Our RP partnership with Ethan and Scott will be forever etched into my memory. Your talent knows no bounds, and when it came to the graphics for Scott's novel? You knocked them right outta the park. I couldn't have wished for anything more perfect and fitting. I appreciate and love you every day, my little Americano friend.

Bob. My fellow prankster. You stuck with me until the end. Your suggestions and positive feedback have been greatly appreciated. Which reminds me... I probably owe you a red pen or three, right? You can cash those in later. Mwah! Not only did you take time out of your busy life to edit Scotty, you also took the time to listen to me. To guide me through one of my biggest challenges of all. I love you so freakin' much.

Franny, Franny, Franny.. What can I say? We've been through so much together, both work and personal. You have encouraged me, and helped me grow as a person and I will always be thankful to you for bringing me into your world. Sod the distance! You have always been there for me at the drop of a hat and it doesn't matter that we're miles apart because I know, hand on heart, that you will always be there. Love you to the moon and back.

Amy. My hot little Bama bird. You bounced into our lives with so much passion and wit that it was hard not to be drawn in by you. You ARE massively talented, fun and so stinking lovely. Thank you for your support and encouragement. I can't wait to return the favour someday ;)

To the ladies over at Bare Naked Words: Wendy and Claire. You guys have supported us from the beginning. You gave us your time, patience and loyalty. I can't even begin to express the amount of gratitude I have for you both.

Kat. I couldn't write my acknowledgments without mentioning you and your outstanding eye for detail and grammar errors. Your words of wisdom will always stick with me. Thank you.

To the real life Darcie. You'll always be his number one *peaches.*

To my best friend. The other half of me: My moo. I love you more than I love red bull and Prosecco. You have literally been there for me through it all. You witnessed my meltdowns and outrageous behaviour and you didn't even bat an eyelash. You know me better than I know myself and that is scary. You held me up when I could have easily fallen, and you gave me the strength through kind words and your epic wisdom. You're like a sister to me and I will love you forever.

To my beautiful, caring and funny little family. Sam, my best friend and future husband. I will always be grateful to you for the amount of work you gave up so I could fulfill my ambitions. I'm sorry I wasn't always there to cook the dinner and I promise you'll never see another pizza or kebab again. EVER! To my three little beauts, Keira, Madison and Benjamin. You have kept me sane through this journey. When life got tough, you made me laugh and when I felt like crying, you hugged the hell out of me. I love you more than words can say.

Last, but by no means least. Our epic Wonderlanders. For travelling on the Wonder-Bus, following along on life-changing journey and for always being there.

I love you guys epic amounts.

CHAPTERS

Acknowledgement	09
Dedication	15
Prologue	17
Chapter 1	27
Chapter 2	36
Chapter 3	46
Chapter 4	56
Chapter 5	69
Chapter 6	79
Chapter 7	88
Chapter 8	96
Chapter 9	108
Chapter 10	115
Chapter 11	120
Chapter 12	128
Chapter 13	136
Chapter 14	146
Chapter 15	155
Chapter 16	160
Chapter 17	166
Chapter 18	174
Chapter 19	180
Chapter 20	190
Chapter 21	199
Chapter 22	204
Chapter 23	215

Chapter 24	219
Chapter 25	224
Chapter 26	231
Chapter 27	238
Chapter 28	247
Chapter 29	258
Chapter 30	270
Chapter 31	280
Chapter 32	286
Epilogue	299
Playlist	309

Dedicated to...

All you Wonderlanders out there.

May you live, love and dream…

Prologue

August 1991

Summer holidays. They are the best part about being an eight-year-old. The second the school bell rings out through the halls, everyone knows it means we have a whole six weeks to enjoy being kids. No homework, no early morning routines and no having to be home when the street lights come on. Six weeks to do whatever we want. Within reason, of course. School is too serious. I want fun. I want to wake up and enjoy the warmth that floods through the open window of the bedroom I share with my big brother, Liam. I want to wake up with that tingling feeling inside my tummy because I know that today will be a new adventure. Another day to make new memories that I will remember forever and always. I like making new memories. I love having fun. I like being free.

It's the first year we aren't going on a family holiday, and as much as I enjoy them, I don't mind staying home for once. It means I have more time to do cool stuff and hang out with my best mate, Ethan. We're practically joined at the hip. Mum says we're as thick as thieves, whatever that means. I'm not sure. All I know is that we are best friends and always will be. I haven't told him yet, but he's my hero.

"What's that?" I ask, pointing at the dirty blue rope bound around his wrists.

"It's a piece of rope." He laughs, shaking his head as if I've just asked the dumbest question ever.

"I know, but what's it for?"

He bends down, brushing a hand across the dirt and fallen branches. "No good," he mutters to himself before jumping to his feet. "We'll need bigger. Much bigger. Here, hold this," he orders, tossing the rope at me.

I catch it easily and hold it out with a frown. "What are we doing, E?" I sometimes call him E because his younger brother does, too. It's kind of stuck with us now.

"You'll see, Scotty," he replies with a grin. "You'll see."

It seems to take forever for me to realise what he's doing, but I'm soon staring up at Mr. Bakerman's tree in awe, the excitement coursing through me, forcing me to bounce on the tips of my toes as my anticipation builds. I'm smiling so hard that my cheeks are beginning to ache.

"You wanna go first?" he asks, clutching the branch with both hands.

It's really high. I'm not sure if I can even get on it, but I do want to try.

Ethan passed another house last night on his way home. It was a normal house, like the houses we live in, only this one had a tree house in the backyard – a tree house with a rope swing. We've always wanted to make one but none of the trees in the woods at the back of my house were good enough. My next door neighbor, Mr. Bakerman, has a big oak tree at the back of his house. Not even Ethan has ever been brave enough to climb it until now.

I think he must have grown superpowers overnight, because he insists that Mr. Bakerman's tree is now perfect for our rope swing. I'm not so sure, though. It really is big. But he wants it to be bigger and better than the one on the tree house he passed last night.

I shuffle my feet against the dirt and shrug. "Sure," I answer, pretending I'm not scared. I don't want Ethan to think I'm not brave, like a soldier or a knight. He doesn't look frightened at all. Then again, he's just climbed to the top without falling and even managed to tie the rope to the thick branch above, just for me. I wonder if he's scared of anything.

"I'll hold it while you jump on. Don't forget to get a good run up, otherwise you'll go too slow and it won't be any fun."

"I can do it," I reply, nodding my head eagerly.

My heart pounds in my chest as I hook a leg over the branch that's barely big enough to fit on.

"I'll pull you back, Scotty. That way it'll be like you're flying over the pond up ahead."

I want to fly, but the rope creaks as I lift my other leg up and over, and I glance up to make sure it's secure. "I'm not sure the rope is safe enough, Ethan. What if it snaps?" I ask, trying desperately to hide the quake in my voice.

"It's safe. I won't let you fall," he promises, holding the branch tightly in his grip as he starts to run backwards, his trainers kicking the mud out from underneath them, making a perfect track mark.

I close my eyes for a brief second, the cool summer breeze hitting me in the face. My breathing calms, and suddenly I don't feel afraid anymore. I can do this! I can do this because Ethan is always by my side, like a brother – a brother that looks nothing like me with his brown hair and hazel coloured eyes, compared to my thick, black, curly hair and bright green eyes, but he's my brother no matter what anybody else says… and he believes in me.

See, Dad, I am brave, I say to myself.

I let the moment take over, like the time I rode my bike down Pierces Hill. The thrill of the wheels picking up speed, the way the wind whipped through my hair – it was rip-roaring, and I was flying.

Flying…

Flying…

I'm flying.

My eyes pop open and my head spins as I try to take in the scenery whizzing past me.

Squeezing my eyes shut in excitement, I let out a *whoosh* and a *whoa*, my eyes opening just in time to see the pond coming into view. I glance up at the clear blue sky and release a contented sigh.

"You're flying!" Ethan yells from behind me.

"I'm really flying!" I cry out, laughing as pure happiness pours out of me.

I close my eyes again and wrap my legs tightly around the rope, throwing my arms out to the side.

I can't stop laughing as the swing flings me from side to

side, the wind taking my breath away with each gust. I'm flying and I don't even need a cape.

"Look out!" is all I hear before the rope snaps above me and I land with an almighty thud.

Mud and water cascade over me. The shirt that Mum bought me for my cousin's birthday party is now soaked, covered with brown stains and forgotten leaves.

Easing my hand into the cloudy water, I dig deep. "I've got it!" I cry. "I've got it, E," I repeat, holding the branch in the air.

"Shit! Are you okay?" he asks, panting heavily with his hands clutching his hunched knees.

"That was..."

"Scott?"

"That was..."

"Your dad is going to-"

"That was the best!" I cut in, pushing up onto my knees.

"Your dad is going to kill you."

"So..." I shrug. "It'll be worth it."

"Come on." He laughs. "Let's fix it."

And I know that no matter what trouble waits for me at home, everything will work out alright. It always does when Ethan is around. He saves me; I save him. Nothing can come between us. Or at least I don't think it can, not until I hear an angel speak from behind us.

"What are you boys doing?" the voice asks.

We both turn our heads and I drop the branch, letting it swing out.

Wow.

I've never seen an angel before. Before now, I've never

even been sure they exist.

I swallow loudly and shuffle my feet along in the dirt.

"What does it look like, stupid?" Ethan replies, making a run for the swing.

She digs her white sandals into the grass and pushes up, brushing away the green stems that have clung to her dress. A daisy chain hangs loosely around her neck, swaying in the light summer breeze.

The sun shines down on her, making a halo appear around her head. She really is an angel. She has long white hair curled into ringlets, a flowing dress that stops just above her knees and bright blue eyes that look like the sea.

Maybe she'd like a go on the rope swing.

"Do you… Would you…" I stutter, pushing my hands into the pockets of my shorts and forcing my eyes to the ground as I fumble with my words.

Ethan comes barrelling over, branch in hand. "He means do you want a go?" he asks, offering out the swing.

A sad smile washes over her face and she shakes her head. "No. I'd better not."

Her eyes fall to the ground where her skipping rope lies.

"Scaredy-cat," Ethan sings.

"Am not," she barks, her head whipping up and her eyes landing on Ethan with a hard glare.

"What's the matter, princess? Worried you'll ruin your dress?"

"No. My mum… I can't. I have to go anyway."

I watch as she bends down, picking up the pink skipping rope. "C'mon. Just one go? Show us you ain't a scaredy-cat."

The angel looks back and forth between the swing and the gate, seeming lost. I wonder for a second what her problem is and why she keeps looking up ahead, until her soft voice cuts through my thoughts.

"Fine. One go, but then I really have to leave."

Ethan looks at me with raised brows. "Help me lift her, Scotty."

I grab the branch to steady it as Ethan pulls her forward.

"I can get on myself, you know."

"Well, it's easier this way. Wouldn't want you to ruin that pretty dress of yours."

She doesn't hesitate and lifts both hands out, her small fingers curling around the thick blue rope.

We grab behind both of her knees and lift until the angel is firmly on the branch.

"Ready?" Ethan yells, giving me a silent nod.

We don't wait for her reply as we push back on our heels and run backwards.

"Go!" I shout, and then we let go of the branch.

We both drop to the ground and laugh as the angel speeds ahead, squealing and kicking her legs out. The swing darts from side to side and my eyes follow the movement while Ethan rolls around in the dirt, laughing.

"Amelia Elizabeth Chamberlin, what on *earth* are you doing?"

Our heads whip to the side at the harsh sounding voice, and we don't waste a second, pushing off the ground and diving behind a tree.

"Jeez, who is that? She's scary," I whisper.

"Yeah, worse than your dad."

I'm not sure that's true but I nod anyway.

"Where did she go?" I ask, craning my neck so I can see better.

I can't see anything other than the wicked witch and the rope swing thrashing backwards.

The lady looks angry, and she's shouting something I can't make out while marching in high heels towards the pond.

Ethan and I exchange glances and follow behind the witch.

There she is.

The angel.

Sopping wet and covered in mud in the middle of the pond. She's a little way from where we're stood but close enough that I can make out the tears streaming down her face as her lips quiver, releasing sobs.

"Whatever were you thinking? Look at your dress. What will your father say?"

I peek at the girl again and we lock eyes. Something familiar flashes through them – a sullen sadness that reminds me of someone I know. From the outside she looks perfect, but inside, she just wants to be liked. There's a need to be perfect, but she seems to know she will never actually be able to reach her goal. Or maybe I'm wrong. Maybe, like me, she doesn't want to be perfect at all. Maybe she just wants to ride her bike down Pierces Hill, never knowing which way the wheels are going to wobble. Or jump a rope swing, not caring if her dress will be torn and no longer pristine. Maybe, finally, there is someone else in the world just like me.

Maybe that's why she looks familiar.

Even dripping in weeds, she's perfect to me.

I continue to stare as the wicked witch leads her away, still shouting.

My eyes land on the patch of grass where I first spotted her making daisy chains.

"Hey, your skipping rope," I call out, bending down to pick it up.

"You are never to play with those young boys again, do you hear me? Tearaways, the pair of them. Their mothers may not care what they get up to, but I care about you. You do not need boys like that around you. Bad influences. Look at you. Your dress," the scary lady shrieks.

I hold my breath and drop the hand holding the pink rope.

"C'mon," Ethan calls, ruffling my hair. "Let's get out of here. Tomorrow, I'll raid my dad's garage for some more rope. Better rope this time," he promises.

I sigh and glance down at my now brown shirt, suddenly feeling bad.

Ethan notices, nudging his shoulder against mine. "Don't worry, Scotty. I'll tell your dad we were helping my mum in the garden. He'll believe us."

"Do you really think so?" I ask, my eyes following him, hopeful.

"Sure." He shrugs. "If not, my mum will tell him so."

I'm not so sure Dad will buy it, but if Miss Julia tells him so then I guess it will be okay. I smile and nudge him back, suddenly feeling okay again. I'm only eight years old. I don't know much.

But two things will stay with me from today. Two things

that I will hold onto forever.

I want to see my very own angel again sometime soon, and Ethan Walker is definitely my hero.

Chapter One

August 2002

The early morning breeze nips at my skin, causing the hairs on my arms to prickle and stand to attention. I shrink inside my yellow vest. It reeks of dried cement and congealed mud, but that doesn't stop me from enjoying the sudden sense of warmth I get from it as I bury myself in the thin, bright material, comforting myself in even the shittiest of situations. Only it doesn't last long. It never does.

I hate mornings. Despite the sun peeking out from the horizon, threatening a blistering day, I feel nothing but emptiness, a hollow feeling that I've grown accustomed to over the years.

Every day I promise myself that changes will happen, that today will be the day that I finally open up to my father. But I break that promise to myself every damn day. I've planned the whole scene in my head ten times over. I tell my father that construction isn't what I want to spend the rest of my life doing. In my head, he smiles as he looks down on me. He smiles instead of frowning as he looks down on his youngest son with nothing but pride and joy. He holds that comforting smile as he says, "That's okay, Son. You should never be afraid to be open about your hopes and dreams. Whatever you decide to do, I will be proud of you. No matter what."

My head is stupid. If and when I pluck up enough courage to voice my ambitions, it certainly won't go the way I've hoped and dreamed it will.

The ground cracks beneath my feet as I walk. Broken tiles and off-white pebble-dash line a path towards our newest project. An empty shell sits disheveled upon a slight hill that overlooks plush fields and forest. In eight months' time, that empty shell will be no more. In its place will stand a proud, four-bedroom house, with a high-pitched roof providing shelter for what will soon be a play room for two excited children. I should feel a sense of warmth at that thought alone. Every child should have a place they can call home, where they feel safely guarded from the outside world. Instead, I feel that familiar sense of emptiness creeping in. I try to push it back and imagine the laughter that will play out behind the bricks and mortar, but not even thoughts of a white picket fence or adventure playground can ease that unwanted feeling.

I've been working with my dad since I left school almost three years ago. I finished my final year with a handful of GCSEs that, at this moment in time, are useless to me. I studied hard for the best part of a year to achieve the grades I got, but the sleepless nights and panic over whether or not I would get through them only left me feeling foolish. I spent an entire year fretting over something that, in reality, was pointless. It's only now I realise that a decent grade in maths won't make for a successful or happy future. Not that that matters. My dad has had my life mapped out for me from day one of my existence. I will work for him in his rundown construction company that, at the very most, might leave us with enough money to pay the mortgage on the three-bedroom townhouse we live in. We aren't poor by any means. But we aren't rich, either. The last few years have been hard on my dad. The jobs haven't come in as frequently as they've needed to. The business is now suffering and my dad has been finding it hard to keep the staff, especially during the months where the workload decreases considerably. We've relied on last minute work because without that, the company would have no income, but even that isn't guaranteed. Needless to say, it has probably been a good eight months since I've received a pay cheque for my work. In the beginning, I was happy to help out. My parents worked hard to raise us. They gave us life, clothed and fed us, and never once resented us for having taken away their freedom, even if they do have ridiculously high expectations of me. We are their world, and even though my father has always been a bit of a hard arse, wanting me and my siblings to conform to his ideals, I still feel like I owe it to them to stick around and help out.

But as the days end and mornings come to light, I slowly begin to feel as though I'm suffocating in a world that's constantly on repeat. I'm only nineteen, but it's almost as if this is it for me. This is the peak. This is how my life will always be.

I want to wake up on a summer's morning and look

forward to the future, to relish the warmth instead of being assaulted by the bitter cold as I settle into work. I want to feel like a teenager – live a little, screw a lot – but mostly, I just want to work and get paid for it, not be taken for a ride because I'm the son of the owner. Dad's excuse has always been the same. "Sorry, Son, we're still waiting on the cheque to come in from Mr. Robinson. It's been a rough few months. Maybe next month will pick up." His excuses are almost as tiring and aggravating as listening to Liam chomp his way through a bacon butty. Sloppy fucker.

Sighing in frustration, I use all my strength to lift the loaded barrel and throw myself into work. *Only seven more hours, Scotty.* That thought only makes me sigh again as the wheelbarrow jostles and struggles to stay in a straight line.

As promised by the weatherman, the searing sun has now settled upon us. The humidity clings to my skin and the day's grime has mingled with the damp, sticking to me in little clusters that make me feel like I have the weight of the world clinging to different parts of my body. I unload the last bricks, placing them in even piles on what will be the new driveway. Exhausted and dirty, I look forward to climbing in my beat up car, that's hanging on to life by a thread, and heading home to shower.

"Nice one, Son," my dad says from behind me, slapping a rough hand to my shoulder. "You did an outstanding job on the Henrys' conservatory. Thanks to you, they've given us the go ahead on that outhouse they're planning on building. Work starts first thing Monday. Just try not to be late this time. It doesn't look good for me, or the company for that matter."

Never a compliment without an insult.

I want to argue that it was one time – one time being late and it wasn't really my fault at all. Fucking car. Shit happens, right?

"No worries, Dad," I call out, but he doesn't acknowledge me as he jumps in his *Ford* truck and speeds off in a cloud of dust, kicking up debris in his wake.

I let out a sigh and wipe at my brow with the back of my hand, no doubt leaving more dirt that I'll have to try and scrub clean later.

Liam's cocky form filters out through the archway, his head hung low, amused at whatever has caught his attention on his phone. Shaking my head, I tug my belt loose and unfasten my cargo pants before pulling them away. Unlike me, Liam loves this job. Not that he actually does much work, unless you call sitting around on the bed of his truck and stuffing his face while playing Snake on his *Nokia* phone, work.

"Hey, Scott," he calls out from a few feet away. "Hold the fort for me, would you? I got a text from Meli. Her parents are away for the evening and we–"

Ah, Meli. Amelia: the girl on the rope swing. The angel I swore I wanted to meet again, only to find that when we did come face to face later in life, she was an epic bitch who somehow ended up with my brother.

"No," I cut him short, shrugging my arm out of the luminous yellow vest that comes with the job. "I'm not doing it, Liam. I've been here since the crack of dawn working my arse off without a break. I'm going home for the day."

"Dad said–"

"I don't care what Dad said. He's not here, and in thirty seconds, I won't be either." I grit my teeth and shake my head in annoyance, refraining from telling him exactly what I think of him. Not that it does any good. Once a lazy bastard, always a lazy bastard. My hands clench into fists at my side, and for a fraction of a second, I imagine him sprawled out on the deck with a bloody nose and me looming over his pathetic body with a smug smile on my face. I despise my brother, most days. I know that's partly due to the fact that he seems to get away with murder whereas I get a clip on the back of the head if I so much as sneeze in the wrong direction, but the hatred it there and it's real.

He grins up at me, shoving the phone in his back pocket. "What's crawled up your arse today? You've been whining like a bitch since you got here."

"You wouldn't get it," I mumble, pausing briefly for a second to take in my surroundings.

"Try me," he challenges, crossing his arms over his chest.

It isn't just the lack of pay that makes me hate my job. Nor is it the early mornings and manual labour. It's him. If he isn't sat on the bed of his truck, chewing my ear off about his latest conquests, he's standing here trying to pull the shit he's pulling now. I'm tired of being everyone's skivvy. See, my parents think I'm perfect. Everyone thinks I'm perfect, mainly because I just get on and do what needs doing. I'm not perfect, though. Far from it. Perfect means I have to maintain a façade that I don't believe in. Sure, I'm polite and respect my elders. I get along with pretty much everyone that enters my life. But that doesn't make me perfect. I swear like a trooper, fuck like a whore and lie through my teeth when I tell my dad I want to work for him. Truth is, I despise it.

I've always tried to be a good son, following the rules that are set out for me, very rarely breaking them. When I do, though, they come down on me like a ton of bricks. They say it's for my own good, that they want me to succeed in life. I can do that by myself. I don't need a helping hand or shitty rules to help me reach my goals.

My problem? I like an easy life. I like to maintain quiet and order.

I usually like to avoid confrontations and pointless fights that I know I'm going to lose.

Sometimes I wish they'd treat me like they treat Liam. He goes AWOL for days and they don't bat an eyelid. He could rob an off-licence at gunpoint and probably get away with it. He is, what Gran would call, a tearaway. He's always getting into trouble with the Old Bill and hanging out with the wrong crowds. My parents seem to turn a blind eye when it comes to him. I guess they consider him a lost cause or something. But either way, he's happy. Despite having a job and a family that, in their own little way, love me, I'm *not* happy, and I feel a bit shitty about that fact. I envy Liam, in more ways than one, because I don't remember a time when I ever really was happy, unless it involved my best mate, Ethan, and a few tins of *Bud*. I'm happy in those moments. In those few hours of obliteration, I'm able to push the sensible Scott to one side and just be me. The real me.

"Scott?" Liam interrupts my thoughts, shoving at my side.

I'm tired of being good, and my patience is slowly wearing

thin. I need an out. In layman's terms? I need to grow a pair and man the fuck up. I'm nineteen. I don't need to be stuck in a dead-end job, taking orders from my shit of a brother. I need a change. Starting with the career that has been forced upon me.

"You know what?" I say, croakily.

"What?"

I pull open the passenger door of my car, toss my bag in the foot well and turn to my brother. "Sort it out yourself. I'm done."

"What do you mean you're done?" he asks and frowns.

"Exactly what I just said. I'm done. Outta here!" I yell, tossing the hard hat against the tailgate of his truck. Stick that!

"You mean for today, right?"

"And tomorrow. And the day after that, the one after that... Oh, and all the rest of the fucking days you want me to do your shit for you. You're on your own, mate."

"You fucking idiot. Dad is going to..."

I let his words linger in the air before tuning them out and sliding into the driver's seat. Pulling the door shut, I shoot a quick message to E, telling him I'm done for the day and for him to meet me at the local boozer.

As usual, the drive to the The Crown pub takes no more than ten minutes. In those short minutes, I dodge rocks and fallen branches that litter the single track dirt road. If I'd thought about this properly, I would have suggested we met somewhere in town, but that's the problem. I'm not thinking. I never think. I just need to escape.

The car is whining and making some sort of strangled cry as I pull into the only available parking space. The exhaust bellows out, a thick blanket of smoke surrounding me. E insisted on fixing it up for me. I'm almost certain he only suggested it because he was concerned how I'd pay for a new car. He knows about Gramps' inheritance that's sat in my savings account, but he isn't about to sit by and watch me piss it away on a new car when he can so easily fix the old one. He always has liked to father me in a way. I've never really understood why.

The driver's door flies open and E's face appears behind the grey smoke.

"Mate," he chokes out, using his shirt to shield his face. "Drop this pile of wank at my old man's garage on Monday. It fucking stinks, and quite frankly, I'm embarrassed to be seen talking to you in it. Maybe it really is time to get rid of it. I can't polish a turd anymore."

I laugh and switch off the ignition before climbing out. "It's a classic. Quit fucking hating." I shake my head and shove the keys in my back pocket. Maybe he has a point. The thing is an embarrassment. It's far from the chick magnet it once was. Ethan's offer suddenly sounds a whole lot more appealing.

"Whatever. Look, Jake's throwing a house party. I said we'd go after here so we're only stopping for the one. You can leave your car here and we'll hitch a ride with the others. I'll sort your car out on Monday."

"Sound." I shrug in response. I'll think about how to get to and from work tomorrow. Then it dawns on me and I let out a small laugh. I quit. I don't have to worry about how I'll get there. I'm free to enjoy my night and I'll worry about Dad tomorrow.

Chapter Two

K ey in lock and turn. Sounds easy enough. Well it would be if you could actually see the damn key – or anything else for that matter.

I fumble around again, squinting to find the lock I know is somewhere in front of me. My vision becomes a blur of haziness, forcing me to lose my footing and stumble backwards, the key scraping against the glass panel as I try desperately to correct myself.

Cursing under my breath, I run one hand through my black, curly hair and press the other against the red stained door for support. I wonder for a moment how much booze I actually got through last night as I groan through the pounding in my head.

Thud.

Thud.

Thud.

"Fuck!" I groan, losing my footing. I'm vaguely aware that I'm moving, or maybe the ground is moving, and I'm falling forward and forward and...

The door springs open and a rough hand grips my arm.

"Jesus Christ, look at the state of you," my Dad forces out

through what I can only assume are gritted teeth. Or fangs. Yeah, fangs. I laugh under my breath and point to the two heads. Two heads? Shit! One Dad is enough. Now I have two to deal with. What the actual fuck?

"Do you even care what the neighbours think?" he scolds, lowering his voice cautiously.

The smell of bacon wafts through the hallway and out onto the porch. Frowning, I swallow the bile rising in my throat and grip the doorframe, pushing my feet over the threshold. A rough hand is still gripping my forearm, but not for support. Oh no, never support. Bed. I need my bed. And juice. Cold. Juice.

"You're a fucking joke, Scott. The one time I thought I could count on you and you go and let me down. You let us all down. Do you realise how long it took to haul that shit around?"

I stare blankly as he speaks, my eyes shifting to each mouth. It makes me dizzy. Am I going to be sick? It's a possibility. My father is inducing nausea. How does my mother cope sleeping next to him?

Or maybe it's the alcohol, I think while I hiccup. Yeah, it's probably that. And you'd think my father would show some compassion, huh? Can't he see I'm hanging out my arse? Maybe he does. I guess that makes sense. I'm already suffering so why would he pass up the opportunity to torture me some more?

"You left us in the shit, boy. You come home stinking like a stale brewery, acting as though everything is fine, and you don't even have the decency to apologise to me like a real man. Did I teach you nothing? And what do you mean you quit? You can't just fucking quit. No son quits on their father."

I don't even have the strength to argue back. *Don't say anything, Scotty. Nod and look as though you're actually sorry. He might ease off you, lad.* This is what I tell myself. Fuck if it works. It seems to piss him off even more. There's no way in hell I can even contemplate giving it back. My brain and mouth aren't in sync and my tongue is as dry as a nun's... You get my point. I mumble something unintelligible and shake my head. I don't need to listen to this. He's hurting my head. Fuck! I'm thirsty. Where's all the water?

I turn my back on him and push up the stairs, taking them two at a time. Or at least I try to. My legs are shaky, making me falter, my body swaying back and forth. I will them to cooperate as I use the banister for support. My head feels heavy – a dead weight against my lifeless body. I somehow miraculously make it to my room in one piece, flinching like I'm under attack as I close the door.

Why is everything so fucking loud?

Dropping to the edge of the bed, I kick my trainers off, allowing the heavy weight of my head to finally fall back and hit the pillow once I'm out of them.

Tomorrow. I'll deal with my dad tomorrow. A sense of déjà vu hits me right before I close my strained eyes and get pulled down into a dark, deep sleep.

Ah, peace.

******

I'm not sure how long I've been out. Not long enough,

I'd say, considering I still feel like death. My head is fuzzy and I wrack my mind for any recollection of last night or how the hell I even made it into my own bed, but my brain is unresponsive, probably on strike for all the shit I undoubtedly pulled last night. I focus hard and finally remember the pub, the party, and the fuck hot brunette with amazing tits. Ethan and I in the taxi... I crashed out and woke up... here.

Digging my elbows into the mattress, I push myself up as my eyes scan the room.

"Fuck. My dad," I curse under my breath as all the memories from the night before hit me like a sack of shit. The text I sent to Dad telling him I quit.

Groaning out loud, I cradle my head in my hands. If I didn't ache all fucking over, I'd kick myself for getting so wasted. The same shit, minus the text to my dad, happened last weekend and I swore I wouldn't repeat it. Man, I'm such a dick. No wonder they give me grief.

A soft tap on the door pulls me from my own misery, and I'm almost thankful that it isn't my dad. If it was, he'd have flown through the door like a tornado – angry and loud.

The handle turns slowly and my older sister's head pops around the corner, her hair flopping around her face, covering her eyes. She doesn't say anything. Then again, she never really does in situations like these. I note the tall glass of orange juice in her outstretched hand and my eyes bulge out. I salivate, almost tasting the cold liquid already.

Slumping down at the foot of my bed, she hands it over before reaching down and pulling out two controllers from the cabinet. She chucks one on my lap and goes about making herself comfy by tucking her legs under her arse. I want to tell her that I'm not in the mood for gaming, and that I just want to be left alone to wallow in my own self-pity. But it won't matter what I say because Beth is a stubborn little shit.

I've never really gotten my head around how different Beth is from every girl around here. Most of the lasses her age are only interested in looking good or having a decent lad on their arm. Not Beth. It's not that she's ugly or anything. As far as sisters go, she's alright. She's tall like me, but not too tall, and her hair is normally a muddy brown, almost black in colour like mine, but during her rebellious stage, she started dying it jet black. It's been like that ever since, but now she's given up on the black eyeliner and heavy mascara, allowing her grey eyes to shine that little bit brighter again, like they always did as a kid. I always thought it was weird that neither of us have the same eye colour. While Beth's are grey, mine are green, and Liam, well he has dad's eyes. A deep, dark brown.

I remember the first time Beth waltzed through the living room like a stroppy teenager, face caked in make-up with thick black rings around her eyes. I'd never seen Dad pale to the extreme he did that day. Mum took one look at the lip piercing and broke down in tears. The whole scene amused the hell out of me. It was such a Beth thing to do. She doesn't care how she looks or what others think of her. She's smart as hell and isn't afraid to make a statement. "What? Who died?" was all she asked, not hiding her 'I'm not really all that bothered but I'm being polite' shrug.

I envy that about her. For years I tried my hardest to be everything everyone wanted me to be, to be looked at by my folks with love and not disappointment, but it wasn't long before I gave up hope and stopped trying altogether. Deep down, I know I'm a decent guy. I do, and if they can't see past my mistakes then they aren't worth my efforts. Besides, it could be worse. I could be like Liam.

Growing up, he was only ever really interested in chicks, and despite his lack of manners, he still manages to charm the pants off them. A ruffle of his dirty blond hair and a glimpse of his smarmy good looks is all it takes. That all stopped a little while back now, though. He's been on and off with Amelia since he left school.

Amelia Chamberlin happened to be in my year, though, not his. Her parents were on the school council, owned a ton of businesses and were only ever seen socialising at the country club. She was a stuck-up bitch, even at school and I guess not much has changed over the years. I hated her back then, and I still do, despite that first impression I had of her that day with the rope swing. She pretty much made up her mind about me before we'd even spoken again, way back in year eight. She was too good for me. She looked down her nose at me like I was a piece of gum stuck to the bottom of her designer shoe, just like her mother had done that day. She was probably the only chick at school that wouldn't give me the time of day. That suited me just fine. I wasn't all that keen on her anyway. Don't get me wrong, there was a time many years ago where I had thought differently of her, and I still thought she was the hottest chick around, but she knew it, and that was enough to make my dick shrivel in zero-point-five seconds. Major turn off in my books. Still, I'd be lying if I said I haven't pictured her face while knocking one out. Only the once, mind you. When Leanne Taylor joined us in year nine, she replaced the queen bee instantly. Poor Amelia. Her face was a picture when she realised that she no longer held the crown.

She and Liam are a lot alike in many ways. Maybe that's why I've never really got along with either of them. I sometimes wish I had the same relationship with Liam as Ethan has with his brother Dean. They actually get along, whereas, I find it hard to engage in any conversation with Liam at all. I'm not sure when we drifted apart. I honestly can't remember a time when we ever really got along.

My sister, however? She will sit at the edge of my bed for hours upon end playing video games. She's always taken an interest in my accomplishments and dreams, and in return, I let her chew my ear off about all the boring crap that no one else wants to listen to. I've always admired her. She's not just smart; she's funny, too, and I have a feeling she'll be the one out of the three of us that makes a difference in the world. I respect her and trust her with my life. She's fiercely independent and strong willed. Doesn't stop me from trying to protect her, though. She might be older and wiser than I am, but there's still a bunch of dicks out there who think they can take advantage of her. I know how their sick little minds work and fuck it to hell if they even so much as lay a fucking finger on her. Not a chance. At least not while Ethan and I are still alive, that is.

This has become sort of a routine – her showing up in my room not long after I've gone two rounds with our parents. As much as I feel comfort in knowing at least one member of the Jenkins family sympathises with me in some way, it's one routine I really wish never existed.

"Do you want to talk about it?" Beth asks, interrupting my train of thought. It's only when she speaks that I realise my mushroom has died and *Mario* is currently in the process of defeating the dragon. Still, her eyes never leave the screen and her expression remains blank, her fingers still tapping away eagerly against the buttons on the grey controller.

"Nothing to talk about," I reply with a shrug, because there isn't. Same shit, different day.

I watch her shoulders slump, almost in defeat, before she cranes her neck and shoots me an apologetic look. "He's upset now, but it won't last long. I'm sure they just want what's best for you, Scott, and you know, maybe it is time you stood on your own two feet and sorted yourself out," she says through a sigh. "And quitting your job by text? Really, Scott? How the hell did you think he'd react?"

I want to tell her how wrong she is. Part of the problem is not having a say in my own life. How can I stand on my own two damn feet when I'm attached to a permanent leash? So maybe I should've spoken to him first instead of sending a drunken text. I know my dad, though. He wouldn't have listened even if I had.

Not feeling the need to explain myself, I nod through a yawn and drop my head back against the pillow, hoping she'll take the hint. The alcohol from last night is still in my system, and the start of what I know will be a two-day hangover from hell is beginning to kick in. Sleep. That's what I need: an afternoon siesta to fight this bitch of a hangover.

I wake up around three hours later, almost hangover free. But as the clearer head settles upon me, memories come flooding back. The girl I fucked and left without as much as a goodbye. The text to Dad... Quitting my job.

Fuck!

The silence creeps in, but so does the guilt.

I hate to feel bad for something that I feel passionately about and I shouldn't feel guilty for voicing my dreams. Still, I know the difference between right and wrong, and the way I went about it was bad, even for me. I only hope he won't come down too hard on me. Maybe after a few days he will have got his head around the idea. Besides, he still has Liam. If he wants that father-son business he's so hell bent on having, then that still remains safely intact.

I still have the inheritance from Grandpa, which isn't a huge amount, but it's enough to keep me going until I find a job. Preferably one I'll actually enjoy. The car will have to wait. Maybe Ethan can fix it up enough to last a little while longer.

I've already decided that I'll head into town tomorrow. Maybe they're hiring bar staff at the The Crown, or one of the clubs. Staff don't tend to stick around long enough to palm their first pay cheque. I'm sure to find something. Anything beats working for my dad, and besides, it won't have to be for long. One day E and I are going to own our own business and to hell with every other fucker that thinks we won't make it happen. Call it a pipe dream, but we are deadly serious. At least I am, anyway. I'm not so sure E really believes we can make it happen, but I do. Mainly because I believe that he is capable of anything, and he'll never leave me behind. We're brothers for life, just without the DNA.

Chapter Three

I've only ever cried once in my life. Well, twice if you include now and the time I jammed my ankle in next door's fence while trying to get my ball back, only to be bitten not once, but twice by their fucker of a pit bull.

I've cried twice in my whole existence and I already know this time, it will stick with me forever.

My hands ball into fists at my side while my back remains stiff. My vision is a blurred haze as my mum's words play through my mind like one of Liam's shit CD tracks. Over and over, the words are still the same, yet the story tears me apart with each heart-shattering repetition. Each chorus knocks the wind out of me, stealing breath after breath until I'm gasping for that tiny piece of oxygen. Anything, no matter the measure, just as long as it will see me through until the next one is taken... Which it will be. That's how loss works. And the pain and hurt? They're inevitable.

"I'm sorry, Scott. There was an accident. It's Julia. She's dead."

That's it. So simple. Those few, short sentences are enough to bring me to my knees, cursing God. And they do.

Ethan has just lost his Mum.

I'm not talking misplaced. He's lost her forever. She's gone. The one woman who was the constant in all our lives, and she's fucking dead. Just like that. No longer here. Lost to this shitty little world.

Everything has changed in an instant. Time seems to stop as all those silent tears wrack through me. I'm suffocating in grief and gasping for air. I'm a child again, seeking comfort from my mother. Lost in her own world of pain, she doesn't reach for me. No comfort, no words of sympathy. Nothing. Just emptiness and the distant sound of cries from downstairs. We've all lost someone we loved, an extended member of our family.

Two hours later, my eyes still sting from the pain that seems to have no filter. Anger, hurt and confusion consume me. How can she be gone? I saw her just yesterday, standing in the doorway wearing a smile that I knew was only for me. Even though I looked like shit and was wearing my clothes from the day before, she hadn't frowned at me. She was just Julia. She was like a second mum in my life. One who, more often than not, knew me better than my own flesh and blood did.

I can hear the sound of ringing coming from the hallway. I know it will be the women from Mum's club wanting to know if it's true. We don't live in a big neighborhood so it's inevitable that word will get around sooner or later. Julia was loved by everyone in the community and by the pupils she taught. She was so damn nice it was unfair.

And I'm already referring to her as a *was* rather than an *is*. That alone cuts me in two.

Behind the tears and violent string of curses, my thoughts drift to Ethan. What is he doing? How is he feeling? Does he need me? How the hell do I help him through this? I'm not sure what I'm meant to say or do. Other than Gramps, I've never had someone I love die before.

The hours keep ticking by and still I sit here, not knowing what to do. All my life I've looked out for him, been there for him, regardless of whether he was in the wrong or not. So many times I've put Ethan before myself, sacrificed so much, because to me, he's always been more important than anything I've been going through or any situation I've found myself in. But how, someone tell me, how do I help him through this? What am I meant to say? How do you even begin to say how sorry you are? Sorry isn't enough. It will never be enough.

As much as I want to see him, I don't think I can. At least not while I'm like this. I'll only say everything I shouldn't and become what I hate – a fumbling fool.

I will myself to get it together, but it's no use. See, Julia, she looked out for me, fed me, and kept me on the straight and narrow when I could have so easily slipped down the wrong path like Liam. I've never had that bond with my own mum. Don't get me wrong, I know Mum loves me in her own way, and that she cares for me when she thinks I need it. I know my mum would crumble if she thought there was someone else I would run to in an emergency, but the reality is, Julia was that person for me. She understood me. And now she's gone.

I think back to when I was sixteen – when I had locked myself out of the house. I didn't want to call Mum and Dad. They would have had to have left work to come and let me in and I didn't want that to happen. I remember I was fucking starving. At sixteen, there weren't many things a lad needed. Booze, babes and sex were the obvious, but food wasn't something I could live without, either. I'd rocked up to the Walker's house, hands shoved in my pockets, wearing only my charming good looks and my cock-sure grin for good measure.

My jaw drops when I hear Mr. Walker grumbling about something on the other side of the door, but when Mrs. W answers, my smile grows wider than ever.

"Again?" is all she says on one of those little eye rolls of hers before stepping back and waving her hand for me to come in.

I don't have to play up to Mrs. W. Okay, maybe I do a little, but whatever, it works.

"It wasn't my fault this time. I sw–" My words are cut short when I feel the faint sting at the back of my head, causing me to shrink into the collar of my jacket and leg it upstairs to Ethan's room without another word.

"Dinner will be ready in five. Go wash up." I catch wind of her soft chuckle as my fingers circle the door handle and I slip into the safety of Ethan's room.

"Your mum is an angel. Wanna swap?" I ask hopefully.

"Not on your life, mate, and don't even think about it," he retorts, my smirk clearly registering as he tosses a sports mag in my direction. "She's off limits, you sick fuck!"

Feigning a gasp while dodging the dirty mag, I plonk down on the leather desk chair and stretch my arms above my head, mumbling, "Dude, I've already told you. I wouldn't go there."

Running my hands suggestively over my puffed out chest, I deadpan, "Not unless she begged me, anyway,"

He shakes his head, clearly not amused. "You've got serious issues, bud."

"Boys! Dinner's ready." Our heads whip around at lightning speed before we make a mad dash for the door at the same time, pushing and shoving our way down the stairs.

Frowning, I rub at my elbow and slide into my usual spot at the table.

Mrs. Walker's gaze falls on me, then on Ethan, and then back at me before it finally fixates back on her son and a stern expression mounts her face. "Ethan, leave the boy alone."

"Don't worry, Mrs. Walker. I'm used to it."

"How many times? It's Julia. Mrs. Walker makes me sound so old."

"Sorry." I glance at Ethan, waggling my brows before mouthing her name suggestively and popping a potato in my mouth. I shrug my shoulders and grin.

The word 'dick', followed by a swift kick to my ankle has me choking on Aunt Bessie's besties, but it isn't long before we're both laughing at our private joke and poor, sweet Julia is none the wiser.

It wasn't just that she defended me against her son. I always knew she was kidding. If anyone was used to our behaviour, it was Julia. It wasn't even that she fed me, though I was fucking starving. No, it was that she knew I probably deserved my parents' actions, yet she took me in anyway. She believed in second chances – or third in my case. She saw beyond the teenage banter and petty behaviour. All she ever saw was me.

My forehead drops to my knees as silent cries tear from my chest, and they continue to do so until I have nothing left to give. I cry for my best mate and his brother. I cry for Mr. Walker, and I cry for myself. I'm not ashamed to admit my selfishness in all of the wailing, because even as I think about how Dean and Ethan will cope with the loss of such a strong women, for the longest moment, I wonder how the fuck I'm going to make it through life without her, too. I'm not sure I can.

There is one thing I'm sure of, though...

I've just lost the only person in this fuck awful world, besides her son, that ever truly believed in me. Faults, floppy hair, fuck ups and all.

******

The light slowly creeps through the gap in the curtains. Already I want this day to be over and it hasn't even started yet. I need to push my feelings aside for one day and concentrate on what's important: The Walker boys, and giving Julia the send off that she so rightly deserves.

As hard as it's going to be for me, it's going to be ten times harder for Ethan and Dean. I can do this, for them. I have to. It's time to be a man.

The light around me changes almost in the blink of an eye. Moving my head to the side, I glance at the gap in the curtains while the sky silently mocks me. It's grey, almost like a storm is brewing somewhere. That's when the rain begins to pound against the windowpane and I laugh humorlessly. What is it they say about rain on the day of a funeral? It's fucking inevitable. I shake my head and will my stiff legs to cooperate. I need to haul my arse out of bed and get ready. The funeral isn't for a few hours but I need to make a pit stop before I can face that.

I change into my black trousers and matching jacket, accompanying it with a plain black tie. Mum insisted on buying it for me last year when we buried Gramps. At the time, I thought it was a complete waste of money since I'd only be wearing it once. I didn't know back then that I would be pulling it back out of my wardrobe so soon.

I flatten my palms across the crisp, white shirt and tug at the sleeves of the jacket before fixing my hair into a sensible mess. It's unruly at the best of times, but having slept like shit last night, it has somehow turned into a mass of tangles and unwanted curls.

Blowing out an exaggerated breath, I take one last look in the full-length mirror and sigh.

I fucking hate life. Cruel mother fucking world.

"Scott?" Mum calls from outside the door.

Lost in my own thoughts, I must have missed the floorboard creaking outside. It's always a telltale sign that someone is about to knock, only this time, it wasn't.

"Yeah?" I call back before pulling my bedroom door open to find her standing in front of me.

"You're up early. The funeral isn't for another–"

"I couldn't sleep," I cut in.

She nods silently and pulls her gaze down to my bare feet.

"It's expected, love," she says with a sad smile before continuing. "I polished your shoes last night. They're in the hallway, but they should be dry by now."

"Thanks," I mumble.

"Will you be riding to the church with us, or do you have other plans?"

"Actually, I do. I'm gonna head over to E's house."

"Good idea. Mr. Walker is great and all, but Julia would have a fit if those boys were late for her funeral."

Mum pretty much thinks everyone is great. But we both know Mr. Walker's really a twat. Still, today isn't about judging people for their mistakes. It's a day for remembering the woman that made everything right in the world.

Nodding, I pull open the door and slip past her. "I'll see you there," I whisper before leaving her stood in the doorway.

I have no idea what time it is when I leave the house to make the short, five minute journey to Ethan's, but by the time I get there, the curtains have already been drawn in the living room. It surprises me a little, but I don't think too much of it as I turn off the engine and pull the matching suits from the backseat.

The rain stopped on the way over and the sun is now beginning to make an appearance. It's already warm and humid and I wish I hadn't got dressed so damn early. I'm sure that if I pull my jacket off, my shirt will be drenched through, but that's the least of my worries. I have two hung-over teenagers to deal with.

I called around yesterday to check on them both, and it was a bloody good job I did because the boys were fucking wasted.

I don't know where Mr. Walker was at the time – most likely in the same state as them, I would guess. After watching over Ethan while he chucked his guts up in the toilet, I tended to Dean, who was heaving over the sink. I would've laughed if the reason behind it hadn't been as serious. I finally left them to it once they swore they wouldn't touch another drop after I'd gone.

I cautiously push open the door and peer around the corner. The place stinks of booze again, and I'm pretty sure I could get pissed just from the fumes. Lying fucks.

Taking a deep breath, I go in search of Ethan. It doesn't take me long to find him sprawled out on the dining room table.

It's still early, so I let him sleep it off a little while longer. I don't have the heart to be a thorn in his side today, even if I know he will regret it some point later in his life. He'll probably still have a decent amount of alcohol in his system, but at least this way he might be able to walk in a straight line if I let him sleep as much of it off as he can.

Mr. Walker makes his way downstairs, moaning about flowers or some shit. I'm not really listening. I'm more concerned about the empty bottles littering the house and wanting to get rid of them before he notices. He isn't stupid. He's bound to notice them the second he comes down, and if not, the smell will be a dead giveaway. Luckily, he leaves soon after coming down and doesn't bat an eyelid in his son's direction.

I finish cleaning and take out the three bags of rubbish I've collected from downstairs. Dean woke up a little while ago and I shoved his suit at him without a word. His face said it all.

"Mate, you fucking stink," I shout, kicking Ethan's foot with my own.

Turning my back to the lump of muscle on the table, I start to hang his suit on the door to save from any further creasing. A groan followed by an almighty thud has me whipping my head around to find Ethan in a heap on the floor.

I'm not sure if he's ready to hurl or shit his pants, but the noises he's making are enough to set me off. I laugh lightly, despite the situation, and shake my head.

"What. The fuck. You doing, Scott?' he heaves out, panting between breaths.

"Waking your drunk arse up, you smelly tosser. You think your dad was gonna do it?"

"What the fuck are you on about?"

I roll my eyes and sigh. "Mate, it's Tuesday."

Ethan looks confused once he's finished grunting and shoving his face into the carpet. I'm not sure he even knows which room he's in, let alone what day it is. Yeah, so much for laying off the booze.

Today needs to be over already.

Something tells me this is going to be harder than my worst nightmares could have anticipated.

Chapter Four

It feels like only yesterday we said our goodbyes to Julia. The days are whizzing by at lightning speed, and yet, everything is still as grim as it was the day we found out about the accident. The funeral went as well as it could go. The church was full to the brim, and it appeared that the whole community wanted to pay their respects to Julia and the family. Mum was a huge help. She had prepped and packed all the food so Mr. Walker didn't have to stress over it. The boys didn't say much, but I knew they were thankful, even if they didn't voice it.

But the funeral is only ever the start of it. The grief that follows is a long journey. Longer than any of us can truly prepare ourselves for – especially three fucked up lost boys from Manchester.

So it's no surprise that Ethan isn't dealing with it very well. I can't blame him. I'm not sure I could cope if I lost my mum, but this is different. Things have changed, and I'm not used to Ethan shutting me out the way he suddenly seems to be doing. How do you help someone who doesn't want your help? How do you find the line between being supportive and being a nuisance? I know he needs time, but I'm not used to feeling helpless around him. The days following the funeral are mostly spent in an uncomfortable silence, not knowing whether I am coming or going, not knowing if Ethan really wants me around. Another thing I'm not accustomed to. He's always been the one solid thing in my life, and it feels like now… now all of that is being tested before either of us is ready.

"Where the fuck are we going, Scott?"

I'm lost in my own thoughts, somehow forgetting that E is sat in the passenger seat beside me. I guess that happens a lot lately, too. I seem to be trapped in my own bubble of thoughts, none of which are ever any good, trying to figure out what to do and how to do it. I spend most of my time cursing God for taking a good life too soon, or battling an uncontrollable anger inside of me, one that's burning to break free. Nothing makes sense anymore.

"I thought you said we were going to a party?" he chimes in, craning his neck so he can see past the car in front.

I've dragged him out this evening, and although spying on Liam isn't exactly my idea of fun, it's something to do that doesn't involve hiding away from the world. Like me, E loves nothing more than winding my older brother up when he gets the chance to, and Ethan needs a distraction – one that doesn't involve him reliving the day he lost everything. He doesn't need to be holed up inside with only thoughts of Julia's death to keep him company. I don't know much about grief. I'm learning every damn day, but I do know that drowning yourself in torturous thoughts can't exactly be healthy. But the longer I think about it, the more uncertain I become about us heading out tonight. I'm not sure this is a great idea, after all. Our crowd of friends are never tactful when it comes to real life shit, and Julia's passing is a sore subject for anyone to engage in. Still, it's taken me almost two weeks to get him out of the house and I can't back down now. He needs to be back out in public. He needs to find himself.

He needs to remind himself he hasn't died, too.

Rolling my eyes, I shake my head. "We are, lad, but Liam's been acting weird as shit lately. More distracted than normal."

"We're following your brother?" he blurts out in question, a hint of confusion settling across his forehead before realisation sets in and a smirk that matches my own curls his lips.

Quirking a brow, I shift gears. "Exactly what I thought."

I knew he'd jump at the chance to spy on my bro. Liam is beyond confusing to most people. He's so fucking evasive, no one ever knows the backwards shit that's going on in his head, and this is an opportunity neither one of us can pass up. Normally, I wouldn't give a toss what Liam gets up to, but lately he's been acting differently. He spends more time in front of the mirror than I do, which doesn't seem possible, and his attire has changed completely. He actually does this whole double take thing while ruffling his hair. Prick! The weird thing is, I know none of it is for Amelia's benefit. He's never made this much effort with her, which only adds to the mystery. Who the fuck is Liam meeting and why does he hide it from Amelia?

We tail Liam and his Vauxhall as far as we can, not that it's hard, what with his car's disgusting brown exterior and those lime green lines all over the place. He looks like he's driving around inside a fucking mint *Aero*.

"Where is he going?" E muses out loud, and the two of us throw a few ideas around, but no matter what we come up with, none of it sits right with me. I'm pretty sure my brother is being a shady fucker again. Ethan is convinced it has something to do with surprising Amelia, whereas me? I have lower expectations of my older brother than that.

After a while, we pull up behind him when he finally draws to a stop. Not close enough to get noticed, but not too far away so we can't see shit, either. I don't recognise the building he parks outside of, and before Ethan or I can figure anything out, we are both carefully climbing out of my not so trusty *Beetle* to get a good look at what is going on. Liam is standing there, staring up at another building I have never seen before. I'm so lost in trying to work out where we are that I almost miss Ethan pulling out the hip flask full of alcohol that I gave him at the funeral to get through the worst few hours of his life. He doesn't see me eyeing him warily. He doesn't need to, and despite the prickling of unease that rolls down my spine, I don't let on that I'm worried for him. He's just a lad having a drink, right? What harm can he come to? I'm just about to look away when I see Ethan's expression change completely as he looks over at my brother. A spark of life comes back to his face all at once, like someone has just turned the lights on in his eyes for a second, as he lowers the hipflask from his mouth and blatantly stares, open-mouthed.

Frowning, I turn to see what has caught his attention, and when I see two girls walking closer to my older brother, I can't help but smirk. One of them, probably the cute little blonde, has clearly just caught E's eye. Ethan has never had trouble pulling the chicks. In fact, there's a long line of reserves that he could call and get satisfied by at the drop of a hat. A longer list than mine, the fucker. But the look on his face as he watches her – well, I've never seen that shit on him before. He wears it well, and I can't help but smile.

Then he moves forward, and if I wasn't so determined not to get caught out by Liam, I would let him go to her. But I can't risk it, so I step over to him and grab his arm, laughing as I do to bring him out of his love-struck trance and back to me.

"You got it bad, lad." I chuckle.

"What are you talking about?"

"Whatever, loser. You can lie to yourself but trying to lie to me is just useless."

He doesn't argue, instead choosing to throw some curse words my way, which make me smile even more. For one moment, it's like the old E is back here with me, and as he takes one last look at blondie, I know it's probably her I should be thanking for it. Instead, we both give it up as a bad job and head back into the car.

An hour later and we're waltzing through the open door of a house party I got wind of, my nose instantly screwing up in disgust at the distasteful music spilling out through the dodgy speakers. Despite our efforts, we're no closer to finding out what the fuck Liam is up to so now I need to find another way to keep Ethan busy.

We head to the kitchen, trying our best to tune out the depressing lyrics that make me want to slit my wrists, then do it again just to prove a point. I don't even get to smell the first whiff of alcohol before my eyes land on the town's very own she-bike.

Jessica fucking Gregory.

I love women as much as the next guy, but this lass is something else for all the wrong reasons. Sure, she's got a decent pair of tits and her arse isn't too shabby either, but she's a walking, talking disease who'd do anything to reel Ethan in and use him for whatever she can get.

I've learnt to block out her noise, which sounds more like nails running lengths on a damn chalkboard than the husky, you-know-you-want-me, seductive tone she tries to use to bait him. It's taken months of practice, but I've managed to perfect my technique enough that I don't have to listen to it anymore. Any other time and I'd probably let her get on with it, but not now when Ethan is so fragile. I can't keep quiet when her game plan is written all over her face.

"Go back to whatever hole you crawled out of, Jess. The answer is still no," I say for him, gritting the words out, shaking my head in sheer and utter annoyance.

Now I wish to fuck we'd followed that blonde girl he was crushing on. Ethan might've already staked his claim on the unknown blondie, but her brunette mate wasn't half bad either. In fact, she was perfection compared to the talent, or lack of it, in this joint.

"Fuck off, Scott. What are you, his conscience?"

"No. I'm his friend, and he doesn't need the likes of you sniffing around." I take the beer from Ethan's hand, and we make a quick exit from the kitchen to scout around, leaving Jessica's whiney noise lingering in the distance.

Weaving through the cramped hallway, we try our best

to dodge the clouds of smoke that definitely aren't caused by cigarettes. My eyes eventually land on a head of dark hair. I don't have to see her face to know she's a stunner. I've seen her around before but haven't yet had the pleasure of getting to know her. Her groupies practically hang off her every limb as they giggle and attempt to dance through their drunken haze and six inch stilettos.

"Fuck me, mate. Look at her," I whisper to Ethan, my gaze traveling farther down... and down. Legs that go on for miles beg for my attention. The shit I could do with those bronzed pins. My dick clearly has the same idea, straining against the zipper of my jeans as it wakes up, reminding me I didn't put any pants on this evening. *One less item in the way*, I think to myself.

I lean in, my eyes still locked on those legs. "I'll be right back."

My foot hangs in mid-air, almost taking the first step, but I stop abruptly and turn back to Ethan. *Shit!* I came here to cheer him up and keep an eye on him. I can't do that when I'm buried inches deep in some random lass. I look over my shoulder at the brunette and then back to Ethan, unsure what to do. I don't want to smother him, but I also don't want Jessica fucking Gregory getting her claws into him. I open my mouth to speak, but I'm quickly cut off.

"Mate, I don't need a fucking babysitter. Go get her," he instructs, nudging me back with a laugh. I give him a silent nod and glance towards the door leading to the kitchen to see if Jessica Gregory is lurking around. Maybe she's already found a replacement. Ethan should be safe, for now at least. With a final glance at E, I duck through the crowds once more, only acknowledging the few people I know that are actually worth my time. I down the rest of the bottle in one, sliding the empty on the shelf. It's like she can read my damn mind. Her big brown eyes find mine and suddenly no other fucker is in the room but us. I blow out a breath, almost cursing when some chancer slides up next to her, his sleazy hands groping her arse. My anger doesn't last long, though. She shoos him away with a flick of her long, dark locks and her eyes are back on mine again. A sexy little smile tugs at her lips while her friends scoot left and right, clearing a pathway that has us in direct line of one another.

"Alright, sweetheart. The name's Scott," I tell her, leaning in close.

"I know who you are, Scott," she says, rolling her big doe eyes, and I pull back, tilting my head in confusion. Clearly unimpressed, she shakes her head, her hair spilling over her face as she juts her hip. "Jake's house?" she adds, raising a perfect brow.

Nope. Still fucking confused.

"You don't remember, do you?"

I frown. "Of course I do. Ja… Lea…" *Shit!*

"Paige. It's Paige," she grinds out, shaking her head. "We became acquainted… In the bathroom… You wouldn't let me leave unless I showed you my–"

"Whoa! Okay, I get it," I cut in, tossing my hands in the air.

Dammit! I was so fucking hammered that night. But I'm sure I would remember if I'd had some lass in the bog – especially one who looks like a Greek fucking goddess.

My confused thoughts are interrupted by a full, enthusiastic belly laugh, causing me to frown and peer down. The girl, Paige, is hunched over, clutching her stomach.

"You should've seen your face," she says through short bursts of laughter. "I'm sorry. I couldn't resist."

What the fuck?

I guess that serves me right for getting completely fucking wasted. Maybe she was lying about already meeting me. I hope she is, because if there's one thing I've always found to be a guaranteed cock riser, it's a stunning looking woman who can match me pound for pound with her wit. Something tells me, I may have just found one.

******

"So what happened when his wife walked in?" I ask curiously.

Shrugging, Paige pulls the straw between her teeth, her eyes dancing with amusement. "She asked to join in."

"No way?"

"Yep," she says, popping the *p*.

Well that explains her "never engage in a one-night-stand" rule.

I chuckle and continue to smile at the lass who has got me completely fucking mesmerised. Unbelievable just doesn't cut it. She even manages to hold a conversation without the need to grope me every few seconds. It's oddly refreshing. I've learned a lot about her in the last hour, so much so that it almost feels like I've known her for years. I'm noticing the little things about her, too, like the small dimple that appears in her right cheek whenever she smiles a genuine smile, and how her deep brown eyes glisten when she speaks of her Uncle Keith back home. I can tell he's her favourite person in the world and that she clearly adores him. I also love how her little button nose scrunches up whenever another lass pays me even an ounce of attention. I'm glad I'm not the only one that finds it annoying. I've also learnt that she despises players and would never indulge in a one-night-stand, regardless of how hot the dude was and how well she knew him. I wonder for a second why she's still talking to me, but I shrug it off. I'm obviously not getting anything from Paige other than friendly chit-chat tonight, and I'm surprised by how much this doesn't seem to bother me for once.

The beers flow freely, the topic changing to high school and what happened after we left. Turns out she only moved here six months ago after being offered a job at the DVLA. I get the impression there's more to it than just moving for a chance at a new career, but I don't push her on it. I'm not in a position to ask questions. We all have skeletons buried deep within our closets, details we keep hidden from others in fear of the knowledge breaking free. Still, her smile doesn't break the whole time we speak, and man does she have a beautiful smile.

We talk, flirt and drink some more. I'm wound up so tightly I can almost hear my limbs beginning to snap under the pressure. I'm horny as fuck, and watching her pearly white teeth graze the pink of her full bottom lip is driving me crazy. I want to taste her lips to see if they're as sweet as they look. Enough is enough. I snatch the red solo cup from her hand

and toss it to the floor amongst the others, capturing her lips between my teeth.

"Scott?"

I was right. Sweet as fuck! I want more. I don't give her the chance to speak again. My dick is as hard as a steel rod, and fuck if I can take it anymore.

Her lips part, surprising me as she grants my tongue access to explore her even more. I grip her hips, tugging her close. All the while, her fingers trail down my chest, drawing an invisible path to my groin. A hot as hell moan escapes her that does nothing to ease the ache behind my jeans and fuck if I don't want her to touch me again.

"Fuck!" she groans out, nipping my lower lip with her teeth as I push her back against the wall, caging her in with my arms.

"Can you feel what you're doing to me?" I ask, pressing my erection against her.

"Mmhmm. Upstairs. Please," she pleads between hard kisses, her voice turning to pure sex.

"I thought you didn't do one-night stands?" I ask, pulling back slightly.

Shrugging, she fists my shirt in her hand, tugging me closer. "People change."

I search her eyes but they don't waver. Either she's good at lying or she really means it. I don't question her any further. I'm already pushing her out of the door and up the stairs before she has the chance to change her mind.

As we near the top, I jerk her hips flush against mine and take that hot little mouth again. Our tongues and hands become sloppy and misguided as we search aimlessly for an unoccupied room.

I'm about five seconds from giving up, and I curse more than ought to be possible, until I shove open the last door on the landing, revealing nothing but darkness. Thank fuck, because if she continues to rub my dick any longer, I'm pretty sure I'm going to come in my damn jeans.

I grip her arse and haul her off the ground, her red dress riding up just enough for me to see the tiny lace thong she's sporting underneath. "Damn, sweetheart. I'm gonna enjoy peeling this off you." I growl, hooking a finger through the small piece of fabric and letting it snap back into place.

Paige hisses under her breath and I push her back onto the mattress, settling myself between her legs.

"I want you, Scott. I've wanted you since I first laid eyes on you."

Pressing my hands flat to her thighs, I push her legs farther apart, grinding my hardness against her heat. "Now you can have me," I reply with a smug grin, pushing her dress up and around her waist.

"Shit!" I curse, shaking my head in wonder. "I'm really, really going to enjoy this."

Her lightly bronzed legs fall limply to the side and I run my fingers along the underside of her thighs to see if they're as soft as they look. A light speckling of goosebumps breaks out over her otherwise flawless skin and her eyelids flutter closed.

Dropping my elbows to rest above her head, I lean in, pressing my lips to her ear as I begin to nibble and kiss along her jawline. Fuck, shit, fuck! I curse inwardly and press a hard kiss to the corner of her mouth. "I'll be right back. No glove, no love."

"Please hurry," she purrs, propping herself up on her elbows and spreading her legs wider.

"Fuck!" I growl, darting out the door and down the stairs like a horny virgin.

I hunt around for Ethan but don't see him, so after robbing a condom off a guy called Ben, I leg it back up the stairs, taking them two at a time. Knowing E, he's probably getting lucky, too. I know his story won't be as good as mine, though. I have the hottest girl at the party, and she's waiting for me with open legs. Damn, I'm one lucky son of a bitch.

"Sorry it took so long. I couldn't find a–" I freeze in the doorway, both hands clutching the framework as I study the beauty currently sprawled out on the bed, snoring softly. "Condom..."

Nice one, Scotty! Blowing out a breath, I kick my shoes off and crawl onto the bed next to her, releasing a soft chuckle.

I can't contain my goofy grin as I close my eyes and tuck my arms under my head.

So tonight hasn't exactly gone according to plan, but funnily enough, I'm not pissed about it. For the first time in my life, I find myself enjoying the moment. No expectations. No worrying whether I'll regret this in the morning. We've had a great night, and I'm about to fall asleep next to a beautiful girl who I haven't had to have sex with in order to forget the shittier things going on in my life. And isn't that a new feeling for me?

Chapter Five

Life is different now. Getting my head around how quickly things have changed in just a few short weeks is a task in itself. I've tried everything to keep the Walker brothers going – checking in on them and making sure they get up for work. Even chucking dirty laundry in the machine has become a sort of routine lately – only I'm not sure they appreciate me being there most of the time, but someone needs to be. Someone needs to quietly step in and show them that they aren't alone. Mr. Walker certainly isn't doing shit. E's younger brother, Dean, surprisingly, seems to be coping. He doesn't really talk much or show any ounce of emotion, but then again, that's Dean all over. He's always been the same. It's like he isn't sure if it's even real, and that's an emotion I can definitely relate to. As for Ethan, he doesn't talk about Julia at all now that she's gone. I thought that once the funeral was over with, life would start to slowly ease back to normal. Well, as normal as it can be. It would be different, sure, so I wasn't expecting miracles. Grief is dealt with in different ways, and at one point, I was certain that Ethan's coping mechanism would be booze. That thought alone scared me enough, but the night of the party proved that alcohol isn't the only drug that exists in this world, and I hate myself for leaving him alone.

I should have covered all bases when I walked away. E said he didn't need a babysitter, but that was a load of bullshit, and deep down, I think I knew it. I guess because he's always been the strong one, I thought that he could still say no. I thought that he would cop off with a beautiful, leggy brunette, or maybe, at worst, that redhead chick he once had a thing with back in high school. I thought he'd probably drink himself into a deep sleep, fall flat on his back and snore the night away. What I never, ever expected to find the morning after, was Ethan looking at me like he'd just seen a ghost. I didn't expect him to tell me that, while I was off getting my groove on with Paige, his drink was being spiked by Jessica fucking Gregory. What I didn't expect was for Ethan to tell me he'd slept with her, that she'd fucking tricked him into seeing her as something she could never be: desirable.

I feel like going straight to the police, and all I can think of as the events go through my mind is that if their roles had been reversed and a guy had done that to a girl, all hell would break loose, and rightly so. But what's the fucking difference for my mate? Why should she get away with doing what she did to him?

Why is everything so goddamn messed up?

I can't seem to catch a break, or find a way to help. No matter what I do, I mess things up, and in the process, my best buddy is slipping further and further away from me. It's like I'm trying to cling on, but his hands are greased up and I just cannot find a good grip to hold on.

I've let him down.

I've been doing the same thing all week since the party – driving out here, dimming the lights, cutting the engine and sitting here for hours on end just to make sure he's alright.

Drugs...

Since the night of the party, things have changed. Ethan has changed. I know he secretly found some kind of numbness in that disgusting, drug induced moment with Gregory – a state of calm that he probably hasn't felt since Julia died. I should never have left him so I could pursue Paige. The girl is unbelievable, but it wasn't worth the shit Ethan has found himself caught up in. Fucking drugs? I've never been against them myself. Each to their own and all that. At least, I wasn't against them, not up until now. I've never dabbled in them, having never really felt the need to. I live off life, challenges and individual moments. They give me a buzz that I'm pretty certain not even drugs can match up to. Alcohol, yes. But even then I know my limits, and it never really makes me feel unlike myself. I don't need any substances to turn me into something I'm not.

Watching my mate slowly slip away from me, from the world... Well, it's hard to deal with, let alone watch. But what other choice do I have? That shit that E got a taste of? It isn't going to work. It isn't going to help him forget. It's not easing or removing the pain. It's just freezing it, putting it on pause, but when that shit wears off... I can't bear to think about what he will do. The buzz of drugs only lasts so long before the reality of what's happened kicks in with a sodding big bang.

Before I realise it, I'm secretly checking up on him more than I'm taking care of myself. The house always looks the same, but whenever I see him, his eyes seem to have lost that little bit more life than the last time I saw him. He can deny using all he wants, but I know what's happening. I'm not stupid. I just don't know how the hell to save somebody that doesn't want to be saved anymore. I'm too young for this.

I've not really had much time to grieve for what I've lost. It still sits raw. But just watching my best mate buzzing off his tits is enough to push any sort of grief aside so I can deal with the inevitable.

All I can do is be here, even if he hates me for it. If he's adamant on using drugs to keep him afloat, he's going to have to get used to me acting like his surrogate mother.

As the weeks roll on by, I make sure he gets up for work on a daily basis, forcing my way into his house and food down his throat because I know the second my back is turned, it won't be food slipping down that fucking neck of his. Seeing him so out of himself is the scariest, hardest thing I've ever had to witness, and the decline seems to happen so quickly. How come only a few weeks ago we were living a fairly normal life? How can so much go so wrong in such a short space of time? I've seen shit, but nothing like this. Witnessing it firsthand just makes me hate the stuff even more. The worst thing is, it's like he doesn't care at all anymore. Not about himself, not about Dean, not about what his mum would think of it all…

Sometimes, when I'm not looking out for him or making sure that skank Jessica stays away from him, I can't help but go there in my mind and wonder how Julia must be feeling from up above. Can she see what I'm seeing? Is she as disappointed in Ethan as I am? Is she cursing me for not doing enough to help him?

Again, I find myself pulling up outside his home and cutting the engine. The Walker house is dark, the curtains almost always drawn these days, with no sign of life ever really appearing behind the oak-stained door. Sliding my phone off the dashboard, I peer down at the text message displayed on the screen.

PAIGE

THANKS FOR BEING A GENT. I PROBABLY WOULD HAVE HATED MYSELF THE MORNING AFTER FOR LETTING THINGS GO TOO FAR. I'M NOT NORMALLY LIKE THAT. HONEST. ANYWAY, SORRY IT'S TAKEN ME SO LONG TO GET IN TOUCH, I JUST HAD TO WRAP MY HEAD AROUND IT ALL, BUT I NOW FEEL LIKE I SHOULD MAKE IT UP TO YOU. FANCY MEETING FOR A DRINK? NO REPEAT. BROWNIE'S HONOUR! X

I did the unimaginable that night of the party and gave Paige my number. She's different, and at the time, the thought of seeing her again seemed like a good idea. Now, though, I'm not so sure. It's because of my lack of resistance towards her that Ethan's found himself in this mess. I don't have time to engage in any sort of romance. I need to focus on Ethan and Ethan alone. But as I stare down at the message, my finger idly stroking the reply button, I can't even attempt to hold back a frown.

No repeat? I'm not sure whether I should feel pissed or thankful. For once, my charm hasn't worked. I don't know why, but it feels kinda good and I can't help but feel a challenge coming on. E is under the impression that I fucked her, and I need him to believe that. I can't tell him that since his mum died, I've found it hard to indulge in anything good. I can't make his mum's death about me when it's not. Not that my lack of sex drive is completely down to that, and who knows, if Paige hadn't fallen asleep, maybe I would've taken her, and suddenly, I can't seem to help the reply that I eventually find myself sending back.

FUCKING SOMEONE UNDER THE INFLUENCE ISN'T EXACTLY MY STYLE. IN SOME PLACES IT'S DEEMED AS RAPE. WHEN I FUCK YOU IT WILL BE BECAUSE YOU BEGGED ME TO. WHERE AND WHEN? SCOTT.

Lie.

Of course I have every intention of eventually fucking her, but I also need her to believe that I'm not a complete arse. Even if we aren't going to fuck, I still want to keep her around – for distraction purposes only, of course. She's a nice girl. We have a lot in common, and to be honest, I could really do with a reliable friend of my own right now.

******

I sit across from Paige, grinning. After getting over the initial awkwardness at having to face me again, she seems to have relaxed and the conversation has, thankfully, turned into laughter. As soon as I had spotted her at the bar, I'd remembered why I felt instantly drawn to her that night of the party. The white denim jeans she's wearing hug her curves in all the right places. I couldn't help but stare as she leant over the bar, searching the drinks cabinet. Her hair is pulled down again and flowing across her shoulders in loose waves. The summer has obviously agreed with her. The black, off the shoulder shirt she is wearing exposes the sun-kissed glow to her skin. She really is beautiful. Add in her obvious stunning looks and the way she comes out with the most random and inappropriate shit, and I've got myself a right little gem here. I'm not sure if she's rambling because she's nervous, but I really hope it doesn't stop. Light-hearted fun is what I need right now, and Paige is doing a cracking job at giving me exactly that. For the first time since Julia's death, I don't feel the need to check my phone constantly. I'm always on high alert, awaiting a call to say that Ethan has got himself into trouble or that he's done something outrageous while high. I'm always waiting to hear the name Jessica Gregory again.

"So, you left pretty quickly that morning. Not that I care. In fact, you did me a favour. I don't deal well with rejection, or that awkward morning after the night before scenario. Was there a reason behind the quick exit, or should I just take it as you being... well, you, I guess?" She shrugs, pulling the drinking straw between her teeth with her eyes trained on mine.

I chuckle against the rim of the bottle I'm drinking from, and shake my head. "You want the honest truth?" I ask with raised brows. "Ethan. The mate I came to the party with?" I pause, allowing her time to recollect. She nods, prompting me to continue. "Let's just say, he doesn't exactly cope well with the whole morning after the night before thing, either. Especially waking up next to a lass that spiked his drink to get him in the sack."

"Jessica?"

"You know her?" I hit back with a frown. Damn. Paige is sweet and I struggle to think how the hell the two girls, complete opposites, could be friends.

"Eh, no. Not really. I mean, I've heard of her, but I tend to stay clear of vapid bitches like her. No brains, just tits, you know the type? I'm pretty sure her double D *Wonderbra* hates her, too."

"Well, it's good to know I'm not alone in my feelings for Jess. Anyway, what was I saying?" I ask, shuffling in my seat.

"You were about to come up with some dumb arse excuse as to why you left me," she says nonchalantly while quirking a perfect brow.

I don't normally care what women think of me. I've never claimed to be any different or something special. They know what they're getting into, but somehow, hearing cynicism about me from Paige has me feeling like a dick, and I quickly find myself wanting to correct her, reassure her that I'm not as bad as she thinks I am. "No excuses. Like I said, Ethan needed to get away and I was driving, so..."

"Bros before hoes, right?"

"Something like that. Although, you should know he's not usually someone who needs looking after. That morning was—"

"It's okay. I'm not mad or anything," she interrupts. "I get it. He's your mate. I'd have done the same thing if I were you."

"You would?"

"It shows you're a good guy."

I sink back in my chair, relieved.

"He's okay though, right? Ethan, I mean... After the drugs and all?"

I'm not sure how to answer that question. Is he okay? No. But maybe things aren't as bad as I think. I could be overreacting.

"He's good. As good as anyone who's just lost their mother can be anyway."

"Wow. I'm sorry. I had no idea. For what it's worth, Jess is a bitch. If it wasn't your friend, it would've been someone else."

She's right. Jess doesn't back down from anything. If she wants it, she'll get it. I nod and tilt the bottle to my lips, swallowing the last drop.

"You're right," I agree, pushing my back against the chair. "And you've just reminded me... I'm sorry. There's somewhere I need to be. Thanks for the drink, though. It's been real nice to catch up with you," I say, taking a stand.

"Oh yeah, sure. I didn't realise it was so late. My bad. So, we're friends?" she asks, her eyes hopeful.

"You think you can handle me as a friend?" I smile.

"I think I can handle anyone." Her eyes are bright and filled with mischief, and it makes my grin grow even wider before I shake my head and laugh in response.

"Okay, buddy. Friends," I agree as I lean down and press a kiss to her cheek. "I'll see you around, Paige."

"Definitely! And Scott?" she calls out. "I'm still not sleeping with you."

"Did I ask you to?" I hit back, raising a brow.

"No, but you will. They always do."

"You sure about that, sweetness? I'm not like every other guy out there."

"You're definitely one of a kind, Scott Jenkins." Something about the way she says that has me feeling like I've done something right with someone for once.

"This isn't over." I point.

"Go see your friend. Get outta here." She laughs.

I chuckle back and shake my head again as I push through the door into the open air. The darkness taunts me like a nightmare, swallowing me up. I shrink inside my jacket and unlock the car.

Ethan might be using drugs as an escape from the real world, but it's still early days. I can still pull him back from this. I can make him see me through the fog. If anyone can make him see sense, it's me. It's time to start believing in myself a little bit. No other fucker is going to do it for me.

Chapter Six

September 2002

"How is Ethan holding up?" Mum asks, handing me a bottle of my favourite liquid while trying her damnedest to ignore the shouting that's coming from upstairs.

Shrugging, I dig my nail into the label and begin to peel it away. What can I say that she doesn't already know?

"It's expected, love. He needs time to adjust. It's been a huge shock for everyone. I'm glad he has you, though," she says, nudging my arm with a soft smile.

"And Kev," Dad chimes in, his attention solely on the football game showing on the TV.

"Yeah, 'cause he really spends all his time concentrating on the boys and not the empty pint glass down the local," I reply, sarcasm dripping from every damn word.

"He's grieving, too, Scott. Remember that."

I do remember that. It's hard not to. Mr. Walker hasn't given Ethan or Dean the time of day since Julia passed away. He would rather hide himself away in our local boozer than console his grieving boys.

"Yeah, and they're still only kids," I mumble to no one in particular.

The shouting continues to grow deafeningly louder.

"Seriously? Are they gonna carry this on for the entire evening? If so, I'm outta here," I say, rolling my eyes for the fourth time in a matter of minutes and wishing I had taken Paige up on her offer to head into Manchester for the evening.

I glance at Mum who has her head tilted to one side while her eyes search the ceiling. Sighing, she shakes her head and looks to my father, who doesn't appear to be all that fussed with the shouting and screaming coming from upstairs. "Brian, maybe you ought to go and see if everything's okay up there." It isn't a request. She's just as annoyed as I am.

"Does it sound like it's fucking okay up there?" I mumble, pushing to a stand.

"Language, Scott," my dad warns, boring his beady eyes into me.

My language? You have got to be shitting me? My vocabulary is extensive when it comes to cursing, but I'm pretty sure Liam has stolen my crown for how many swear words you can spit out in the last half an hour. Not that I'm surprised. My dad has been permanently pissed at me since quitting.

I've stayed true to my word and never returned to the job. I went into town last week and applied to a few articles in the local paper. It's mainly bar work and the odd delivery job, but it's a start. When my dad found the pile of application forms on the kitchen counter he just laughed. The dick didn't think I was serious but I proved him wrong yesterday when I got a call from one of the bars I applied to work at. It's a student bar that has been around as long as I can remember. It's run down and in need of some serious work, but it has potential. I didn't think twice about my answer, and my dad's been pissy ever since.

Amelia hasn't even been here an hour yet, and she and Liam are already at each other's throats, kicking off and throwing shit around in his bedroom. If they aren't fucking, they're arguing. Their whole relationship is pointless, if you ask me. Who wants that much hassle in their life? It's enough to put me off having any form of relationship, ever, not that I have any desire for one anyway. No. Meaningless hookups I can do, but hearts and flowers just aren't my thing. I'm too young for that shit. I can't seem to take care of myself, let alone a damn chick who wants cuddling and spooning all night long.

"I guess I'll go up and sort them both out then," I mumble against the rim of the bottle pressed to my lips.

More yelling.

More smashing.

I pause on the bottom step. A door slams.

Leaning against the banister, I take a swig of my drink and wait for it. I know what's coming.

Her legs are the first thing I notice. Then again, she has always had a great set of great pins. It's hard for any hot-blooded male to ignore them, especially bare, with the exception of a jean skirt that could be pulled off as a damn belt. It's just a shame about all the other shit that goes with it. Nice legs, bad attitude. I refrain from rolling my eyes when I hear her dramatic sobs begin to filter down the stairs. I wonder what Liam has done wrong now. Then I remember that I couldn't care less.

"Trouble in paradise?" I say, smirking as the rest of her figure comes into view.

It takes a few seconds for her to notice me, but when she does, her lips pucker and her brows dip into a frown. "Fuck off, Scott."

I chuckle and wave a hand. She scurries past me, tripping on the welcome mat. "Might wanna check your face before you leave, darling. You look like shit." She doesn't listen to a word I'm saying, but it would seem out of character of me if I didn't partake in teasing Amelia fucking Chamberlin.

"What's up with you two?" she yells, wafting her hand around in the air. "Is it in your genes to make my life hell? To be absolute arseholes?"

"We take after our dad." I shrug. "And you're just too easy to piss off. What can I say?"

"Well, I am so fucking pleased you find this amusing, Scott. Now, why don't you run along and find your next whore and leave me the hell alone?"

She blows a strand of blonde hair from her face and huffs out in annoyance.

Sucking in a quiet breath, I push a foot forward and stalk towards her.

Her eyes widen and she takes a step back just as I take another step forward.

"You know, if I didn't hate your prissy arse so much, I'd wipe that attitude and anger right off your face."

"Threatening a girl? Wow! I didn't know you had it in you," she retorts, crossing her arms over her chest and jutting her hip.

I hold back a grin and trail the rim of the bottle across her bare shoulder. "Trust me, sweetheart. That wasn't a threat. And you have no idea what I'm capable of."

Her mouth opens but quickly closes.

I lean in, pressing my mouth to her ear. "Don't think I haven't noticed the way you look at me. You're angry with me because you want me."

She shivers against me, causing me to chuckle and pull back. "You sure it's not you who wants me?"

"No, babe. You're not my type. I wouldn't touch you with a borrowed dick."

"I…"

"Mum? Dad? I'm going out," I call over my shoulder before swatting Amelia's arse and leaving her standing there, frozen in the doorway.

****

"What did you say to Amelia? She's been blowing up my phone all night, cursing your motherfucking arse." Liam says as soon as I walk back into my bedroom an hour later.

I try to keep a straight face but the twitch at the corner of my mouth doesn't hold out. "Not sure what you mean, brother. I saw her come down the stairs, said hello and left right after," I lie. "Why? What did she say now?"

Liam blows out a breath that almost sounds defeated and I

busy myself by rummaging through the wardrobe.

"Fuck knows. She's been acting crazy as hell lately."

Shrugging, I pull a fresh towel down from the top shelf and glance sideways. "And you haven't done anything to make her that way?"

"Not that I can think of. I dunno. I just don't get it. She used to be sound, you know? Always let me do what I want. The old Meli wouldn't check up on me twenty-four/seven. Now I can't catch a damn break. All she wants to do is stay in, watch movies, and fucking cuddle. What the hell? I feel like a fifty-year-old stuck in a twenty-one year old's body."

"Maybe she's on to you."

"On to me? What the hell are you talking about?"

"All I'm saying is, I've noticed. Ethan's noticed. Maybe Amelia has, too."

"Noticed what?"

"This." I point out, gesturing to the pressed shirt that hugs his torso and the light wash jeans. "You've changed, mate. You trying to impress someone else?"

He narrows his eyes at me, shaking his head. "You're just as bad as her. I didn't realise I needed your approval when it came to my wardrobe, *Mum*. And so what if I've decided to smarten myself up. It's not a damn crime."

I toss the towel over my shoulder and throw both hands up in surrender. "You're right. It's none of my business… even though it kinda sounded like you were asking for my advice, but what the hell? I'm gonna take a shower. That's if there's any hot water left."

I make quick work of stripping out of my jeans and boxers,

and run the shower, turning the dials to the correct temperature before stepping under the spray. Despite it being cooler than I'd like, it's enough to wash away the day's grime and leave me feeling refreshed. Only it doesn't last long.

"What the hell?" I growl out, cradling myself from the ice-cold downpour.

"I think I might call things off with her," Liam says casually, turning the tap off over at the sink.

"Great. Could you not have waited for me to finish my damn shower before throwing that shit on me?"

"Do you think I should?" he asks, like I'm not stood butt naked right in front of him.

"What?" I squint.

"Call it off with Amelia."

"Are you shitting me, right now?"

"Just answer the question, Scott."

"Who the fuck cares? Get out of here," I curse, whipping the shower curtain from the pole and hugging it tightly to my chest.

He chucks his head back, laughing at my awkwardness. Only Liam could laugh after announcing he's splitting from his long-term girlfriend. "I just want your advice. No need to be a twat about it. Anyone would think it was your time of the month, you big girl."

"Go fuck yourself. There, that's my advice."

"Wouldn't life be simpler if we could actually do that shit?"

"Okay, fine. You want my honest advice?" I ask, reaching for the towel at the dry end of the bath tub. "Do us all a favour and get rid of her. I can't stand the woman and it's not like you love her or anything, right?"

"That simple?"

"That simple." I nod.

"Her mother will kill me."

"You big fuckin' baby. Now who's the big girl?"

"Fuck you, man. You've met her. You can't tell me you ain't scared of her."

"You're right," I agree, tucking the towel around my waist. "She scares the shit outta me. Not enough to make me stay with the lass, though."

I brave the biting cold again and switch the shower off.

"Fuck, I don't know what to do. She's a pain in my arse, but I can't be bothered with all the aggravation that'll come with a split. Amelia cries like a fucking monkey. She never stops. I'm just gonna stick it out for a bit. Besides, she gives great head," he adds, shrugging.

That's my cue to tune him out. Too much info, dick.

"What? It's not like you'd turn her down," he says with a smirk.

"Not my type, kid."

"You have a type?"

"Not really, but I avoid bitches, whiners and drama queens."

"Whatever. Trust me, if she got down on her knees in front of you, you'd be converted."

"You're sick."

"It's all part of my charm." He laughs.

With that, Liam finally turns around and leaves me, and as I dry myself off, I try not to think about Amelia's lips around my cock. The way she shuddered against me was, admittedly, fucking hot as hell. It did wonders for my ego, but then again, any form of reaction from any decent looking woman would have done the same. I refuse to think about her like that, though. She's the least of my current worries. Tomorrow I start my new job. I need a clear head and to not be distracted with disturbing thoughts of my brother's missus.

Chapter Seven

The following day...

I've woken up this morning feeling refreshed and ready to tackle my first shift at the bar. I've almost forgotten about Liam's comment until his girl in question struts into my bedroom like she owns it, her tight little arse swaying from side to side in heels that have to be at least six inches high and have been worn to be noticed. If I wasn't still horny from my relentless thoughts last night, I most definitely am now. Her hair cascades around her shoulders in soft waves and she's wearing more makeup on her face than I usually like on a girl. But even I have to admit that she looks damn hot. Liam is in so much trouble. There's no way he's going to be able to let her go. No way at all.

I leave them to it, and for the first time in my whole existence, I find myself a little thankful that I am forced to share a room with my brother.

Perks of the prison sentence.

I throw on a pair of jeans and fitted grey t-shirt, accompanying the outfit with a black leather belt. Then I'm all set for work. Or at least I think I am.

Des – my new boss – calls me ten minutes before I am due to leave to ask if I mind changing my early shift to a late one. I tell him I don't mind, not wanting to sound like an awkward employee before I've even begun working for him. The evening shifts are always busier, anyway. Unlucky for me, it also means I have a whole seven hours to kill before that shift starts.

The day doesn't drag nearly as much as I think it will, though. I try to call Ethan but it goes straight to voicemail. I leave him a message, telling him my plans for the day, not really knowing if he will even listen to it. The sad thing is, I'm not even sure he's aware that I've landed myself a new job, so I tell him all about it, and I even tell him of my not-so-secret hopes of him somehow stopping by during my shift. Moral support and all that. It feels strange not having that from him anymore. As the night rolls on by, and the longer I get into my first shift, the more I realise that I haven't been thinking straight about any of it. It was dumb of me to invite him here, especially around all these high people. Especially if *he* is high. I'd lose my job before the night's out for dragging in the wrong clientele and then I'd be back at square one. Des seems like a decent enough boss so far, but I can tell he doesn't stand for drugs in the bar and I can't argue with that.

"You're doing good. And no spillages. The boss will be pleased," the pretty blonde whose name I can't remember says as she slips past me with a tray of dirty glasses.

"Thanks. As far as first shifts go, this one's been a breeze."

"Yeah? Well don't get too comfy. It's normally busier than

this. We started you on a good day," she says, flashing me a smile over her shoulder.

I lean against the bar, folding my arms across my chest. "What? You don't think I can handle it?"

"Oh, I'm sure you can, pretty boy." She eventually grins, slamming the door on the dishwasher once it's loaded up. "I wasn't talking about the workload. I'm almost certain you can handle that," she compliments me flirtily, tossing her long blonde hair over her shoulder. "Have you noticed how there aren't any females in here tonight? I mean, other than me?"

I furrow my brows. "Yeah. What's with that, anyway?"

Shrugging, she leans forward and pulls a tumbler from behind me, her fingers lightly brushing my arm. "It's Tuesday. Males only night."

"What, is that even a thing?" I ask, ignoring the way her eyes graze over my groin.

"Not really, but D likes to mix things up, try new ideas. He thought it would make this place a safe haven for the guys, away from nagging women and cheap whores, even if only for one night of the week. Eventually he'll scrap it when he realises it's just another one of his shitty ideas."

"So you did this on purpose?" I ask incredulously, hiding a hint of amusement.

"Like I said, it's a males only night. Less temptation for the male staff and less punters for the newbie to wait on. Makes sense you'd start tonight, I guess. We've all seen how Tom Cruise fucks it up in *Cocktail* on his first night." She giggles.

Nodding, I quirk a brow, having no idea what the fuck she's on about Tom Cruise for. "So, when's female night?"

She throws her head back, laughs and shakes her head. "You've got a lot to learn, pretty boy."

"What does that mean?" I whine as I follow closely behind her, picking up glasses along the way. "When is it?"

"There isn't one," she deadpans, dumping a stack of pint glasses on the few I've already collected.

"Where's the equality in that?" I grin cheekily.

"Do I need to remind you that you're here to work, not ogle the women?"

"Are you always this hostile to men, or is it just me?"

"No, it's just you," she says flippantly.

"What did I do?"

"You ask too many questions."

As the bell rings for last orders, I follow the girl, Darcie, around as she reels off a list of to-do's at the end of the night. It's all fairly simple really. Collect dirty glasses, wash, polish and put shit away. Sweep and mop the floor. I'm not entirely thrilled about that part but I'll do it if it means I get to hold down this job. I need this job, for security and for my own sanity.

By the end of the shift, Ethan still hasn't shown. A hint of disappointment settles within me but is quickly gone as Des and Darcie come back out from the kitchen and both congratulate me on a great first night.

Beside Darcie's outspoken demeanor, she actually seems like an all right lass. Her answers are always fiery and directly to the point, which is surprisingly refreshing. She's funny as hell which will no doubt make the painfully slow nights pass by at a more tolerable pace. I'm almost certain she's gay, but I figure we don't know each other well enough for me to ask her that outright so soon into our working relationship.

"Thanks. It was ace," I tell them honestly as I pull my keys from the inside pocket of my jacket.

"Good. So we'll see you tomorrow?" Des asks, raising both brows as if he isn't sure he will.

I nod. "Tomorrow."

On a final salute, I push through the red door and step out into the open air.

I have survived my first shift and I'm already looking forward to the next one. I just hope it isn't another "males only" night; otherwise that shit is going to get real old, real quick.

Males only. What the hell is he thinking? That he runs a damn strip joint?

******

Sleep came easily for me last night. Or this morning… whichever way you look at it. By the time I pulled up outside the house and crawled back into bed, it was after two in the morning. I guess it will take a while to get used to the different shifts, turning nocturnal in the blink of an eye and seeing less of the daylight than I'm used to. Still, that's better than early morning rises and days spent covered in grit and filth with my annoying brother.

After learning the initial layout of the joint and the rules, I easily settled in and found my feet. It helps that I've had Darcie there to keep me on my toes. I can already tell she wants to pull me under her wing and protect me. From what, I'm not sure, but she has that whole "motherly" instinct about her. That whole, "I'm gonna make your life hell, but you'll thank me for it," attitude. I guess I should be grateful that I haven't been partnered with a complete bore. Sure, she makes me work my arse off and whenever she sees me leaning against the bar, bored, she tosses me the stink eye, which is enough to have my feet moving quickly again.

I shower, dress and eat the breakfast mum has prepared for me. It's been, or at least it feels like a long time since she has cooked for me during the week. I normally have to fend for myself so when I see the already made-up plate of food in the kitchen when I come down the stairs, it takes me by surprise.

While she sits there reading a magazine, she asks me questions about work and how I got on. I half expect her to lay into me like dad would, but she seems genuinely interested. This morning is full of surprises and, unbeknownst to me, there are more of those little fuckers to come. My phone ringing cuts through her questions and I hit the green button absent-mindedly.

"Yep?"

"Scott? Is that you?" the voice on the other end of the phone asks. The signal isn't great and the line seems distorted.

"Who is it?" I frown.

"It's me," he answers roughly.

I push the phone closer to my ear as if it will help and say, "Yeah, E, I hear you. Where are you?"

"At some party, mate. Fuck knows where, but there are loads of chicks. You need to get your arse over here."

I don't have to ask; I already know that he is wasted. I guess that explains why I didn't hear back from him last night, too. Knowing Ethan of late, he's probably been out of it for days. Fuck.

Glancing at the clock on the wall, I ignore Mum's curious eyes and whisper, "I can't get there. I've got work, mate."

"Don't be a dick, man. I've got a beer here with your name on it. C'mon. I ain't seen you in ages, you ugly prick."

I want to ask him whose fault he thinks that is, but I can't form a single word that will sound aggressive or push him away, so I shake my head and inhale a deep breath. "Sorry," I reply. It's all I can manage to say as I scrunch my eyes shut.

"Your loss. In that case, I gotta go. There's this hot–"

The line goes dead and I stare down at my phone in disbelief.

Who the fuck is that man?

Not a single question about why I have to work tonight or where I'm going to be? The insults, the bored tone of his voice when he's speaking to me… It's like the Ethan I once knew has gone, and in his place is a fucked up, drugged up, male version of the very woman he used to despise: Jessica fucking Gregory.

One day she will pay for what she's done to a good man. One day, I hope karma makes her sorry for ruining so many lives, just so she could get her hands on Walker. If there was any kind of justice in the world, Julia would still be alive and it would be people like Jess who would die too soon.

But the more time goes on, the more I'm beginning to realise…

There is no justice.

Nothing seems fair.

We're all just winging this shit. We're all struggling to survive, each day at a time.

Maybe it's time I found a way to wing my own life without Ethan by my side.

Chapter Eight

May 2003

I blow out a breath and dump the last box on the granite worktop, taking a look around.

The musky, unused scent of time stood still clogs my lungs, and I push off the counter to open a few windows. My trainers squeak against the freshly-laid wooden flooring as I cross the open-plan living room to the wall of windows.

It turns out I can't save Ethan at all, and here I am, eight months later, without him. You can't save anybody that doesn't want to save themselves. I've learned that the hard way. Yet, I've always thought about this day, even hoped this day would come sooner. But I didn't realise back then that Ethan would be so elusive and lost in a new life of drugs, sex and partying to numb his grief. We should be doing this together, right alongside owning our own business some day, or at the very least, making plans for it. Having a bachelor pad of our very own was also at the top of our to-do list, and here I am, achieving it all on my own. It just doesn't feel as sweet as I imagined it would, because he isn't here. Every plan we made doesn't seem possible anymore. Things have changed and I'm not sure we'll ever get back to that place again – that place where all our dreams fell in line, and were mapped out in our adolescent, naïve little heads. That place where the only thing that mattered was proving that we could make something of ourselves.

Proving everyone wrong.

Now it's May already.

Blossom litters the roads, and daffodils line the grass verges. Everything is coming to life right in front of my eyes. Yet, not even the spring can fill me with fucking joy. I'm stuck in an everlasting winter. Cold nights and emptiness.

I've hardly seen E since his dad kicked him out back in January. He's moved in with some stoners downtown. I tried to persuade him to move in with me, but he wasn't having any of it. He barely even registered what I was offering him, the thought alone proving enough for him to push out a short laugh and walk away. Above everything that he seems to stand for lately, the only thing that's really left of him is his pride. That remains firmly intact, and I wish it didn't. Despite him being adamant that he doesn't want to burden my parents with his troubles, I know deep down that he really needs help, even if he won't admit it to himself. The only hope I can cling on to is that if there is some pride still left deep down inside of him, one day he might just wake up and realise what a mistake he's made by going down the road he's chosen, and he'll come back to all of us. Me, my family, but most importantly, his little brother, Dean.

On the odd occasion when I do speak to him and he seems

slightly more sober and compliant than usual, he talks in tired slurs and exhausted groans. One time, I actually got him to admit out loud that he was an addict even though we both already knew it. I guess I thought hearing himself say it might have been enough to wake him up, but he was just resigned in his admission, like this was his life now, this was all he knew, and there was no going back. I told that fucker I loved him, that I was here for him and no matter how long he decided he needed to be away from me and what he used to know, I will always be around when he decides to come back. He's an addict, not a leper, and I need him to know that he's my brother. I may hardly recognise him, most days yet every so often I'll catch a glimpse of my best mate, the Ethan we all know and love, and my hope burns a little brighter those days.

But once that darkness flares back to life in his eyes, burying the good guy away again, I leave and force myself not to look back, even though it burns holes in my conscience every single time.

Today… today is about me now, and I'm moving into my swanky new apartment. I should be happy, celebrating even. Yet here I am, lugging box after box inside, staring blankly at the crates of *Bud* stacked on the kitchen counter and wishing for nothing more than to have Ethan here. But instead, I've got to act like I'm building a life for myself, just to please every other Tom, Dick and Harry. I'm existing, but I sure as shit ain't living yet.

You selfish bastard, Walker, I think to myself. *You selfish mother fucker. Look what you're doing to me. You're making me miss my own life because I'm so damn worried about you and yours, you prick.*

"I think this is the last one," Beth says, interrupting my thoughts, puffing out a breath and dumping what I hope is indeed the last box we have left to bring in.

"About damn time. Remind me never to do this again," I groan out, running my hands through my damp hair. "Moving sucks."

"Trust me," she says, pausing to dust her knees off. "If you do this again, don't expect me to help."

I chuckle and pull her down into a headlock. "Don't worry. I promise I won't ask for your help again."

"Get. Off. Me," she grinds out, trying to break free.

I release the hold I have on her and shake my head. "Seriously, though. Thanks for today."

"Not a problem, little brother. Anytime."

"Anytime?" I ask, lifting a brow in question.

"Nope. Ignore that last part. Never again! Not ever." A grin tugs at the corner of my mouth and I pull her in for a hug. She doesn't try to break free this time. Instead, she squeezes me tightly and smiles up at me. "I'm really proud of you, Scott. I know you have tonnes of shit going on, and I know you aren't one for opening up and all that, but I am here for you, you know? If you ever want to talk, that is."

"Thanks, sis. Duly noted, but really, I'll be fine."

Sighing, she claps my back once and pulls away. "Well, the offer is there. Just holler if you need me."

"Will do. Now get your scrawny arse outta here. I need to shower and rid myself of this day."

"Yeah," she interjects, scrunching her nose up in disgust.

"You do sorta stink."

Pointing to the door, I give her my best glare and mouth, "Go."

"Okay, okay," she says in a sing-song voice, throwing her hands up in the air. "Consider me gone."

As much as I don't want my sister hanging around on my first day in my new apartment, I can't help but feel the loss of her presence the second she leaves. I try to busy myself with unpacking and rearranging the artwork Beth took it upon herself to display, even after I insisted that I hated it. Having only accumulated enough boxes to fill a small room, it really doesn't take all that long to unpack. I've ordered the essentials – kitchen appliances and a top of the range flat screen and sound system – but they won't be here until late tomorrow. I've showered, moved the three-piece sofa for the third time, and cleaned the bathroom, but still the emptiness lingers. The crates of *Budweiser* on the kitchen counter silently mock me and I tug at the long strands of my hair in exasperation. I'm not in the mood to socialise, but a house party is the only way I'll stand any chance of pulling myself out of this woe is me hell I've fallen into.

****

I've rung round a few of the lads and arranged a get-together. I need some fun in my life. For one night, I need distracting. It doesn't take long for word to spread, and soon the place becomes Health and Safety's worst nightmare. The communal stairs are littered with tanked-up lasses and lads, and

I have to manoeuvre my way through the cramped hallway just to get through my front door after making a mad dash to the off-licence to pick up more beer.

I don't care that the neighbours have shown up more than once to put an end to the noise. I don't even care that the first impression they will be getting of their new neighbour is that he's a paralytic drunk who mistakes them for Jehovah's Witnesses yet still goes on to offer them shots long after they've confirmed they are, in fact, simply seventy-five and sleep deprived.

"Hey, Scott. There's some old chap banging on the door. He looks pissed as hell," Jake yells, zoning in on the peep hole.

"Ignore it, mate," I call back, grabbing Paige by the waist and nuzzling into her neck. "There're more bottles in the spare room. Help yourselves, just don't disturb me."

"Where you going?"

"Bed."

"Ah, c'mon, you ain't turning in already, are you? It's fucking early."

I have no idea what the fucking time is but I'm pretty certain he's right. It is early, and it's late. But it's definitely damn early. Daylight is slowly creeping in through the gaps in the blinds and the bloody birds are already chirping their tits off.

"I'm sure you can amuse yourself, Jay. I'm taking my girl to bed."

"Your girl?" Paige asks beside me, grinning up at me like she actually likes the sound of that.

"Damn right you are," I reply, kissing the top of her head

and pulling her to the bedroom, not really caring about the implications of what I've just said. Paige is comfort to me. She's warm, she's soft and she makes me forget all the bad stuff. It makes sense right now. Everything makes sense for just a moment of my time.

Stripping out of my trousers, I tug my shirt over my head before slipping under the covers. When I pat the spot beside me, Paige slowly slides in, still fully clothed.

"You okay?" she murmurs against my neck, her fingers trailing down my chest in lazy strokes. "You seem distant tonight. Not really here, even though you're next to me."

Paige is different to most of the girls I know and I like that. I like the fact we can lose track of time after spending hours talking about random shit and never get bored. Even after all the months I've known her, she's still a breath of fresh air – air that I seriously need right now. I can tell her anything and she won't judge me. Not to mention she's fucking hot. No, she listens, cares, and unlike the others, she takes an interest. She doesn't pretend to listen to me, or try and distract me with her tits. She understands me. I've told her all about Ethan and how I struggle to make him see sense. She knows he's a sore subject but that doesn't stop her from asking about him, and surprisingly, I tell her. Maybe because she always seems to ask the right questions at just the right time. She's becoming more like a friend and less like a lass I want to sleep with. Sure, I'm attracted to her. I'd be an idiot to feel otherwise. She's smart, funny and caring – all the qualities I need around me right now. We're yet to cross that line of being more than friends. She won't put out for just anyone, which makes me like her even more. We've done stuff. Foreplay, mainly. It only happens when we drink too much and need a release. If her blow jobs are anything to go by, I know that sex with Paige will be even more mind blowing than I can probably handle. Still, I knock that thought out of my head each time things get too heated because I know, the second I bury myself inside of her, things will change. She wouldn't just be another notch on the bedpost, and I'm not sure I'm ready for anything more.

She deserves someone who will look at her like she's the only woman in the room – the only one that matters. She deserves that hearts and flowers stuff. Right now, that isn't me. I can't be that for her. My head isn't in the game and I'd only end up hurting her. I've tried to back away. I've tried so fucking hard to ignore her, but the truth is, I need her. Whether she realises it or not, I need her, just not the way she deserves to be needed.

Without E, I have no one. There's no point in talking to him about my life and how I'm feeling. The fucker probably wouldn't remember it the next day, anyway. Obviously I keep tabs on Dean, but knowing the shit that I know, I need be careful around him. One slip and everything Dean has worked hard to fight off could break loose. He doesn't need the worry of his brother's drug addiction to knock him back. Sure, I have people in my life that care, but none of them let me be me. The closest person I have right now is Paige, and although having her around makes me feel good about myself, my true intentions will always outweigh that. I'm using her to fill a void, and one day soon she will realise that.

"I'm good. Tired. But good," I say on a yawn, lifting my

arm over her head and tugging her closer.

"I'm tired, too – tired of waiting for you to make a move on me. A girl can only wait so long, Scott."

I chuckle against her forehead, my lips barely brushing her hairline before I answer her. "You're a good girl, Paige."

"Yeah, so you keep telling me."

I don't have to see her face to know she's rolling her big brown eyes. She does it every time I tell her.

We've both had a skinful tonight, and although I've somehow managed to sober myself up, I still can't do that to her.

"Scott. Stop overthinking. We're both adults here, and I'm not naïve enough to think you want anything more than sex. It's just sex. Sex between two consenting adults."

"You don't know what you're saying."

"I know exactly what I'm saying. I want you."

"But…"

"I want to fuck you, Scott. Even if it only happens once."

Fuck! Why'd she have to go and say that? No lad in their right mind could turn down an offer like that. No strings sex with a Greek goddess? This girl will be the death of me.

"Just sex?" I ask with raised brows, challenging her. "You think you can handle that?"

"Just. Sex." She nods, a little too eagerly. "And I know I can. I'm not made of glass. I won't break if you drop me."

As I wrack my brain for an excuse as to why this is a really bad idea, soft fingers skim across my hip, tracing a pattern down to my groin.

"Paige…" I warn her.

"Scott..." she counters, curling her delicate fingers around the base of my cock through my boxers.

I groan in frustration as she tightens her grip and does this weird flip of her wrist that has my cock jolting and trying to break free. "Fine. Okay," I sigh in defeat. "Just remember it was you that asked for this. I simply gave you what you wanted. Don't hate on me when this is over." I groan, grabbing her thighs and lifting her to straddle me.

She wastes no time in removing her shirt, exposing her ample breasts, and I shift my hips, pressing my erection against her. At first the movements are slow and torturous. I take my time, savouring each whimper and soft moan as my mouth closes over her breast. My teeth clamp over her hardened nipple while my other hand comes up to the other, gently stroking and massaging the soft, pink flesh there.

"Wait..." I start to protest, something not feeling quite right, but her mouth seeks out mine again.

"Relax, Scott."

"Shit. I can't... We can't."

"No. No. No. No. This can't be happening."

I pull back and shift from beneath her, running my thumb across the corners of my mouth. "I'm sorry. I can't do this. It's not right."

"What do you mean, you can't? You've done this heaps of times, Scott. What the hell is wrong with me?"

"Excuse me?"

"Am I that disgusting to you?" Her frown is heavy, loaded with hurt feelings and bruised ego.

"What? No. It's not like that," I start to protest but my mind goes blank. There's so much I want to say. I need her to know this has nothing to do with her, but I can't. "I can't... I just don't... you're all I–"

"Scott?"

"Nothing."

"Scott."

Everything in me screams to get out and as far away from this girl as I possibly can. She doesn't need someone like me screwing with her head and giving her false hopes. I don't need it either. I'm already plenty screwed up over Ethan. I need Paige to be by my side, not against me, which she will be if I let things get too far.

I gaze up at her. Big brown eyes meet mine and I tug my bottom lip into my mouth, grazing it with my teeth as I wrack my brain for the words to make this right.

"What is it, Scott? Please, talk to me. What did I do?" Her voice quivers and the slight tremble of her lower lip has me feeling like a total jackass.

"Nothing. You did nothing wrong. You never do anything wrong. I'm sorry. C'mere," I say, pulling her close. "Those twats out there are sorta killing the moment. That's all it is. And I'm wasted. It's not right."

"We don't have to do anything. We don't. This... It's okay." She gazes up at me through long, thick lashes and I fight the urge to kick myself as her eyes glisten with unshed tears.

"Don't be silly," I say, pressing a kiss to her forehead. "I want to."

And that's it.

With three small words, my world has just got a whole lot

more complicated. I've promised her something in the future that I'm not sure I am ever going to be able to deliver.

Nice one, Scotty.

Chapter Nine

Between working shifts at the bar and looking out for E, I'm becoming not only physically exhausted, but mentally, also. I'd kill to go out on the lash, or have a few mates over to watch the footie. Fun... relaxed fun where I don't have to make promises of free booze, loud music and broken bottles. I'm not even sure I know the meaning of the word fun anymore. Even I wouldn't want to hang out with myself, these days. I'm miserable and moody, all the things I'm not used to feeling.

My body is worn out. I'm drained, at a complete loss with the world.

Having a few days off would normally bring me fucking joy, but as things are right now, it's giving me anything but. I know I'll be spending my free time worrying about that inevitable phone call about Ethan, or making sure he's coping, which of course, he won't be. I also know I have nothing around here to provide me with a distraction from everything that has happened these past nine months.

I've told Paige that I'm busy tonight, so there's no way I can let her know that I'm suddenly free. I had thought for a moment that I could force myself to do the right thing and walk away from her for good. I've never had to force myself to have sex before, and truthfully, I felt weirded out by my hesitation when she first asked. I felt awful about the sadness in her eyes when she assured me it would be okay. I felt bad that I had promised her something and I didn't know if I could deliver, so I did the only thing I could do. I closed my eyes, took in a breath and told her we could try. That one look of disappointment from Paige left all my own hesitations hanging in the back of my mind as I eventually gave in and buried myself inside of her, granting her the orgasm she so greatly pleaded for. For the first time in my life, I felt like I was being used, even though I knew that wasn't her intention at all. It felt wrong, so wrong, and I know that there's no way on this earth that I can ever go back there again.

Despite her saying she knows where she stands, I can't help but feel like an arsehole. Who knows how a chick's mind works? She could say one thing and mean another. I can't risk getting that close to her again and giving her false hope that we can have a repeat performance, when in reality, for me, it was nothing more than sex. Sex with an incredibly fucking stunning lass, sure, but I needed more than that. I still need more. The second she took my dick in her mouth, her tongue teasing the tip like a damn lollipop, I knew she was a keeper... for someone else. It's just a shame I can't be the one she eventually claims.

Don't get me wrong, I love women and yeah, someday I can see myself settling down with a beautiful girl. Maybe even have a few kids running about the place. But I'm a long way off having either of those. I'm determined to make something of myself first. I don't deserve to have that kind of happiness until I've made a decent life for myself. I'm only twenty years old. I have all the time in the damn world.

Twisting the remote between both fingers, I let out an over-exaggerated sigh and kick my feet up on the table. I wonder for a moment how life has become so incredibly complicated. I'm not sure when it started, but I know something has to give, and soon. Miserable isn't really my style, but I've been sporting it repeatedly since the long, torturous weeks after Julia's death.

I can just hear her now.

"Scott! What on God's earth are you doing moping around that apartment? Get up, get dressed, and live your damn life. And, son, while you're at it, get that damn mop of yours cut. You can't just win a girl with that over-confident, boyish charm of yours."

Chuckling, I run my fingers through my hair, tugging at the ends. I started letting it grow a while back. I needed a change, and long hair seems to work. I'm not going to get it cut.

Tossing one leg over the other, I nestle back against the leather and blow out another breath. My eyes are scanning the channel listings for something other than shitty old soaps and game shows when the buzzer rings out, echoing through the apartment.

A brief smile appears on my face. The thought of it being Ethan is enough to increase my strides, but only for a fraction of a second before my hopes sink to the ground with a drawn-out thud.

I haven't heard from him since a night at the pub when I left him to make an arse of himself. He was out of it – more than I've ever seen him before. It was embarrassing to watch, but surprisingly, I was more embarrassed for him. I gave him shit and walked out. I'd had enough. I wanted to take him out, buy him a few drinks and tell him about the apartment I'd brought for the both of us. As usual, he was too wasted to care and continued to grope some random lass' arse. He was pissed 'cause I was pissed. Basically, it was one big piss fair that I just didn't need.

My hand falls lazily against the lock, sliding it down as I pull the door back, a frown instantly lining my forehead.

I tilt my head in question. *"Amelia?"* My eyes rake over the length of her. Her tight denim jeans and cream flowing shirt look out of place against the sadness etched on her otherwise flawless face.

"I'm sorry. I didn't know where else to go. Can I...?" Her chin drops to her chest and her shoulders sag in defeat.

"Can you what?"

"Come in."

"In here?" I ask, completely confused.

"Yes. Yes, please."

"I... Sure."

Opening the door fully, I lift a hand and gesture for her to come inside. My frown sits firmly in place as she shuffles past me in her designer tan boots, not saying another word as she makes her way to the sitting room and slumps down on the couch, crossing one leg over the other.

She's clearly not hurt. At least not on the outside, but having her show up here at all is enough to piss me off. If she's boo-hooing about something, you can bet your life it won't be of any interest to me. There's no love lost between the two of us. I could go as far as to say I hate her with a passion, but the truth is, I don't really hate easily, unless your name's Jessica fucking Gregory. It's a strong word that's used too often without any real intent. Nah, I don't hate the lass. Despise, maybe. But hate? It's a step too far in my books.

I find myself clock watching for the next two hours as she sits and sobs like a two-year-old who hasn't got her own way. I listen for two whole fucking hours while she bitches and whines about Liam. The lass is an attention seeker, spoiled and selfish to the core. This girl is probably Liam's biggest mistake to date. She comes from two rich parents, a house the size of my whole apartment complex and a family name that means something in the community… apparently. I don't care to know anything about them. My parents love her but I have always struggled, even to this day, to see why. She's just a prissy little bitch who happens to have a cracking arse. Why she is here is beyond me, and my mind begins to drift off as I think about what food I have in my apartment that I can munch on. Pretty sure I have some steak in the freezer. Hmm. Maybe a nice jacket spud on the side. I could try making some of that peppercorn sauce that Ma was always so good at, too. Fuck me. I'm drooling. Is that drool? Better wipe that shit away before Miss High and Mighty disapproves.

Snorting a laugh at mine and E's term for her royal highness, I quickly gather myself again and hide the smirk that tugs at the corner of my mouth.

I peek up at Amelia who is openly glaring at me. Did I mention she's scary as hell when she wants to be, too? "You think I'm being stupid, don't you? I knew it. I shouldn't have come here. You two are just the same. You go around treating women like–"

"Huh?"

"Are you even listening to me?"

"Of course I am."

"Talking shit must run in the family. You're exactly the same as Li–"

"Whoa!" I cut in, raising both hands in the air. "Do not compare me to my brother. Ever." I growl the words out, laced with more anger than intended. One thing I won't stand for is being compared to Liam. "Look," I begin. "I'm sorry for snapping, but don't go there. I'm not like him. Not in the slightest, and for the record, I treat women how they treat me. No more. No less. Got it?" Raising both brows, I lift the half empty bottle of *Jack Daniels* and tilt it towards her. She needs to loosen up a bit.

"You're right. I'm sorry. I shouldn't have come here and taken it out on you. It's just... My parents are away on some last minute cruise and Amie was out with Marc. I just... I..."

"Forget it." I shrug. I couldn't give a flying fuck if I was the last person to cross her small, dumb arse mind. In fact, I don't really give a toss what she thinks about me at all, which contradicts my outburst a bit, but fuck it! She's in no position to judge.

Realising she has no intention of leaving anytime soon, I

head to the kitchen, grab two glasses from the cabinet and fill them to the brim with the amber liquid.

"Here, this will help." I hold out a glass, which she takes eagerly, and I sink back into the sofa.

"Thanks, Scott. For the drink and for letting me hang around here."

I nod. "No problem." I don't add the *'when the fuck you leaving?'* that I'm thinking.

"I just wish he cared more about my feelings instead of his own. He promised last week that he would take me out tonight to make up for missing my birthday. Is it so bloody hard to stick to your word? It was my damn birthday, Scott."

"I'm sure he didn't mean to let you down," I find myself saying, defending him.

The silence grows thick and I wonder how much longer I have to sit here pretending to care. Blowing out a breath, I reach for the two controllers on the table and offer one out to her with a grin. "Fancy a game?"

A weak smile touches her lips as she tugs it from my grasp with a small huff. I shake my head and laugh before pressing the on button at the side. For the first time since she shuffled through my door, I feel myself begin to relax, probably thanks to the whiskey. Maybe her company won't be so bad after all… As long as she doesn't talk anymore and drink all my alcohol, that is.

Chapter Ten

June 2003

O h my god! I just had the best idea."

"And what would that be?" I ask through a laugh. Her excitement seems to be radiating in beams from the other side of the room.

"Get dressed and you'll find out. Hurry!'

Glancing down at my bare chest and tracksuit bottoms, I shake my head and flash her a grin before heading to my room to change. It's been a week since Amelia first showed up here in a state after having a row with Liam. She's shown up again twice since then. God only knows why. Still, I let her in. I wasn't expecting her to show up this afternoon, though, seeing as she was only here last night, but I can't help but feel a little relieved by her presence, too. I'm lonely, she's lonely, and it's surprising who you'll let into your life when it seems you have no one else. Paige is away on some training course and Ethan is nowhere to be seen. I feared I'd be holed up in the apartment all day, twiddling my thumbs on my day off, and that would've sucked. When I answered the door, I was slightly taken aback to see her stood there, looking lost but trying her absolute damnedest to hide it. Liam was due back from London this morning, but I'm guessing he must have stayed on the job longer; otherwise she wouldn't be here getting excited over whatever it is she has planned.

More often than not now, I seem to find myself feeling sorry for her, which is just straight up weird as hell. It's amazing how your opinion of someone can change when you actually take the time to get to know them. I never gave Amelia a second thought in the past, at least not in recent years. Not unless it was to slate her. Now, I just feel like a prize prick. She's actually pretty decent. In small doses.

Tugging a white, sleeveless shirt off its hanger, I slip it over my head and pull out a pair of jeans from the shelf. I have no idea what the lass has planned but this will have to do. Shaking them out, I bend to place one leg in just as the door bursts open and Amelia bounces through.

"Come on. The tables will be–" she stops mid-sentence and clamps her eyes and mouth shut while covering them with both her hands. "Oh shit, sorry." She frowns with a cringe before turning her back on me.

I stifle a laugh and push my legs the rest of the way in before pulling the zipper up.

"Eager much?" I shake my head and nudge her out the room as I follow behind. "Where are we going anyway? It better not be to one of those hoity-toity joints you hang out at." That thought alone is enough to make me stop in my tracks and frown. "It's not, is it?"

"No, and they're not all that bad. Actually, you should

tag along next time. You might be surprised," she says with a playful grin on her face.

"Never gonna happen, sweetheart."

"You're so stuck in your ways."

"I know what I like and what I don't like."

"Whatever. Come on." She tugs on my hand, trying to move me along. "Scott, please? There won't be a free table if we don't hurry the hell up," she whines, stomping her foot like a five-year-old.

And there she is – the Amelia we all know and loathe, sticking her head back out into the world again.

Thankfully, we end up at the local pub, and after ordering our drinks, we make our way to a side room where the pool tables are lined up in a row, only leaving enough room to manoeuvre a pool cue when we need to. It's a Friday night and the room is packed out, so I lean my back up against the wall, watching as she eyes an occupied table curiously. A foreign look crosses her face. It's a look I've not seen before, yet one I instantly know I don't like.

I tilt the bottle to my lips and take a swig, giving her time to get her thoughts together.

"Liam promised he would teach me to play one day," she mumbles, and I almost struggle to hear her over the fleeting banter being thrown around between a group of lads on the far table.

"Snooker?"

"Huh?" she asks, spinning to face me with a confused expression.

"Liam. He plays snooker. This is pool," I correct her,

pushing off the wall before taking a few steps forward. "There's a difference."

Her mouth forms an "O" shape as she glances back at the table, looking even more confused.

I chuckle and run my fingers over the green cloth before picking up a pool cue and holding it out to her. She takes it cautiously, studying it like it's made out of glass.

"Don't worry, it won't break." I chuckle.

I tug at the knees of my jeans and bend down, placing a coin in the correct slot. "It's pretty simple really." Pushing the metal to engage, I flash her a wink as the balls drop to the base, making her jump back. I've never seen Amelia look vulnerable before, but right now, that's exactly how she looks.

Grabbing the black triangle off the table, I rack up the balls, placing them in the right order, and cast a glance at Amelia before placing the white ball in the middle of the D.

"Come here," I order, crooking a finger at her. When she hesitates, I smile reassuringly at her and I'm awarded with a childlike grin in return.

She takes slow, unsure steps towards me and I tug her hand quickly, forcing her in front of me before pressing myself against her so she's leaning forward.

"I'm going to suck, just so you know." She sighs.

I cock my head to the side and peer down. "Here's hoping," I mumble too loudly. I regret it instantly, though. I regret it the second I'm met with a harsh blow to the gut, causing a girlie yelp to erupt from deep within me.

"Sorry," I choke out. "But you really need to watch how you word your shit when you're around me." I half groan, half laugh while feigning injury. "Everything is dirty in here." I groan, tapping the side of my head lightly.

Her eyes take in the scene before her as she fists the cue in her hands, causing me to curse inwardly and become slightly uncomfortable in my pants.

"Whatever. Just show me what to do with this thing," she bites back, twisting the cue between her fingers.

I suck in a deep breath and shake my head, refraining from telling her exactly what I'd like her to do with my massive one.

Placing my hands on her hips, I bend her over into the correct position. Heat surges through me at the small amount of contact but I brush it aside. *Brother's chick, Scotty. It's your brother's chick.*

Her breath hitches as I lean in close and pull the cue back to line it up. "Firstly, you need to line the white ball up with the red. Once you're happy you've done that, slowly pull back the cue, and shoot!" I fire out, hitting the white ball with a force so hard it sends the once perfect triangle into a scattered mess while my chest leans flush against her back.

There's silence. A silence that feels kind of thick and awkward, but neither one of us moves, and it's with just one small, tiny inhale and rise of her chest that Amelia Elizabeth Chamberlin first lets me know that I'm affecting her more than she's letting on. The shit-eating grin that flashes across my face in that instant is nothing short of a fucking sharp surprise to me, but I can't pull away, even though I know here and now that that's exactly what I should be doing. Shit.

Chapter Eleven

I've discovered that there are, in fact, two versions of Amelia Chamberlin that exist in this world. There's the too grown up for her own good Amelia, who dresses perfectly, speaks correctly and holds true to her family name. Then there's the youthful Amelia who slobs around in tracksuit bottoms and oversized t-shirts, wearing a pair of old Chucks on her feet. She's a girl who's had no choice but to grow up in order to be accepted by her family, yet a girl who loves to swear like a trooper and drink beer from a bottle. Who knew that side of her existed? Not me.

Since Liam started up his own business, I've been spending a lot more time with her. She rocks up two, maybe three nights a week if Liam's working away, pizza in one hand, four pack in the other and her smile perfectly in place The truth is, since the first night she came here, I've started seeing a different side to her. I see a girl who craves acceptance – a grown woman who is too scared to make her own decisions for fear of letting her parents down. A young woman with a heart as big as the ocean, who shields it from exposure because it's deemed as weak. Before, I saw nothing more than a spoiled brat who had somehow managed to sink her uppity claws into my brother. I never really understood what the lad saw in her. But as of late, that opinion has changed considerably. We laugh and fool around like friends, and I enjoy her company. I no longer roll my eyes and grit my teeth when I see her pull up outside in her swanky *Mercedes* convertible. Now, I look forward to those days when I can lose myself in a few bottles and talk absolute bollocks. She's nothing like the person I judged her as. She's different. Fresh, even.

Having Amelia around has helped fill a huge gap in my life that I never really knew existed. The idea of suddenly not having her around makes me feel sick to the pit of my stomach. It's a feeling so alien that no matter how many times I try to tell myself it really is just innocent, deep down, I know it's far from it. I think that's partly why I haven't mentioned it to E. Other than him being miles away from the person he used to be, he'd also have a lot to say about it and none of it would be good. I know I'm playing a dangerous game, yet I can't seem to stop myself.

She stopped by yesterday with three bags of shopping. I just looked at her like she'd grown two heads or something. I've never had anyone really look out for me before, besides E. So when she explained that I needed to take better care of myself, I didn't argue with her. She was right.

After filling the food cupboards and refrigerator, she ordered me to sit my arse down. I tossed her a look that showed I was clearly confused and did as I was told, sitting on the floor with my back pressed against the sofa. She followed behind, carrying a purse or some shit in her hand and sat on the chair behind me.

"I saw this style in a magazine the other day and I've been desperate to try it out. Hope you don't mind being my guinea pig," was all she said before she started doing some weird shit with my hair that felt surprisingly good at the time.

I didn't have the heart to take out the thin braids that lined my head once she'd finished, even though they hurt like hell from being too tight and had me looking permanently surprised. She looked so damn pleased with herself that I decided I'd endure the pain if it meant I got to see her smile.

"Who's Paige?" she asks me now, out of nowhere.

"Huh?" I huff, confused and a little stumped for words.

"Paige? She's been ringing for the last minute. It's on silent," she says, holding my phone out.

I've never mentioned Paige to Amelia. I'm not sure why. I guess I thought it would complicate things for us. She might've felt awkward about the whole thing. Not that there's really anything to feel awkward about.

"She's just a friend," I half lie, taking the phone from her outstretched hand. "So, what's it gonna be? Jackie Chan or Patrick Swayze?" I ask, kicking my feet up and dumping them on her lap, ignoring the quizzical expression being tossed my way.

"Eh... Whatever. You decide." She waves off my question, bringing the bottle of *Bud* to her lips.

"Nice one! Chan it is." Hitting the button on the remote, I toss my arm over the back of the couch and down the last of the liquid at the end of the bottle. It's the third time I've blown Paige off for a night in with Amelia. I feel like a twat for doing it, but I can't seem to help myself. Paige is great and I like how our friendship is. I knew from the get-go that nothing would come of us and I was under the impression she realised that, too. We've fucked and it was great, but there was no spark, no belt of lightning shooting off in all directions as I sunk inside of her. I love her like a friend but I'm not in love with her. She deserves better than I can give her, so I chicken out, forcing myself to believe that the only reason I haven't tapped Paige again is because I'm too busy keeping my brother's girl occupied. That's only half the truth. I can't go there again. I can't do that to her. I respect her far too much to use her for my own purposes. Still, blowing her off for my brother's missus isn't exactly a great way to treat your mate, and I'd probably be pissed if the shoe was on the other foot.

Needing a change in subject, I push all thoughts of Paige aside. "Where's Liam tonight?"

She coughs beside me, choking on my question, and I suddenly hate myself for asking. A pang of something hits me in the chest, and for something to distract myself from that weird feeling, I divert my eyes back to the TV.

"He's in London until Tuesday. He's struggling to get the staff, which is why he's always having to work away at the minute. It sucks." She shrugs, patting her chest. "Whatever. It is what it is."

A small smile touches her lips but it falters just as quickly as it came. I can't help but feel bad for her. He's an arse for leaving her alone all the time.

Oh, but she's not alone, is she, Scott? my inner me taunts, aggravating the hell out of me.

Fuck it! If she was mine, I wouldn't let her out of my sight... Or my damn bed. My brother is a twat, and it's about time he realised what a good thing he had. Has.

Has.

I quickly remove my legs from her lap and press them to the floor. The warmth from her body is gone instantly, replaced with a sudden sense of hollowness. Glancing at the empty bottles lining the table, I place both hands on my knees and push up off the couch in search of more.

Tonight was meant to be fun. My conscience, however, is being a bitch, and now I want nothing more than to get the hell out of here. I need space and people around us. I don't like where my head is going. It's dangerous.

Closing the fridge door, I blow out a breath and call out over my shoulder, "Hey, fancy heading out? Shoot some pool?"

"Sure, maybe you could teach me to do that thing?"

I'm not sure which thing she means. My mind was elsewhere at the time, but I shrug anyway. "Sure, whatever you want."

******

The drive to the pub is spent in silence. An awkward feeling has settled over me and set up camp. I'm not sure what happened back at the apartment, but whatever it was has me feeling like a piece of shit, and suddenly this whole thing feels wrong. I'm beginning to question everything, and as I park up, shift into neutral and crank up the handbrake, I wonder what the hell I'm doing. What we are doing. If this is innocent then why does Liam not know about our new-found friendship? If I don't want inside of her, then why the fuck haven't I mentioned any of it to Ethan? I've been blinded by a pretty face with a sad story. I want to make her smile and take away the pain hidden in her eyes. Pain that only I am able to see. I want to tell her that I prefer her in her *Chucks* than those damn tan boots, and throw her in The Bakerman's pond, cover her in mud and convince her that even dirty, she's still perfect. Because she is. Just like she was back then.

She's perfect, and my brother sure as shit doesn't deserve her. I don't deserve her either, but at least I know her. I wonder if he even knows her at all.

I chuckle as the cue slaps the side of the ball without it moving an inch. "No, you need to chalk the end of the cue, babe. It'll add grip, allowing the cue tip to connect with the ball."

Amelia looks at me like I've grown another head and takes a step back.

"Here," I offer, shaking my head as I take the cue from her grasp. "See this? Chalk. Rub it on the end and watch the magic unfold."

I chalk the cue and hand it back over.

"So that's it? I chalk the end and I'll be sure to sink the balls?" she asks like it is a sure thing – like that's all that's needed to ensure her a victory.

I laugh lightly and shake my head, rounding the table. "You also need patience and good hand-eye coordination."

"Oh...kaaaay"

"And you need to know the difference between speed

and aggression," I continue. "A clear shot won't need much force. You need to learn how to judge the distance and gain the correct speed without using strength."

She huffs, shoving the cue against my chest. "I can't do this. You may as well just take it for me."

"I didn't have you down as a quitter."

"Let's call it hands-on teaching."

"I can't take your shot. That'll go against the whole point of us being here." I drop my tone and pull her beside me, forcing her back to arch forward. "Choose your next move and line your shot," I instruct, placing the cue against the table. "You can do this," I encourage, taking a step back.

And she does just that.

She hikes her leg up against the corner of the table, her body flush against the hardwood. I let my eyes drift to her arse that sits pert in her jeans. She really does have a great behind.

I shake my head and remind myself for the millionth time that she isn't mine to ogle. She's practically my fucking sister-in-law, for Christ's sake.

Her lips twist in a zigzag motion as she thinks up her next move, carefully aiming the cue towards the top right hand corner and shooting without force but with precision. She doesn't move, and silence fills the air until the red ball sinks into the top right hand pocket with a barely there thud. It was an easy shot, but to Amelia it was a challenge. One she's just conquered.

I wait for her to move, to say something, but when nothing comes, I sidle up next to her and lean in. "See? I always knew you could do it. I had faith in you."

I'm so close to her lips that I can feel her cool breath invading my own. Every sound, every movement around us grows distant until it's only us. I can feel myself inching closer, and in this moment, there's nothing in the world I want more than to taste her.

I cage her in, pressing both hands to the sides of her so we can line up the next shot, and a breathy moan escapes her lips at the closeness.

I wonder for a moment if I'm pushing my luck. If Liam walked in and saw us in this position, what would he say? How would he react?

But her eyes are still lit up with excitement, probably from making a decent shot.

Her breathing hitches and she draws her lower lip into her mouth before grazing the fullness with her teeth. Everything in me screams to take her. I've never wanted something or someone so damn badly before.

Her eyes only leave mine for a short second, dropping down to my hand that has curled around her waist without my knowledge, but then they're quickly on me again. The once striking blue colour has become deep, so dark I can no longer see my reflection in them. When she doesn't attempt to move, I angle my head to the side. I want to taste her. I need to taste her.

Just give me permission, sweetheart. One little sign. Let me have what I want.

Then just like that…

All innocence goes out of the window when she lifts her chin and settles her gaze on my lips.

Chapter Twelve

One Week Later

I stare at my reflection in the bathroom mirror and groan. It was a dumb arse response on my part, agreeing to this. I wonder if it's too late to back out. There are plenty of people going. One less won't hurt, surely?

I smooth over the thin braids that are still left in my hair, stopping at the nape of my neck and sighing. No. I need to quit being a pansy and get it over with. Maybe it won't be so bad. Nothing has actually happened, after all. Nothing ever will. I need something strong to drink, and I need to get a fucking grip.

Thing is, since our almost, not-quite kiss, things have become awkward between us. When she looked at me like she wanted to kiss me, it wasn't enough. I needed permission, so I waited. She was too important to me to misread the signs, and I was, in truth, too scared and too slow to close the distance. I haven't seen her since that night, and while I know she has her own life to live, I also know that the real reason behind her absence is me and what nearly happened. It isn't like I have the "too wasted to know what I was doing" excuse to fall back on. I have no excuse other than at the time, it felt right to hold her the way I did. I was caught up in the moment, the way her body leaned over the table, one leg hooked on the edge as she sank her first ball. Her eyes lit up like a fairground ride and her excitement was contagious. I felt everything she felt and more. I was thankful that Liam hadn't taken the time to teach her to play because I never would have had the chance to witness her reaction. And when her chest rose and fell, like silent pants, I knew I was done for. My body came alive, growing under the seductive stare Amelia held over me. My fingers, flexing and fighting against the urge to touch her, had lost their battle. Tipping her chin and exposing her flushed neckline, I brushed her soft, supple skin, caressing tenderly, like she was the most precious object in the world. If the scattering of goosebumps wasn't my downfall then her obvious shiver would have been enough to do anyone in. I'm only human after all, and I have my weaknesses as much as the next man.

My breath caught in my throat and tightened like a damn choker. Her eyes locked on mine and held them there. I'd always thought Amelia was gorgeous, but in that moment, she was breathtaking.

Her lips parted and her tongue swept across the fullness of her lower lip. I was mesmerised, stuck in a trance. Time seemed to stop, and the once crowded room had faded to nothing. In that moment, it was just the two of us, breathing the same oxygen, inching closer and closer. My heart was racing but it plummeted in a nanosecond as an almighty shattering bellowed out around us, jerking us apart.

Pulling back quickly, I glanced across to the other side of the room. A young group of lads were mucking around, throwing pretend punches while their friends laughed and cheered, ignoring the smashed pint glass that had been knocked over.

But the shattered glass wasn't the only object to fall under pressure. My damn heart had, too.

Amelia laughed about it on the way back to my apartment. Me? Well, my head was still at the boozer, pinning her against the table with my hips. She felt fucking perfect against me. I hated that. I hated how much pleasure I felt from the mere contact, but even more, I fucking loved it. Despite where my head was at, I was thankful I hadn't royally screwed things up between us.

This shit with Ethan is messing with my damn head, turning me into something I'm not proud of. The only time I really ever smile or laugh lately is when I'm around Amelia or Paige. Alone, I'm bitter, angry and distant from even myself. Ethan isn't entirely to blame for my behaviour, though. I've been a shit mate. Instead of helping him, I sit by and watch it happen. Maybe it's easier than watching him withdraw from life. The thought of watching my mate go through that kind of torture nearly kills me. I may as well hand him the drugs myself for all the good I'm doing. I'm not looking for pity. I know I'm not the only one to blame for the situation he's in. Still, I'm not helping, either. He sure as hell wouldn't allow me to destroy my life the way he is doing. He would fight for me, for my life. If it meant knocking ten shades of shit out of me then so be it. He'd do what needed to be done.

The guilt is overpowering, consuming my life day by day.

I haven't lost him, but fuck if it doesn't feel like it.

I miss him. I miss my best mate.

Now I have an extra tonne of guilt weighing heavily on my shoulders and I'm not sure how long I can carry it around before I crumble to the ground, turning into nothing. I can tell myself a million times over that nothing happened between me and Amelia, but the fact remains that I wanted it to happen. I don't feel guilty for what almost happened. I feel guilty because, despite everything, I wanted to claim her mouth and throw every emotion into that one kiss. I wanted to feel free and happy. I wanted to feel something that I haven't in a long time.

Selfish.

Amelia has imprinted herself on me, hitting an organ that up until now has been untouchable. That guilt consumes me, but what's worse is the depth of my feelings towards her. I'm not used to feeling this way and it both scares and thrills me at the same time. I've grown up despising Liam, but it turns out that I'm no better than he is. In fact, I'm worse. He might be many things, but he would never deceive me. Our brotherly code has well and truly been broken.

I run my fingers through my hair again and push back the reminders of how good she felt pressed against me, the way our breaths mingled as one, spiking my nerve endings. It didn't matter that we were only inches apart. It was never enough.

Her scent was like a newly blossomed daffodil in the spring. Like the ones Mum used to grow in the garden. Fresh, pure and so fucking intoxicating. She drew me in like metal shards to a magnet, and I hate that. I hate that I have no control. I want nothing more than to flip that damn magnet in reverse and watch it repel.

Having to spend an entire evening with her is going to be torture. With Liam there, though, it could go either way. It could make things less awkward, or a whole lot more so. I'm not sure I want to be around for either. Scrap that. I don't. I want life to go back to how it was, because hating her would mean I don't have to admit that I feel something else for her.

Yeah, this is a really bad idea.

****

I catch sight of Amelia the second I walk through the door to the club. The hairs on the back of my neck prickle to attention as I take the few strides towards the cordoned-off VIP area at the back. She hasn't noticed me yet, which has my shoulders sagging in relief. I need to catch a breath and remind myself that nothing happened. This is just like any other get-together – just a few mates out having a laugh. Nothing more. But as I take the final step towards the group, there's only one person who holds my attention, and hell if she isn't dressed to fucking kill.

I swallow down hard and adjust my goods, pausing only briefly to allow the bouncer to free the red rope from its holding place to usher me through.

"Hey, bro. You made it!" Liam shouts. Unlucky for me, his words don't get lost through the music that billows out around us. Amelia has cottoned on, her eyes lifting from the tall glass up to mine. A gleaming smile spreads across her cheeks and I nod my head in greeting, turning my attention back to Liam like he's the only one there.

"Yep, and it looks like you started the party without me." I point out, taking in the tray full of shots dumped on the table.

"Couldn't wait forever, kid. Here," he says, grabbing two full shot glasses from the tray and handing them out. "You've got some serious catching up to do."

I roll my neck and take them both from his outstretched hands before knocking them back easily. The burn is welcome and I marvel in the warmth it creates as it travels south to the pit of my stomach. I immediately recognise the taste. Sambuca. I'm thankful. If I am going to be forced to do shots, at least it's with something I can handle. Not that I can't handle my ale or anything. I work in a bar. It's a given. But shots are lethal.

Swiping the back of my hand across my mouth, I clasp his shoulder and begin to make my way around the table.

It turns out tonight isn't just a random night out. It's one of Liam's mate's birthdays, which means they will seriously be going at it. I hear Jake mention a strip club downtown. He and Liam share some private joke amongst themselves and I just shake my head and walk away. I'm not sure what the lad's problem is. Amelia is sat a few seats away from him, talking to Hayley. How she doesn't hear the catcalls and whistles they make as they speak about each stripper, using their first names, I don't know. Even I feel awkward listening. There's only one way tonight is going to end up, and that's in a total disaster with a capital fucking "D". It's the same thing every damn time. They fight, Liam gets angry and Meli will cry and storm off. Normally I laugh it off as entertainment, but tonight I don't much feel like engaging in whatever is about to happen.

After a few mindless conversations and shots, I grab my leather jacket and make a stand to leave. Something has been bugging me this evening. I'm just not sure what, but, judging by the careful whispers floating around the table, I know the boys are about to make an early exit, too.

"You're not leaving already, are you?"

I turn my head at Amelia's voice. Tugging at the hem of her dress, she blows out a breath before dropping into an empty chair, clearly exhausted from all the dancing.

"Sorry, sweetheart, early start tomorrow," I lie. A hint of disappointment crosses her face, and I frown. "Have fun, though, and look after my brother for me." Grinning, I clock him from the corner of my eye, downing more of the clear liquid that miraculously keeps popping up from nowhere. He appears to be having fun so I'm not going to go over there. He'd only rope me into going with them and I just want to go home.

Amelia follows my gaze, worrying her bottom lip as she studies Liam from across the table. I know what she's thinking, and a part of me feels sorry for her having to deal with him tonight. Still, he's a big boy, she's a big girl and none of it is my problem, especially not her.

She doesn't respond, sinking back in her chair as she pulls the pink straw from her drink between her teeth. So I turn to leave, unsure what else I can do or say to ease the situation.

I've done my rounds, saying goodnight to those who aren't too obliterated to respond, so all I can do now is go. Alone. As it should be.

See, Scotty. That wasn't so bad, lad.

Nobody shagged anyone they shouldn't have done in the toilets. Success.

Chapter Thirteen

I'm beginning to take this whole brushing me off thing personally."

"Huh?" I ask, raising a brow.

"Don't "huh" me. You know exactly what I'm talking about. Twice in one week, Scott. What's the deal?" Paige huffs, her eyes peering over at me from the top of her Screaming Orgasm cocktail.

"Sorry, sweetheart. Something came up," I apologise, only it doesn't really sound as sincere as I want it to. Leaning over the bar, I place a chaste kiss to her cheek, hoping it will suffice enough to stop the impending nagging. "I'll make it up to you. I promise."

"Sure you will," is all she offers back before the hairs on the back of my neck stand to attention and a chill runs through me. What the fuck?

Being mid-June, the air surrounding the bar is thick and heavy. Summer is well and truly starting to kick in. As my shirt clings to my sweat-ridden body, I find myself frowning. Maybe the air-con system finally got fixed yesterday. It definitely wasn't this cool in here the day before.

"Scott, are you even listening to..." Her voice trails off into the distance, and another small shiver breaks free from me.

"Hey, bartender. Give me a 1-900 fuk-me-up."

I almost choke when my eyes finally seek out the sweet sound, only to find a bemused Amelia standing there.

Cocking my head to the side, I grin, causing her cheeks to flush a brilliant shade of pink without any warning. She looks hot as hell in a black, off the shoulder dress. Then again, she always looks hot. But a sexy as fuck Amelia, reeling off the name of our most popular cocktail is enough to make my dick twitch. Down, boy! Brother's missus. No looky, and definitely no touchy.

Man, I seriously need to get laid, or at least take a cold shower.

Laughing, I shake my head and stalk across the bar to the other side, giving her the once over with an appreciative grin. "No can do, I'm afraid," I apologise, pressing my palms flat against the sticky surface as I lean in. "All out of Amaretto, but could I tempt you with a Sex On My Face?" I draw out, flashing her with my signature grin.

"A what?"

"I said," I start, leaning even closer as I prepare myself to enunciate every single word, "Sex. On. My. Face."

"Sure." She shrugs, seeming unaffected. Turning to face her friend who I've never met before, she quickly adds, "Make that two fucks on your face."

"Coming right up." I nod, laughing quietly, not wanting to correct her.

I'm grinning like a dick as I mix the *Southern Comfort*

and budget Canadian whiskey together. This is the first time Amelia has shown up here at the bar, and I can't deny, it's left me feeling a little surprised. It's not exactly high class. In fact, it probably feels like a dive compared to the places she's used to. But appearances can be deceiving. Every damn day this place is packed to the rim with sweaty students looking for cheap drinks and dates for the evening. Business has never been better. In fact, since the SU bar closed down, we seem to have gained back our locals, and the best part is, we've brought in enough cash to pay for extra entertainment. I've arranged interviews and listened to all kinds of artists play, and pulled the list down to three bands. I've hired them all and made damn sure I'm working on the dates we've scheduled them for. It beats the old jukebox Des insisted on getting. The piece of shit is out of date and half the artists are long dead. The new bands offered to play for next to nothing while getting the exposure they need, so he can't really complain. It's turned out to be a win-win.

Anyone would think I knew what I was doing.

Pouring a shot of cranberry into the mixer, I continue to shake it before I look up and toss a wink in Meli's direction.

Damn. She's adorable when she blushes.

Adorable, Scotty? Really? Of all the things I never thought I'd think about Amelia, adorable is definitely one of them.

My thoughts are abruptly stopped as a loud slapping sound has me twisting on the spot. I frown, struggling to focus until my attention finally lands back on Paige, still sat at the far end of the bar. For a moment I wonder how I got here. I thought I was... I remember being...

"After you've finished with Miss Sunshine, how about fetching me an Adios Motherfucker?" She snarls, pushing the empty glass away from her.

It isn't a question. It's a demand, or a statement, maybe. I'm not exactly sure. I frown again but turn my attention back to the task in hand.

After it's thoroughly mixed, I pour the foul looking liquid into two tall glasses and slide them across the bar, waving a dismissive hand as Amelia tries to hand the cash over.

"Shut it, Meli. You're practically my sister-in-law. Don't be a tit," I tell her and make my way to the other side of the bar. Paige is clearly pissed and I have a funny feeling I'm to blame. I've been pushing her away like she means nothing. Any girl would be fuming right about now, but this is Paige. She's different – or at least she was meant to be. These days I'm not so sure about either of us.

"You alright?" I ask, raising both brows. It's obviously a dumb question, judging by the scowl.

"Just. Peachy," she spits out on a half-smile, which isn't actually a smile at all. It's more like half death glare, half snarl.

Whatever it is, I don't like it.

"What gives, Paige?"

"You really are a... You know what? Just forget it," she huffs.

Turning her back on me and shoving her purse under her arm, she storms off through the mass of bodies like a girl on a mission. It doesn't take long before her fingers latch on to some preppy looking dude in the middle of the dance floor.

The weird thing is, seeing her with someone else doesn't

seem to bother me one bit. If only she knew how much I just want her to be happy. Whoever ends up with her will be a very lucky guy indeed. Laughing it off, I make a start on cleaning the bar while Paige continues to feast on the poor lad's face.

Chicks! I will never understand them.

My shift officially finished ten minutes ago, but the bar is still packed and with it being only myself and Darcie on this evening, I can't exactly leave her to tend to everybody all by herself. If they have to wait anymore than three minutes for their drinks, they start to get rowdy, and despite Darcie's kick-arse attitude, she won't be able to handle them alone. Chicks are mean when they have a few drinks inside of them, and the men... Well, that isn't something I really want to think about. After a while, I look around, aware that I haven't seen Amelia come back for a refill. It hits me that she's most likely gone off to somewhere a little more to her tastes, and once again, I frown at the thought. She didn't even say goodbye.

"Oi!"

I yelp and jump back as a sharp stinging sensation takes over me. Clutching my thigh, I stare down open-mouthed, then glare up at an amused Darcie.

"What the hell, Darce?"

"Go. I've got this."

I begin to protest when she cuts me off, spinning the tea towel in a tornado like motion. "D's downstairs. I'll get him to come up and give me a hand. Looks like you've got your hands full anyway," she says, shaking her head in annoyance. "She did this last week, Scott. What have you done to her?"

My eyes follow to where hers are glued to Paige, and

I curse out loud while hopping over the bar.   "We're friends," I tell her, my feet landing on the other side. "Just friends. I haven't done anything."

"Yeah, 'cause that's what it looks like," she calls back, but I ignore her and continue to push my way through the crowd towards Paige.

I wonder briefly how Paige has managed to get so hammered when I've only made her the one drink. But with the lack of attention I've been paying to her, she's probably been brought drinks by the group of lads who are currently surrounding her, laughing at the state she's gotten herself into while some use it as the perfect opportunity to grope and fondle her tits. That's when I start to feel shit for not keeping an eye on her. It's like the Ethan scenario all over again. *Keep burying that head in the sand, Scotty.*

"Right, trouble. Time to get you home." I keep my voice calm, using an even tone as I place my hands on her hips to steady her. If I make out I'm pissed off, which of course I am, chances are she'll kick up a fuss, and I can't handle drunk chicks at the best of times. She's ticked off with me anyhow. Adding fuel to the fire would be fucking crazy on my part.

Turning clumsily, she points an unsteady finger in my face and begins to slur. "You don't get to touch me, and you sure as shit don't get to tell me what to do, Scott."

Rolling my eyes, I ignore the heavy protests around me and yank her into a fireman's lift. "Don't fight me on this, sweetheart. Trust me. You'll thank me for the intervention tomorrow." Not giving her a chance to argue, I make my way through the corridor and out the back door, while the dead weight on my shoulder pounds her tiny fists against my arse cheeks.

"Thank you? Pah. I will not. I hate you, Scott Jenkins. You're a gigantic arsehole with funny hair who spends half his time in the clouds. I really, really..."

"No, you don't. Quit lying." I chuckle, swatting her backside. She might be small but she's a feisty little thing when she gets going. Thankfully, though, she's far too drunk, and her hits are sloppy. It isn't long before I hear a faint snore, earning another chuckle from my lips.

I make it into the parking lot where my beat up car awaits me – yet another clear reminder that Ethan still hasn't fixed it like he promised all that time ago. Paige mumbles something above me, although I can't really make it out. The only thing I can concentrate on is the small silhouette currently leaning against my car.

She's here again, outshining everything and everyone else. *Amelia.*

"Sorry, I thought you would be alone," she says, her eyes darting between me and Paige with an unreadable expression.

Lowering Paige to the ground, I place an arm around her waist to steady her and dig through my back pocket for my keys. "Someone took advantage of happy hour. Grab the door for me, would you?" I ask, handing her the keys.

"Umm... sure," she replies, seeming confused, but she takes them anyway and unlocks the door for me. "Is she alive?"

"I hope so. I don't fancy burying any bodies tonight."

"Tonight? Like that's something you do every other night?"

"Need a ride?" I offer with a smile on my face, ignoring

her question completely as I slide Paige into the backseat while Amelia holds the door open. "I'm just gonna get this one home and settled, then I'm done for the night."

"Actually, yes, I was sort of hoping you would give me a lift. Amie went on to another club and I don't much fancy catching a cab all by myself. They kinda freak me out," she adds quietly.

Pushing Paige's legs aside, I close the door and make my way over to the driver's side.

"Whatever makes you happy, doll. Hop in," I say, tapping the hood of the car and climbing in.

The car stays pretty much silent the whole way, and after carrying Paige up three flights of stairs to her apartment and tucking her into bed, I rummage through the kitchen cupboards for a bowl. Coming up trumps, I place the large mixing bowl on her bedside table and press a light kiss to her forehead. If she is going to throw up, there's no way she'll make it to the bathroom. Maybe she will see this gesture as some sort of apology, because deep down, I really am sorry. I just haven't figured out what for yet.

I hate that I've upset her. I should have realised that cancelling on her repeatedly would result in her hating me the way she now seems to do. I know deep down she didn't really mean what she said, but I still feel like shit. She is my friend, and God knows I need one of those right now.

I wonder for a moment what Ethan is doing while I'm juggling women, dodging bitchy evil eyes and trying to avoid the ache in my dick whenever I see my brother's girlfriend. Where is he? Who is he with? Sure, I still have him in my life, and sometimes, for brief moments, life seems normal when we do get together, but there is always this niggling feeling inside that rises to the surface. Do I really know him anymore?

Of course you fucking do, Scott.

He's still Ethan.

Just a lost Ethan.

I hope that's true deep down. If he is still Ethan and just a little lost, I can deal with that. Fuck! We're all a little lost right now. I can deal with him going off, doing his thing, one day realising he's a massive dickhead for giving in to drugs, and then coming back to us all. What I can't deal with is losing him altogether.

For now, I have to deal with it day by day. Just like I need to deal with Paige and find out what the score is. Not to mention Amelia, who is currently waiting in my car for me.

Sliding behind the wheel, I cast a glance at Meli and force my lips into a grin.

"How's the patient?" she asks with genuine and surprising concern.

"She's okay for now. I'm sure tomorrow morning will be a different story." I chuckle lightly before turning on the engine and heading out into the darkness again.

"She's lucky to have you, Scott."

My eyebrows rise up, but all I offer back is a short nod. I'm pretty sure Paige doesn't see it that way. In fact, I know she doesn't.

"Why do you say that?" I finally ask, casting quick glances her way as much as I can without plowing my car and the two of us into a giant fucking tree. Turning down all the country roads has left me with very little light to read her expression, and her eerie silence seems to drag on forever. I'm about to speak again when she inhales slowly before exhaling and turning to face me. The blue and red lights from the stereo flash across her face just enough for me to see the sad smile she's slapped on just for me, and with a few small words, she manages to change my whole opinion of her altogether.

"We're all lucky to have you. You're one of the good guys. One day you'll see it. You'll see that you think about everyone else before yourself, no matter how much you try to hide it."

Chapter Fourteen

Peeling my eyes open, I blink a few times to adjust to the lighting. The softly glowing lamp slowly creeps into focus as music plays through the sound system, but neither can distract me from the sound of soft breathing beside me. Alarm bells start blaring in my mind, almost as loud and obnoxious as the noise I wake up to every morning. I gaze down to find a head of blonde hair tucked neatly into the crook of my neck. A lightly bronzed arm hangs protectively across my bare chest, and I wonder for a moment why the fuck I've not got a shirt on. Until it all comes flooding back to me.

The spillage from last night.

Using my shirt to mop up the mess Meli created.

Somewhere between the shots and bad movie, we ended up asleep on the sofa.

Together.

In one another's arms.

Shit.

I thought about dropping her home, but Liam is away in London again and I wasn't comfortable leaving the lass on her own, especially when she appeared to be so lost. So I took her home to change, and then I brought her back here with me and we drank some more. A whole lot more.

Too much more.

We stayed up for hours, talking. We talked about Paige and her frosty reactions at the bar, and we spoke about Liam and how much she missed him when he was away. We bitched about our issues with the opposite sex and drowned our sorrows in a bottle of *Jack Daniels* after Amelia tried to convince me that Paige was in love with me. It was stupid. I know Paige. If she's in love with me then I'd know about it. Wouldn't I?

The clock on the wall reads 4 a.m.

Carefully pushing my back against the armrest of the sofa, hoping I can move without disturbing her, I cringe as a soft whimper leaves her lips.

As I wait for the panic to set in, her fingers twitch idly at my sides and her hand splays out across my chest, causing me to suck in a breath. Again, I wait, only the panic never happens, and I find myself enjoying the small moment of contact. Her breathing becomes shallow, the air from her lungs dancing across my chest causing an embarrassing shiver to run through me. When I gaze down, blood surges through my veins, filling me with energy. What the fuck am I meant to do? Think, Scott. Think.

Fuck her.

Don't you dare.

But I want to fuck her.

And fuck with your brother's life, too?

Jesus Christ, she smells so good.

Focus, Scott. What are you, fourteen with your first hard-on?

Look at her soft skin!

Don't make me kick you in the balls. Amelia is off limits.

Cockblocker.

You'll thank me for it.

Swallowing down, I shuffle beneath her and carefully place my hand over hers to remove it. She murmurs something incoherent, and it vibrates roughly against me, making the thought of moving impossible. The angel versus devil argument is still going on in my mind, and it takes all I have to focus on what I'm doing. I'm not sure if she's asleep, or just pretending to be asleep to save any awkwardness, but there's something down my pants that definitely isn't asleep and is fully fucking aware.

Fuck!

"Scott?" she murmurs groggily.

Double fuck!

"There's something digging in my side."

Groaning, I reluctantly shift her hand and toss my arm over my head, casually stretching my body out to try and act as though I'm indifferent. "Don't worry, love. It happens a lot. Morning wood is a thing." Her eyelids flutter open, and she looks at me with wide eyes. That's when something stirs deep inside me and I see want flaring dangerously in the pools of her blue eyes, a daring twinkle there that does nothing to remove the swelling downstairs. It has the devil doing a fucking premature victory dance, though.

Silence fills the room as her fingers dance across my skin,

stopping at the waistband of my pants. All I can do is swallow down and follow the movement with my eyes as her touch begins to trail farther south.

My breaths come hard then, the anticipation building.

When her fingers find their final destination and curl delicately around my dick, all thought is gone. I almost lose it. Her touch is like an inferno – hot and needy.

"Meli," I groan, but the silence continues to grow. I find myself shifting, but only to press further into her touch.

I hiss.

I watch.

I wait.

I wait for one of us to wake up and realise how very, very wrong this is. Only it doesn't feel wrong. It feels fucking right, like suddenly, everything in the damn universe makes perfect fucking sense.

The way my heart rate picks up pace whenever I see her propped up against my door frame, how a striking set of blue eyes is the last thing I see before I fall asleep – it all makes sense now that she's the one that's been haunting my dreams.

Paige made me feel things, and at one point, despite protesting otherwise, I thought she could've been it for me had I bit the bullet and given in. This, though… This thing with Meli and I is just ridiculous.

It should be Paige. She should be the one to do this to me. In reality, she's everything any sane guy in his twenties should want. She's smart, funny, loyal. Hell, she stands up to me like no other lass ever has done. She should be the one. Not Amelia.

Not my brother's girl.

Somewhere along the way, though, I've developed some crazy arse feelings towards her, and damn if it doesn't feel fucking good. But this shit should scare me. My own admission should freak me the fuck out. I don't do feelings – at least not of the lovey fucking dovey kind. Yet, I feel alive. As does my dick!

My hands cup her cheeks and I lean over, taking her plump lip between my teeth with a low groan. "Tell me to stop," I breathe out. *Please don't tell me to stop.*

Dropping my hands, I ball them into fists at my side. My heart is screaming at me, telling me to do this, but my head is battling against it. I can't deny what's in front of me. No matter how wrong it is, I want this and I want it with her. Whether it happens now or in ten years' time, nothing is going to stop me from wanting to be here with her. I just know it.

"I can't," she purrs in a husky whisper as she turns her cheek.

I groan as her tongue darts out, coating her pink lips. Her eyes are fixated on my groin, burning with hunger. Her lips brush against my skin, sending prickles of heated sensation across me.

"Fuck." My muscles contort, my breaths quicken and before she's managed to hold a firm grip on my dick, I'm shoving her back and in one swift motion until I'm settled between her jean clad legs.

Her breathy gasp only spurs me on. I don't care how wrong this is. I don't care that this woman is making me feel things I never thought possible. I don't care that I might be about to make the biggest mistake of my life. No. Right now, I need this.

Dropping my elbows to rest against the arm of the sofa, I let my gaze travel down to the small sliver of skin exposed on her hip. The swell of her breasts rising and falling with each shaky breath she takes has me intoxicated. Only a thin piece of material covers what I know will be a perfect set of fucking tits, and I almost come on the spot when she arches her back, pressing against my dick to tease me.

Dropping my forehead, I try to steady my breathing but our lips are only inches apart. I'm only a few inches away from claiming her as my own. Our breaths mingle together as one, and that scent – her sweet, intoxicating scent – consumes every cell of my being until I'm at a loss. I'm left with no other choice but to take exactly what I need. For once, I'm going to be the selfish bastard my dad always says I am.

She grinds her hips into mine, slow, yet hard. "Jesus, Meli," I grind out, biting down on my lip. "I want you so damn bad."

"I want you to want me," she puffs out, her breathing becoming erratic as the air from her lungs sweeps across my neck – hot and needy breaths that match my own. "I've always wanted you to want me."

I pull back and glance down with hooded eyes before lowering my mouth to hers. "You are so beautiful. Do you know how beautiful you are?" The words are hoarse as they leave my throat in an almost pained whisper. She whimpers against my lips and some words vibrate against them, although I have no idea what the hell she just said.

Running my palms along the curve of her waist in some sort of slow dance has me mesmerised before I hook my fingers through her jeans. I don't have time to fumble with buttons. I just need them off. She lifts her hips eagerly, and I use this moment to peel them down, revealing soft, caramel thighs and legs that seem to go on for miles. I sit back on my heels and tug the denim the rest of the way off before tossing them to the floor.

All the air leaves my lungs as I take in every inch of her. It isn't long before my patience wears thin and I tug her closer, my hands pushing her thighs farther apart.

"You're too perfect for me. I'm not gonna last, sweetheart," I confess shamelessly.

"I don't care."

Dipping my head, I run the tip of my nose along her jawline to her ear, pressing soft kisses as I go. "Tell me what you want, Meli." I whisper, tracing a pattern across to her hipbone. "Tell me right now," I order, heading farther south.

Her breaths quicken, her fingernails clawing at my skin. "I need…"

Sitting back on my heels, I gaze down in wonder. Her skin is reddening under my intense stare. Licking my lips, I find her heated centre, only covered by a thin piece of material, and press a finger against her swollen bud.

She's so fucking ready.

Her body writhes under the pressure and my cock hardens even further, trying to break free. "Tell me," I growl, suddenly losing patience and slipping a finger inside the lacy fabric of her underwear. "So fucking wet," I groan, circling her sweet little spot, skin against skin. I can't believe I'm here, finally doing this, finally touching the girl of my dreams.

"God, yes. I need that," she whimpers, throwing her head back. "I need that. I need you."

Pulling her underwear to one side, I push through the slick folds of her sex until I'm buried knuckle deep in pure, blissful heaven. "So perfect," I tell her, pulling out slowly, only to push back in again until my movements become frequent, my rhythm precise and steady.

"Please, God, yes," she cries out. Oh, I am, sweetheart.

Bringing my thumb to her clit once more, I circle her sweet little spot over and over until her body shudders with the impending orgasm. I feel her body jerk against me and I slip a finger inside. Pound after pound, her legs start to shudder. Her muscles tighten around me and I know she's coming. Pushing another finger inside of her, I capture her lower lip between my teeth at the same time with an animalistic growl. "That's it, baby. Come on my hand. I want to feel you all over me."

And she does just that. Her sex clenches, pulsing against my fingers. It feels fucking heavenly, just as I dreamed it would. I slow my pace and push my tongue inside of her mouth, swallowing her cries as she rides out her orgasm until we're both breathless and panting. Only then do I drop my forehead against hers.

"Scott?"

"Yeah?"

"That was…"

She doesn't say anymore. She doesn't need to. Amelia simply releases a contented sigh before she slips her arms around my waist. I'm not even close to being done with her. Her sweet, hot juices coat me, but that isn't enough. I want to taste her. I want to bury my dick inside of her and stay there. I've already decided that being inside Amelia is going to be my favourite place in the world. I have to make it happen. I'm all in now.

Our bodies are slick as I finally manage to muscle up enough strength to peel my arms from underneath her. Her groan of disapproval elicits a smile from me, and I brush her damp hair away from her face before placing a kiss on her forehead. Then I pour all my attention back on to her. I do it until it feels like breathing. I do it until we've been lying here for hours – exploring, tasting, teasing, until neither one of us can take anymore.

Her taste lingers on the very tip of my tongue. Her small gasps and soft little moans still echo through my lust-filled mind, and I can still feel the faint sting from her fingernails where they dug harshly into my biceps while she writhed beneath me, silently pleading for more.

I give her more. Ten times over, I give her what she asks for. What she begs for.

I rock into her and, after what feels like the most intense love making of my life, on a final thrust, her glazed eyes roll into the back of her head and a cry of pleasure tears free from her swollen pink lips. The same lips I have just spent so much time tasting.

In this very moment, I know only two things.

She is like a drug, and I am on my very own Amelia high.

Chapter Fifteen

The morning after

As I listen to the water run, I can't help but envision the woman behind the bathroom door. Her beauty is a rare and precious gift in this world. Her movements are so dainty, yet for the most part, she always seems to be in control. I ache with exhaustion, but knowing Amelia is behind that door, naked, is enough to wake Scotty Jr. up again. You'd think he'd never been sucked before.

I peer down and adjust my pants. Easy, boy. Fucking hell.

Just as I'm set to give Junior his final warning and tell him of the dangers of split foreskin, the door quietly opens and Amelia's long, bare legs come into view.

Cringing as she grips the towel to her chest, she throws me an apologetic look. "Sorry, I couldn't find a bigger towel."

I want to tell her that I don't care. I've spent the last few hours inspecting every inch of her; the less she's covered, the better. Instead, I push off the couch and jog to the bedroom to find another towel to make her feel more comfortable.

Pulling a freshly laundered sheet from the wardrobe, I jog

back and find her standing in the same position. Has she had second thoughts? Maybe she realises that she has just made a huge mistake and now she is ready to run for the hills. The thought alone instantly pisses me off. Not wanting to see the look of shame on her face, I hand the sheet over without a response and head back to my room, smiling flatly as I go so as not to freak her out.

The bed dips and creaks beneath my weight as the first evidence of dawn starts to creep through the curtains. How have I let this happen, and why does it bother me so much that she could be doubting any moment that we've just spent together?

Because you like her, idiot.

Well that much is obvious, I think to myself, burying my face in my hands.

A soft tap on the door fills the silence and I glance up.

"Scott? Can I come in?"

"Just a sec'," I call back, scrubbing my face with my hands. *Deep breath, Scotty.*

Doing just that, I push up from the bed and stalk across the room, sucking in another long breath before I release it all in one long stream and pull the door back. "I'll grab my keys."

"Your keys?"

"Yeah, you know, the small metal objects that unlock and start my car? Keys."

"Oh," she mouths, cradling her chest. "I see."

I scan her briefly – only enough to notice she's fully clothed again.

"You want me to leave?" she asks quietly.

Pausing mid-step, I turn my head. "That's what you want, isn't it? To leave?"

"Leave? No..." She frowns, shaking her head dismissively. "Why would you think that?"

"Because… I mean…" Why do I think that?

"I don't want to go. Not unless you want me to, that is."

My eyes widen and I find myself frozen. I'm just staring at her vulnerability, wondering when this woman in front of me will stop showing me sides of her that I never knew existed. "No?" Shocked at her response, I close the distance and grasp her chin between my fingers, forcing her to look at me. "You want to stay here? With me?"

"Yes." She nods, a hint of a smile tugging at her lips.

Good, 'cause I'm not ready for you to leave me. "I want you to stay with me."

"Shit, Scott. I thought you wanted me gone then." The relief on her face is obvious, and I can't help the small victory smirk that tugs on one side of my mouth. What the fuck am I doing? Right now, I don't know and I don't care.

"Not even a little bit. I want you."

"You do?"

"In my bed. But sweetheart, we have a problem."

"What kind of pr–"

"I'm gonna need these off," I reply, cutting her off as I tug at the hem of her shirt.

"Oh. Okay." She grins lazily.

"Good." I nod and lower my head, pressing a soft kiss against her lips. These lips… these lips will be the death of me.

Later that night...

I couldn't contain the grin that I wore when I left the house this afternoon. For the first time in a really long time, I wasn't distracted by sad thoughts, but with images of the girl I left in my bed, spent and thoroughly pleased. I didn't expect this morning to go the way it did. I wasn't sure how Amelia felt, but knowing she doesn't regret what happened last night is a massive relief. Leaving her wasn't easy, and I've found myself clock watching through my entire shift, just waiting for it to end so I can get back to her. Knowing she's probably naked and in my bed has me going crazy. If I make it through the rest of my shift, it will be a damn miracle.

"Seriously, if you keep smiling, I'm gonna shove this glass down your throat," Darcie warns and I cock my head to meet her eyes.

"Can't a guy be happy?" I ask, frowning.

"Of course." She shrugs. "But you? No."

I guess my sudden change in behaviour hasn't gone unnoticed. She is right, though. It has been a long time since I had anything to really smile about. If I'd known that all it would take was a beautiful blonde to bounce into my life then I would've fucked her a long time ago.

I probably should rein it in a bit. Darcie is nosy as fuck. It won't take her long to figure out the reason behind my erratic behavior, and then I'll have to explain shit I'm not ready to talk about.

"Cheers, sweetheart," I scoff.

"Seriously, though, it's nauseating. You need to stop. Like, now."

Laughing, I cup her cheeks and press my lips to her forehead. "Love you, too, doll."

Planting her hands on her hips, she pouts. "You really aren't going to tell me, are you?"

"Nothing to tell." I shrug.

"You are a shit liar, Scott Jenkins. For that..." She points. "I'm not sharing tonight's tips."

Chuckling, I lift her in my arms and swing her around. "You can keep 'em."

"What?" she yells, wriggling free from my arms. "You are so up to something. I'm telling D."

Pivoting on the spot, she stalks across to the other side of the bar, her ponytail swishing around angrily.

"Nothing to tell, Darcie," I repeat, shaking my head although she can't see me.

"I will find out the truth."

"Yeah, yeah." I roll my eyes and push through the double doors to the kitchen.

I can and will keep this hidden from Darcie. She doesn't need to know why I've suddenly done a complete one-eighty. The longer I keep this to myself, the longer I have with Amelia, and I'm damn sure I am not ready for this to end. Not until she's the one to walk away. She will have to be the one to end it if she decides it's all too much. I have a feeling that from now on, I'm going to be putty in her hands for as long as she will allow me to be.

Chapter Sixteen

July 2003

Watching Amelia sleep peacefully beside me has become my new favourite activity.

It brings me a sense of euphoria in a life that hasn't seen much of that recently. For the most part, I've been living through this hell with a permanent frown-line marred across my damn forehead. The stress and worry about Ethan has taken its toll on me. I no longer recognise myself. I've somehow lost myself along with Ethan, and I'm not sure I will ever feel like the same man ever again. Will I ever feel enough happiness to erase the worry lines altogether? When Amelia sleeps beside me, the anger, confusion and everything else I have been feeling, the constant negatives in my life, well, they all seem to disappear.

I've been watching her sleep for the past hour, unable to move for fear of missing a single moment. Even when she sleeps, she is fascinating to me.

I hope that she won't find it creepy if she ever catches me. It isn't like I make a habit of watching chicks sleep or anything.

I just can't stop myself, especially when a sleepy smile forms on her lips every so often, along with those soft contented murmurs that sound more like a kitten purring. Mostly, I wonder if it is because of me. Have I made her feel like this? Settled? That thought alone is enough to make me smile and brush my thumb gently across her forehead to remove a long strand of hair that's drifted there.

I've never seen anything so beautiful.

Her crazy blonde hair is splayed across my pillow, and the way her delicate hand rests against my chest is just another reminder that she's here. Here with me.

After everything that has happened recently, Amelia is the only good thing to come out of it. It's the little things about her that bring joy to an otherwise shitty situation. Like the way her forehead creases when she laughs, or the way her smile grows warm and genuine whenever she sees me. It takes my breath away every damn time. Now, I'm not a firm believer in God, especially since Julia's death, but I believe that if he is real, it was him who brought Amelia into my life when I needed her the most. It could be fate, but either way, I find myself thankful. She really was my angel all those years ago.

"How long have you been watching me?" her sleepy voice asks, pulling me from my thoughts.

I smile down at her and press my lips to her forehead. "Probably longer than could be deemed sane." I chuckle, pulling her closer.

Sighing softly, she nuzzles against me, burying her face in the crook of my neck. "What time is it?"

"A little after ten."

A soft little moan escapes her lips when her fingertips begin to draw a lazy pattern across my chest. "Mmhmm.. What time do you have to be at work?"

"Not for a while," I growl out before flipping her over and onto to her back. Shifting a leg over, I cage her in, smiling softly as I press a kiss to the tip of her nose.

"Good. This bed is so, so damn comfortable. I don't think I can leave."

"So don't," I hit back honestly, because I really don't want her to leave.

"I wish I could stay but Liam is going to–" We both glace over at the bedside table when Amelia's phone vibrates. Liam's name flashes across the screen like a warning sign, taunting me with every ring.

My brows furrow involuntarily, and I pull my gaze away from the phone and onto Amelia. Liam's name is enough to send Scott Jr. into hiding, indefinitely.

"I'm sorry," she apologises, scooting out from underneath me.

"Answer it. I'm gonna grab a shower, anyway."

"Scott?" her voice calls out from behind me just as I pull the bathroom door open.

"Yeah?"

"Please don't. Don't do this," she begs me.

"Just answer it, babe. He'll only keep ringing if you don't."

I attempt to focus on anything other than her voice as I lather the soap into my hand and scrub vigorously, but I find myself listening in, unable to block out her laugh and the way she coos his name. I close my eyes briefly and remind myself that she isn't actually mine. I knew this from the start so why I am feeling this way? Why am I so damn angry at her?

The water runs cold and I climb out, wrapping the towel around my waist and tying it in a knot at the side. The lengthy shower did nothing to ease the bitterness I feel deep inside. I'm not sure anything can.

I blow out a breath and pull the door open, unable to look at her. I busy myself instead, rummaging through the drawers for clean boxers and shorts. I can feel her eyes on me, but the stubborn side of me doesn't care.

She scoots beside me as I sit at the edge of the bed, my head hung low.

"Say something. Anything. Just please don't be mad at me. I did try to warn you."

"Some warning," I mumble and shake my head like a petulant child.

Straddling my lap, she grips the sides of my face with both her hands and raises a perfect brow. "Don't be moody. Can we just enjoy our time together before you leave for work?"

"I've gotta go," I say dismissively.

"You've got ages yet, Scott. Please," she pleads, fluttering her lashes. That shit might work for Liam but not me. I don't play fucking games… except when I'm playing games.

"Just let me go please, sweetheart."

She dips her head to my chest, and I glance down just as her tongue darts out and licks away a small droplet of water that beads down my torso.

I force my eyes shut and try desperately to gain some sort of control over myself. As usual, I fall under Amelia's spell just like that, and I grip her hips, pulling her flush against me.

"Scott?"

"Hmm?"

"I didn't want to bring this up and I know it's probably crappy timing and all, but it's Liam..."

"What about him?" I ask, glancing down at our joined hands. Her fingers feel perfect against mine. Interlaced and just, perfect. It's almost like they were made just for me.

"With the project now completed, there's no need for him to stick around anymore."

I'm not sure where she is going with this so I turn my cheek to meet her eyes and frown. "What does that mean?" I ask, touching my lips to the soft skin of her shoulder blade.

She smells delicious and I can't help but breathe her in, nuzzling my nose against her skin like I can't get enough.

"On the phone... He's... He said he's coming home, Scott." Her voice is desperate, worried, scared, sad, maybe all three. I'm not sure.

Sighing, I pull her closer and place a kiss on her forehead. "That's not a bad thing for you. I mean, you want him home, right?"

"Yeah, I guess so. He's been away for three weeks, Scott. What if everything is different? What if he doesn't want to be with me anymore?"

I swallow down and shake my head, already dreading my next words. "Not possible, peaches. Any man would be lucky to have you in their life. Liam included."

"Do you really think so?" she asks, gazing up at me through big, blue, hopeful eyes.

"I know so," I assure her.

"Thanks, Scott. You're amazing," she says, leaning up to peck my cheek.

"Yeah, that's what everyone keeps telling me," I mumble. "I'm gonna grab a shower. My shift starts soon and I need to be there before the delivery gets in."

"Oh, okay. But you just had a sho… Nevermind. Do you need me to leave?"

"Nah. Stick around if you want. The spare set of keys is on the counter. Just lock up and slide them through the letterbox when you're finished."

"M' kay," she mumbles, turning her head to face the window.

I hold the door open to the bathroom and drop my forehead against the doorframe. "How long do we have?"

I regret the question the moment it falls from my lips but I need to know.

"Two, maybe three days. He's not entirely sure."

She doesn't add anything further, just snuggles back under the covers.

Jerking the door open and closing it behind me, I let out a sigh and press my back against the cold wood.

Although neither one of us will say the words out loud, we both know that what we have was always going to come to an end. It's only ever been a matter of time. I only hope that when that day comes, I'll be ready to walk away.

I'm not ready to walk away.

Chapter Seventeen

The clanging of metal from no more than a few feet behind me has me rushing to the kitchen to see what all the commotion is about. Sticking my head around the partition wall, I stifle a laugh and use my elbow to prop myself up, crossing one leg over the other.

A curse, followed by another pan hitting the tiled flooring has me cringing inwardly.

Meli stumbles backwards from her crouched position, and her arms fly out either side of her, saving her from her impending fall.

It's been a week since we committed the ultimate sin. Seven days since I handed over my feelings and indulged in what I knew would be the best damn ride of my life. I wake with guilt every morning but that isn't stopping me. I need to be inside of her every damn second. She's quickly become the air that I need in order to survive. Without her, it feels like I don't have a future.

Shaking my head, I try to fight off the grin that is starting to spread, but it's useless.

Man, she really is adorable.

Her arms are about as much use as her fogged out glasses, and all I can do is cringe as her backside eventually hits the floor with a thud.

"Shit!"

My laughter can no longer be contained but my grin is quickly replaced with quiet sympathy and sheer and utter fucking amusement.

Yep. Adorable as fuck.

Tugging at the knees of my jeans, I crouch down in front of her and slip my fingers around the frames of her glasses before I carefully remove them from her face.

My heart does something that, up until a few months ago, always felt completely alien to me.

It grows.

It grows with each second I spend with her and every minute I am away from her. Amelia has crawled under my skin and set up camp there indefinitely.

I'm so screwed.

Gazing down at her, I press a swift kiss to the end of her nose and slip my hands firmly around her waist to hoist her up. Tipping her chin, I brush my thumb against her reddened cheek and a genuine smile spreads widely across my face.

Her eyelashes flutter open and her perfectly plump lips twist into a pout before she blows out a breath. "I guess I still need to get used to the damn things."

"That you do. Best make it quick, though, peaches. I plan on taking you wearing nothing but them." Waggling my brows, I dangle the dark rimmed glasses in the air and toss her a quick wink before forcing myself away to clean up the mess. Her mess.

Amelia has always been nice to look at. I'd be off my damn rocker if I thought any different. But Amelia in glasses? Dammit all to hell...

"Is that right?" she drawls out in a seductive whisper. "Well, I'm only supposed to wear them for reading and stuff, so technically, wearing them for dirty, sweaty sex isn't really a necessity."

"Yeah, well, it is now," I toss back, shielding my eyes as I pull back the glass door of the oven and dip my head to examine the dish. "Looks like it's takeout after all." Shoving a hand under the sleeve of my hoodie, I pinch the edge of the white dish and toss it on top of the counter. "Well done for trying, though."

"Never mind. I'm not really all that hungry anyway. At least, not for food," she coos, fluttering her lashes again for added effect.

Raising both brows, I stalk towards her, taking slow, purposeful steps. "Is that so?"

Pulling her plump lip between her teeth, she nods, her eyes mischievous and daring.

Closing the distance between us, I finally reach her and my hands snake around her waist, tugging her close. I can feel how soft her skin is through the thin material of her shirt and a groan rips free from my chest as I nuzzle into the crook of her neck.

"How long have we got?" I breathe out, my teeth grazing along her jaw. It's a question I've asked myself a lot lately. How long? One day I won't have to ask. One day I'm going to get the girl, and that's enough to toss the pain aside. Patience. That's what I keep telling myself. Patience.

"Long enough," she pants, fisting the hem of my hoodie. "You're capable of many things, Scott. I'm sure you can make quick work of me by now."

Nodding once, I press a lingering kiss against her mouth while my fingers circle the exposed skin at her lower back.

While having her near me has me feeling on top of the fucking world, I'm not stupid enough to believe she is only sleeping with me. She has Liam back now. Every night he's home, she goes back to him. I don't want to think about that. Right now, she can only promise me a few hours, and after my initial worry over him returning to her life full-time, I decided that I would quit whining and simply make the most of whatever she offered me. I hope, perhaps stupidly, that one day, she'll say the one word that will ease this fucking ache in my chest. One word is all it will take.

Forever.

And I want that with her. More than anything, I want to be the one to hold her at night, to walk hand-in-hand in the street without worrying we'll get caught. I want to take her out for dinner and compliment her without feeling bad. I want to fuck her ten shades to hell, minus the guilt. But so much more... I want to be enough for her, not some dirty little secret.

But I'll take it for now if it means being close to her still.

An abrupt knocking echoes heavily through the hall, making us both freeze.

"Are you expecting anyone?" she whispers, clinging to my biceps to support herself.

"No. No one knows I'm here tonight."

Pulling back, I run my fingers through the roots and tug at the long strands of my hair, cursing under my breath. "Just wait in the bathroom. I'll get rid of them."

Fuck! Could they have picked a worse fucking time to show up unannounced?

With my fingers on the handle, I glance back to check it's all clear and ease the door open. My heart plummets as I stare at Liam in complete and utter fucking shock. I'm sure he can see my deer in the headlights look, but I try and shake it off and plaster on a grin instead.

"About fucking time, kid."

"Hey up! What you doing here? More to the point, couldn't you have called first?" I ask, annoyance lacing my words.

"Yeah, yeah," he sing-songs, brushing past me. "I'd be waiting a long fucking time for you to invite me over. Thought it was about time I checked out the bachelor pad."

"Yeah, well I'm kinda busy, mate," I reply, scratching the back of my neck while my eyes peer over at my bedroom door.

"No shit! What the fuck have you been burning? It fucking stinks." He grimaces, his eyes landing on the burnt dish behind me. He chucks his head back and laughs. "Dude, you need to teach the lass how to cook some decent grub. Mind you, Meli can't cook for shit, but what the heck? She makes up for her lack of culinary skills in the bedroom department, if you get what I mean."

My head snaps back and it takes everything in me not to knock him the fuck out. Prick!

"Too much info, lad. Now fuck off! I've got a date to get

back to, you scruffy cunt."

Holding up his hands in surrender, Liam shakes his head and laughs under his breath.

"Right. Soon then? You can't avoid me forever."

"Soon," I lie in a monotone voice that surprises even me.

Fortunately for me, he takes the hint and leaves, while I swallow down the sick feeling that has settled in the pit of my stomach.

Warm arms encircle my waist and I tear my eyes away from the door my brother just left through.

"That was close," Amelia says, stating the obvious as she drops her forehead to my back and sighs.

"Too close," I whisper back, closing my eyes. My brother might be a bit of a modern day arsehole, but he doesn't deserve this. Does he?

She digs in her back pocket, pulling out her phone. "He's not due back until tomorrow. He never called or…"

My mind drifts back to my fifth year in primary school, when Darryl Goodwin stole my ball and proceeded to taunt me with it. I tried so hard to get it back, but back then I didn't have the height advantage that I have now. My stumpy legs jumped as high as they could as my hands tried frantically to knock the ball from his grasp. Gramps had bought me the ball when I went on one of my many weekend stays at his house. I loved that damn ball. Liam must've heard the commotion because he came charging over and snatched the ball back with no effort at all. Darryl Goodwin didn't come within an inch of me afterwards. I was left alone to play with my ball and it was all thanks to my big brother.

"Meli?"

"Don't say it."

"One of us has to."

"Nothing has changed."

"It has. I can't do this." I sigh, removing Amelia's arms from around my waist. "I can't fucking do this anymore."

"Don't say that, Scott." She frowns, ducking her head to meet my eyes. "We'll just have to be more careful next time. We can do this. We can make this work."

Make this work? Next time? There can never be a next time. Not after this. We've just had the wakeup call we need to realise how wrong this is. I'm not about to risk another near miss. No, we need to call it a day. As much as it pains me to know that I'll never get to touch her again, or feel her weightless body shudder beneath me as I push her over the edge, this has to end now. Next time we may not be so lucky. I can't bear to think about it.

"No." I shake my head. "We can't. I can't do this, babe. That right there – that was the fucking reality check. I shit myself, Meli. Can't you see? We got lucky. But luck always runs out eventually and I can't stick around and wait for that moment. It needs to stop now."

"I can't walk away from you, Scott."

"We have no choice."

A small tear trails down her cheek, stopping at her mouth. This thing between us is new – so new in fact, already having these feelings seems crazy. They aren't, though.

I lift a hand, my thumb brushing away the dampness as I offer a small smile. "It'll be okay. He'll never know and you'll be able to get on with your life. The life you had before me."

"I had no life before you."

"That's not true, peaches, and you know it. You've always been in control. You've always been in charge of your own life. You get what you want."

"I want you."

"You have Liam. My brother, Liam."

"But... he's not you," she whispers, turning her cheek in my palm.

I want to shake my head and say, "No. No, he's not," because I could never hurt her the way he does, or treat her with such indifference. I want to tell her that if she were mine, she'd never have to cry, and she'd never have to be lonely. I want to tell her that if she knew how strongly I felt about her, she'd know I was doing all of this for her own good. I want to tell her so many things, but instead, I drop my hand and take a step back.

"Scott?"

I swallow down and force the words out that need to be said. "You need to leave."

Closing my eyes, I force back the unshed tears. Don't cry. Do not fucking cry, you big pussy. Why do I feel like I want to fucking cry?

I don't know when it actually happens – whether it's moments, minutes or hours later – but eventually the door clicks shut, and I blow out a breath, fall into the recliner and drop my sorry head into my pathetic little hands.

Chapter Eighteen

The night has been slow. Most students have now gone back to their parents' homes for the summer, so a lot of our regulars are missing and our guaranteed business isn't so, well, guaranteed anymore. Mix that in with the fact that there's a new joint opened up on the other side of campus, and we're all kinds of screwed. The SU bar is more upmarket, without actually being upmarket. The drinks are watered down to the max, but they're cheap, and that's all that matters to people nowadays. I'm not sure how long Des can keep this place up while not making as much of a profit as he's used to. He's assured us there's nothing to worry about, and I can only take his word for it. Still, it hasn't stopped me circling job advertisements in the local paper just in case. With the apartment and the expenses that come with renting, I can't afford to be out of a job. What the fuck is council tax, anyway?

Darce comes up behind me, slapping my shoulder. "Looks like happy hour's over," she says, nodding her head over to the entry door.

I guess it is.

A group of lads strut through past Jez, our doorman, already half-cut and shouting around like they own the joint. With alcohol grows confidence, and with confidence grows cockiness. I know on first sight of them that tonight is about to get interesting. It's why Des insisted we hire a doorman in the first place. He wants the bar manned at all times, flowing at a high pace. An unhappy customer means a bad review in the press, and this place is D's baby. He isn't about to sit back and watch it plummet to the ground in a pile of dust. So, if it comes to it, and we have to jump ship and sort out the crazy, the bar and the takings will suffer. Voila, D. Jez is built like a brick shit house, and with one look, he'd have any douche bag quaking in their knock-off *Timberlands*.

I throw Jez a look that clearly says I'm not happy with his easy acceptance of the rowdy boys, but he only shrugs in response. I know why he did it. He needs this job just as much as I do. The more customers we have through the door, the better chance we have of earning a pay cheque, and truth be told, Jez needs this more than he will ever let on.

Des called me down to his office one afternoon. He'd already mentioned getting staff for the door, but that had taken him longer than he'd hoped. He was overly cautious when it came to hiring. He could see through anyone, and if he saw so much as the smallest hint of something other than persistence and enthusiasm, they were instantly dismissed. No interview. No chance to grovel or ask for second chances. They were out. I guess that's part of the reason the bar has been going for as long as it has. He eventually found a candidate that met his high standards and he wanted me to sit in on the interview. I'd only been here a few weeks so his request threw me a little. Still, I jumped at the chance. I wanted to learn, and D knew what the hell he was doing, so it was an opportunity I didn't want to miss. Especially if I wanted to be in a similar position to him one day.

It turned out Jez had recently done a stint in the nick: armed robbery and assault. Though this should've been a no brainer, we both saw something in his eyes that spoke volumes. He wasn't asking for pity or a second chance, but he needed one. If not for him, then for his three-year-old daughter, Lillie-Mai.

When the interview was over, we welcomed Jez to the family with a few pitchers of beer. I took a step back and looked on with amazement and admiration. This man had done wrong but he wanted to change. Did I think he had it in him? Hell yes, which led my thoughts to Ethan. Could he change? As bad as life was for him, I did truly believe that he would be okay, that his life would change if only he allowed it to.

It was in that moment of admission that Des stepped beside me, clasped a hand to my shoulder and said, "Son, one day you'll strut your horny arse out of here and open the door to your own dream. One thing I won't let you do, Scotty, is live your days out in my place. You have the potential to make something of yourself. Don't waste yourself in a dead-end job."

He wasn't putting down my role at the bar, nor was he bad-mouthing his own success. He was telling me that I had it in me to make my own success – that I needed to take chances and grab every moment I could.

Those words have stuck with me, even to this day.

They give me hope.

"Oi, mate! You gonna stand there all day dusting that glass or serve us a damn drink?"

Snapping out of my daze, I eye the chancer curiously.

Does this dipshit have a death wish or what?

Biting back my anger, I push the glass to the back of the shelf and slap both hands to the surface of the bar. "What can I get you?"

"Dunno." He shrugs, looking to his mates. "What do you suggest?"

I grin and lean in. "First thing you need to know about drinking is that you should always know what you want. Anything else makes you look like an inexperienced little prick. You feel me?"

The girl beside him chuckles and begins to twirl a red lock around her finger while eyeing me up and down. A satisfied grin spreads across her face and I force myself to at least try to bite back a laugh.

"Fuck you! Get me a beer. Actually, make it four."

"Bottled beer or draught?"

"Bottled. And make sure they're cold."

"Cold. Special, rare order of *cold* beer coming right up."

I shake my head and reach for four bottles from the chiller, sliding them across the bar. "That'll be fourteen big ones."

"What the fuck? Plastic bottles? What sort of bar is this?" He snorts, pulling a note from his back pocket.

Instead of answering, I pull the twenty from between his fingers and go about ringing them up. There's a reason Des insists on plastic bottles rather than glass. Fucker's just lucky they are plastic.

Handing over the change, I move on to the next customer. "What can I get you?"

The redhead next to the loudmouth leans over the bar, giving me a perfect view of her tits.

Head out the gutter, Scotty.

"Hmm... I'll get a spritzer. No ice and a slice of lemon."

I nod and grin over at the lad still eyeing the bottle curiously. Preppy little shit.

"Three-fifty," I say, sliding the drink over.

Taking her fiver, I ring up the spritzer and count the change into my hand.

"You handled that well. I would've kicked him in the balls if he spoke to me that way."

"Yeah? Well, it's not my first time, and just because I didn't act on it, doesn't mean the thought didn't cross my mind. I need the job, and besides, he's just a kid."

"But you're not," she states, running her painted fingernail down my arm. "You're a man of the world. I can tell."

"I am also working. Sorry, sweetheart," I apologise, catching her finger before it attempts to travel any farther south.

"Later then?"

Chuckling at her persistence, I lean in. "See that bald man over there?" I say, pointing to Des. "He doesn't take too kindly to his staff fucking his punters, and like I said, I need the job."

"Oh. Okay, well never mind. I'll see you around, Scott."

I don't have the chance to question how she knows my name before she flicks her red locks over one shoulder and struts off to the dance floor. Fisting the change in my hand, I drop it into the tips jar and get back to work.

Maybe I was a little too hasty in brushing the girl off. I could use the distraction, after all. Amelia has been plaguing my thoughts since I let her walk away three days ago. I've thrown myself into work and catching up with Dean, but still I can't fucking shake her. I know letting her walk away was the right thing to do. Maybe she realises that, too. After all, silence speaks volumes and I haven't heard a single fucking thing from her since Tuesday. Not that I really expected to.

At that thought, I feel my phone vibrate in my pocket. Fishing it out, I glance down at the screen with a frown. Liam messaged me twice yesterday and even tried to call. I didn't have it in me to answer. Something inside me hopes it will all go away. Only I can't forget, and Liam is growing more persistent by the day. It's just a few drinks he's after. No harm can be done. I hit reply and type a quick response to let him know I'm free tomorrow and shove the phone back in my trouser pocket.

I've lost my girl. No point in losing my brother, too.

Chapter Nineteen

July 2003

When I agreed to go for a pint with Liam, I hadn't realised it was going to turn into a drinking session in a club with his work buddies and fucking girlfriend. I should've backed out, but that would make me a pussy. I don't much like that label from other people, even if I do sometimes feel like one in the quiet emptiness of my own company.

I just keep telling myself that I can do this. It's just a few drinks with my brother, his girlfriend and a bunch of people I don't really know. That's all I need to tell myself. Besides, life goes on. I could go back to the way things were before, when I despised everything about her; I can do that, right? Letting her walk away broke my damn heart, and being here with them, *together,* knowing what I know, remembering what we've done… it's going to break me all over again.

It doesn't matter that I find myself staring at her more often than not, or fucking fighting for breath whenever I see her smiling. I just have to repeat the mantra that I've drummed into my head. *This is Amelia, and you hate her.*

It lasts all of ten minutes.

Who am I kidding?

I'm in too deep. There's no rationality left in me. Not when it comes to her. It doesn't help that she looks so damn hot in that red boob tube dress she's wearing. The thin material barely covers her arse and every damn time she bends over, she's giving me and every other fucker the perfect view of her tits and backside. I feel like covering her up and telling every dick around to keep their eyes off my woman. Then I remember how it felt to have my hands on her, to touch her in places that were meant to be forbidden to me. But it doesn't matter how good she felt in my hands. She wasn't, and isn't, mine to touch. Not anymore, anyway. She never really has been.

As I peer up from my pint, my jaw ticks. I don't know what I expected to feel, but seeing them together, wrapped in each other's arms like love's young dream, has me feeling sick to my fucking stomach and causes a sneer to take up permanent residence on my face. I know I need to slow down on the drinking but there's only so much I can take while sober.

Before I know it, the table is lined with empty glasses of various sizes. The booze hasn't numbed any of the pain. If anything, it's made it worse. The joints in my hands ache from repeatedly clenching. Jealousy and rage begin to swallow me up. I'm not entirely sure why I'm so pissed off. I just know I am, and the anger is thrown directly towards Amelia, not Liam, as I shoot daggers across the table.

"Shots!" I yell, tossing my arm around Liam like we're the closest pair of brothers to exist since Ronnie and Reggie Kray.

I can fucking *act,* bitch. That's right.

"Dude, I think you've had enough," he tells me quietly.

I laugh lazily and squeeze his shoulder. "Coming from you, big bro, I'll take that as a compliment."

He shifts, forcing my arm to drop. "I don't know what's gotten into you tonight, but whatever the fuck it is, you need to deal with it, and deal with it quick. Is this about Ethan? 'Cause if it is, now is not the time. I came here for a good night, Scott, not a damn bar brawl." Shaking his head, he stalks off.

Shrugging, I chug the rest of the bottle and stumble backwards. Fucking pussy. I've had a few beers now. So what? And maybe I do feel a little more fuzzy around the edges than I thought. So what again? It's not like the lad hasn't done it before. It's his damn forte. Besides, how the fuck else was I meant to get through tonight without killing someone?

I push my legs to move, only I don't get much farther than the bar stool that's been holding me up for the last... last... however sodding long I've been here.

"He's right, Scott. You've had enough. How about I call you a cab?"

I turn my head at the sound that once had my dick twitching and find myself sneering once again. "No, thank you. I'm good here."

"What the hell is wrong with you? This isn't you. You start an argument with Darren and force him to leave, then you go and hit on Amie when you know damn well she's here with Marc. What's with you tonight? Your attitude sucks, and quite frankly, so do you."

I've done all that shit? Well, fuck. I can't remember fuck

all.

I turn my cheek and hold a finger up to Yasmin for another. I don't need to justify myself to Amelia, or Liam for that matter. Besides, Marc's a prick and Amie definitely wants to suck my boner. Marc has been eye-fucking Meli all night. I couldn't exactly say anything so I did the only thing that I knew would get his back up. It's not like I would've actually gone there... again. Still, it worked. Fucker turned his attention off my... off *Liam's* Amelia, and focused back on his own bird.

"Fine, ignore me. You'll regret this tomorrow, Scott, and none of these guys will be here to listen to your pathetic apologies."

"Will you be?" I ask with a raised brow.

Her eyes scrunch in confusion and she shakes her head. "What are you talking about now?"

"You. Will you be there tomorrow?"

"You know I won't be there tomorrow, Scott," she whispers, cautiously peering over her shoulder.

"That's a damn shame because hearing you curse and beg for me to fuck you really gets me going. I've missed it. A lot, actually. Maybe a little persuasion..." I draw out, trailing a finger along the curve of her hip. "It didn't take much last time. In fact, it was so damn easy I could laugh, if I wasn't so drunk, that is."

"Don't do this."

"Oh, I love it even more when you pretend to make me work for it."

"You really are a piece of shit." She snarls, gripping my thigh and digging her fucking claws in so hard that I actually flinch. "You told me to leave, Scott. *You!* You have no right to say that shit to me anymore."

"I have every right."

"Really? You blame me when you know full well I didn't want to go."

I shake my head and groan. "You know why I did that. It was the right thing to do. Doesn't mean you can flaunt your relationship in front of my damn face."

"How the hell else do you expect me to behave? He's my fucking boyfriend. If I want to snog his face off, I will. If he wants to kiss me in front of you, I can't stop him. I belong to him. Always have."

"Bitch," I hit back before knocking the shot back and wiping my mouth with the back of my hand.

She leans in close, patting my shoulder blade. "Jealousy isn't a good look on you, Scotty."

"And whore doesn't suit your skin tone, honey, but you don't hear me complaining to you."

"Did you really just say that?"

"Said it. Meant it," I lied.

"Poor little Scotty. Is someone's ego a bit battered? Poor baby," she sing-songs.

"Fuck off, Meli. I mean it," I grind out, gripping my glass.

"You're still wondering why I'm with him, aren't you? Well, let me fill you in on a little something." She leans in closer, her scent invading the space around me. "He gives me the best damn sex of my life. And do you want to know the best part? With Liam, I don't even need to pretend."

I know it's a damn lie, but it doesn't stop my anger from

reaching an all-time high.

My cheeks are the first to heat, and it isn't long before my entire body is like a furnace, shaking with a feeling that consumes me. I bare my teeth like a rabid wolf and grip her elbow. "Lie all you want. Just remember I know you."

"And what the hell is that supposed to mean? You don't know me. We had a *thing*. You were merely there to help a girl out until the *real* thing came back home. You're delusional if you think that means you know me."

"Yeah? Reality check, sweetheart. I know you better than you know yourself. I know what makes you tick... What gets you going. I know how to get to you like no other man can. *That* is why you're with Liam. You're scared of me, because I know the real Amelia Chamberlin. That scares you and that is exactly why you're with him. Because despite the years you've been together, he still doesn't know y–" I'm cut off. My words hang in the air.

"You're such a cocky bastard," she growls.

"With one taste, I knew everything there was to know about you, Meli." I smirk.

"Shut up. Shut up right now."

"I held you. I listened to your body say the things you couldn't admit out loud."

"Stop! Will you just shut the fuck up before someone hears you," she seethes, pulling her elbow free from my hold.

"Oh, darling, you really think he gives a shit? Really? I hate to disappoint you, but your boyfriend is otherwise… engaged," I mock with a little sing-song of my own, turning my eye on Liam and the brunette next to him.

Right on cue, Amelia whips her head around and her shoulders slump as soon as she sees what's in front of her. "They're just friends, Scott. Stop looking for something that isn't there."

Disappointment flashes through her beautiful eyes, only it isn't directed at Liam. No. That look is all for me, and I can't blame her. I wanted a rise out of her, and I got it. Now I feel empty all over again because she still isn't mine for the taking.

"Maybe so, but you know one thing that is true? If you were mine, I wouldn't look, let alone talk to another woman. If you were mine…"

"It doesn't matter because I'm not yours."

"Yet." I grin. "You're not mine… *yet.*"

"Never."

"We'll see, sweetheart. We'll see."

Blowing out an exasperated breath, she shakes her head, sending her curls dancing around her face. "That's the thing, Scott. You are so quick to judge everyone else that you can't even see yourself for who you really are. You think you're so fucking perfect. Scott Jenkins has got all his shit figured out. Well, I hate to be the one to piss on your parade, but your life is one big joke and you are a heartless son of a bitch. You may not agree with me, Scott, but there is certainly one woman out there who does, and where is she, Scott? Where is Paige?" she goads, raising both brows and smirking.

"Be careful," I warn her.

"Truth hurts, doesn't it?"

I suck in a sharp breath and clench my eyes shut. "Fuck off, Meli. Please." And with that, I have no choice but to be the one who walks away. We could stand here and do this all night. We could pretend that we hate each other and tear each other apart, but nothing is ever going to come of it.

"Scott, wait!" she calls out as I stumble through the crowd towards the exit.

The fresh air hits me as soon as I push through the door and step out into the open.

"Scott?"

"Go back inside, sweetheart," I tell her.

"I'm not leaving you, Scott. Not like this."

Locking my fingers behind my neck, I drop my forehead against the cool brick and curse under my breath. I don't want it to be this way. I've well and truly fucked everything up. Jealousy has me acting out in a way that isn't like me at all. What the fuck has happened to me?

"I am so sorry, Scott. I never meant..."

"Don't. Don't you dare apologise," I say through clenched teeth. My chin falls to my chest and I drop to my knees right in the damn alleyway. I never meant to hurt her. It was the last fucking thing I wanted to do.

"Look at me, Scott," she pleads, crouching down in front of me.

I lift my head and squint as I try to focus, but it's no use. "I'm sorry. So fuckin' sorry. You didn't deserve any of that and I'm sorry, and my God, you are so beautiful it hurts me to look at you and not have you."

A shy smile falls upon her lips and she dips her head, lifting her hand to tuck a loose strand of hair behind her ears.

"Don't hate me. Be angry at me. Hit me if it makes you feel

better. Just don't hate me."

"I could never hate you, Scott," she says, laying a reassuring hand on mine.

My breath falters and I glance down at her hand with a frown. It feels like it's been so long since I've felt her touch. I was so scared that I would forget what it felt like, but I've been worrying over nothing. Her touch is something I could never forget, even if I wanted to.

Lifting her hand, I brush my lips across her knuckles and offer her a warm smile. "Thank you."

"Why are you thanking me?"

"For not hating me. For forgiving me and proving why the hell I don't deserve you."

"Listen to me now, Scott," she pushes out, gripping my chin between her fingers. "I was angry back in there. You wound me up and I bit back. I didn't mean any of what I said. You... You deserve to be happy. You deserve to have a good woman in your life – one that you can take out to dinner and not worry about being seen together. I don't make you happy, Scott. If anything, I've ruined you."

"You've definitely ruined me, peaches. Just not in the way you think," I admit.

Our eyes lock and her fingers loosen their hold on my chin before they fall to my chest and stay there.

Dragging my teeth across my bottom lip, I chuck my head back and force my eyes away from hers. "Please don't kiss me. It'll kill me, sweetheart."

Minutes pass.

The silence grows unbearable.

And when I open my eyes, I'm all alone again.

Chapter Twenty

Twenty-four hours later.

I woke up this morning not only with a raging hangover and banging headache, but with an awful sense of guilt settled in the very pit of my stomach, too. I'm not sure what got into me last night but the way I behaved towards my friends and family was nothing less than fucked up. Seeing Amelia and Liam together was always going to be an issue. I should have known that. The way I went off at Darren, and then hitting on Amelia's girlfriend – It was all a bunch of bad moves on my part. It was easy to think that I could bury my feelings away by drinking, only I didn't think about what would replace those feelings I wanted to keep hidden. Anger and rage consumed me last night, turning me into someone I'm not. I wanted to make Amelia jealous by hitting on her friend and that went down like a wet fart in a church. Not only was she *not* jealous at all, but she's now extremely fucking pissed off at me. I'm not too proud to admit how ashamed of myself I am. The man I became last night is someone I wouldn't even piss on if he were on fire. He was a piece of shit drunk, a guy who had no remorse or compassion for anyone other than himself. I vow, right here, right now, that I will never unleash that monster again.

I sidle up behind Darcie when I finally arrive at work, planting my hands on the bar either side of her. "Darce?"

"Hmm?"

"How long have they been sat there?"

"Who sat where?" she asks, eventually lifting her eyes.

"Them in the corner," I say, nudging my head in their direction discreetly.

"No idea. They friends?"

"No."

"Trouble?"

"Who knows? Just keep an eye out, would you?"

"Sure thing. Need me to give Jez a head's up? Or I could sort them out myself?" she says, flexing her invisible biceps.

I snort out a laugh and shake my head. "I'm sure you could. I don't think it's necessary, though."

"Whatevs. Just holler if you need me. I've been waiting for the day when I can try out my new tricks."

"Still taking classes?" I ask, raising my brows as I refer to her self-defence classes. "Thought you quit?"

"I did. For like, a week. He begged me to come back, so I did. I'm a good girl."

"Unbelievable," I say with a small laugh thrown in for effect.

"What? I'm a natural," she says matter-of-factly, before skipping off to the other side of the bar, her ponytail swishing from side to side.

She busies herself serving the customers and I use the opportunity to risk another glance across the room. I can't see their faces properly, but I know they are looking my way and sharing a private joke between themselves.

I note the two empty pint glasses on their table and do something I haven't done since the first day I started.

Lifting the bartop, I signal to Darcie that I'll be back in a second and head over to their table.

"Everything okay, lads?" I ask, reaching for the empties.

They exchange glances and the meathead on the end cocks his head to the side, as if he's examining me or something, and says, "Just enjoying a pint."

Nodding, I stack one glass on top of the other and head back to the bar without another glance in their direction.

Something is off, and an uneasy feeling settles in the very pit of my stomach. A hundred different scenarios play out through my mind and none of them are any good. They look like loan sharks, or some other dodgy shit, from what I can see of them, anyway.

Does Des owe them money?

I know the business has been suffering lately, but surely it isn't bad enough to make him go to a loan shark for the cash.

I think about calling him up, but quickly push that thought aside as quickly as it comes. These guys could do him some serious damage. D might be built like a brick shithouse, but he's fifty fuckin' two. His reflexes and judgment aren't as quick as they used to be.

No. I'll let the night play out before I do anything too hasty. Besides, we shut in an hour. They'll be gone soon.

"Since when do you collect the dirties?" Darcie says as I hop over the bar.

"Since I let curiosity get the better of me," I hit back, tugging on her ponytail.

"Curiosity killed the cat, my friend. You'd be wise to remember that," she teases me, tossing in a wink before she saunters off, leaving me standing there, feeling like I have two pairs of eyes staring holes in my back again.

****

"Hey, wait up, I'll walk with you," Darcie calls out and I pause, my fingers falling from the handle of the club door.

"I don't need a babysitter, Darce."

"No, but I do," she says, wrapping her arm around mine.

I chuckle and push the door open, stepping out into the darkened alleyway – the same exit we make most nights, so I have no idea why tonight feels stranger than usual. "Where did you park?"

"Just over there," she tells me, nodding her head.

Nodding back, I pull the zipper up on my jacket, tucking my chin inside the leather, and start to make my way to her car with her. I'm going to have to speak to her tomorrow about how far away she parks. It's not safe out here. Anything could happen to her, even if she is taking fancy self-defence classes these days. She's still a vulnerable woman out here.

"You okay? You seem out of sorts today."

I glance down to the side and grin at her. "Nothing for you to worry about, sweetheart."

"Okay. If you say so."

A strange feeling settles over me, an unwanted feeling that increases with every step I take. I look ahead and narrow my eyes into the darkness, unable to shake off this suffocating panic that's creeping up my spine and threatening to take my throat hostage.

"What was that?" Darcie suddenly whispers, coming to an abrupt stop as we both hear the clanging of what sounds like metal hitting the ground.

"I dunno," I say, holding my arm across her chest protectively. "Listen, I need you to do something for me."

"I don't like the sound of this, Scott."

"It's nothing to worry about, I promise you. I'm just going to need you to go back inside and wait there until I come back in. You hear me?"

Her eyes widen in horror. "What? No," she says, shaking her head.

"Darce," I warn. "Just do as you're told, please."

"What's going on, Scott? You're scaring me."

"It's nothing. I told you. Can you please, just for once, do as I say?"

"You're serious, aren't you?"

I don't answer, but my straight face and serious eyes tell her everything she needs to know. I'm deadly fucking serious.

She nods silently and cautiously turns her back on me. "Hurry up," is the last thing I hear fall from her lips before she reluctantly walks away.

I know what's coming before anything actually happens at all, but in some kind of defiance, I keep my eyes trained on

Darcie until she disappears from my line of sight altogether. Then I wait. I'm unmoving to the eyes of whoever is nearby, but inside, I'm tensing, my body rigid and my hands curled into fists ready to fight back.

Even though I like to think I can handle myself, I've never been a fighter. That has always been Ethan, but when you feel the eyes of the wolves on your back and you know that you have no choice but to fight, that's when the adrenaline kicks in. And it has definitely kicked in.

Just not in time for me to fully prepare for the harsh kidney punch that instantly has me grunting as my body doubles over to one side and my eyes scrunch together tightly.

"Mother fucker," I push out through gritted teeth, trying to ignore the spots in my vision as I open my eyes again and swing my arm around in the air wildly, like that's going to connect with anything and make a decent impact.

The disorientation sends me stepping forward twice before I turn around and try to find some kind of centre of balance, while also trying to remember how to breathe. In the dark, I can't see for shit, and no matter how many times I blink and widen my eyes, I can't see the fucker who has just got a hit on me.

"I take it hello is an old fashioned custom these days," I croak to the invisible arsehole.

Nobody speaks for a while, and the only sound I can hear is the controlled slap of shoes against the concrete before the guy on my left comes into focus, thanks to some light shining out from the bar.

He's not what I expect at all... and it's not one of the guys from the bar, either.

A towering beast of a fucker, dressed like he's the pimp daddy himself in a floor-length, black tailored coat, crisp white shirt and red tie moves closer towards me, tugging on the edges of his leather gloves as he does. I've seen evil bastards before – Ethan's dad can be the biggest prick on the planet when he gets into one of his moods – but the only place I've ever seen anyone with a face like this guy is on TV. He looks like he's stepped right out of *The Godfather*, and his eyes look hungry for my fucking blood.

Shit.

This isn't good.

Stepping closer while I cautiously retreat, he shakes his head in disgust and opens his mouth to speak, revealing a mouthful of missing teeth, apart from a few gold nuggets here and there.

"Scott Jenkins, I believe?" he growls – and it is a growl. He sounds like he's smoked fifty a day since he came out of the womb. There's an eerie calm to his voice, something that doesn't feel right, and for the first time in my life, I'm not too much of a dick to admit that I am absolutely petrified.

"Listen, mate," I start. "I don't know what the hell I'm supposed to have done to you, but I can assure you, you got the wrong guy."

"I never get the wrong guy."

"Never?"

"No."

"Just my luck."

Our eyes meet then, mine unsure of what the hell I've done

wrong, or whose wife I must have shagged, his completely in control, zoning in for the kill.

"You want to know how I know you're the man I'm here for?" he asks, his crooked, humourless grin pulling up into one of his cheeks.

"It's the hair isn't it?" I cough roughly, still feeling the sting from the ten tonne kidney punch. "People always recognise the hair."

Shut the fuck up, Scott, you dickhead. I can hear E saying it in my mind, but where he has muscles and power to fight off this kind of attack, all I have is bad humour and the ability to – usually – talk myself out of this shit.

"I know it's you because they told me you were a pussy who would run, and it looks like you're running."

"They?"

"You can thank your friend."

"If this is some kind of early Christmas present, it's pretty fucking shitty."

"That mouth is going to get you killed, boy."

"Agreed."

"Make sure Walker sees this."

I'm just about to ask him what the fuck he's talking about when I'm stopped abruptly in my tracks, my back slamming into another towering wall of muscle that feels as tall as The Eiffel Tower.

When another pair of hands reaches up from behind to grab hold of my biceps, I know I'm in big fucking trouble.

Epic trouble.

The kind of trouble where you end up in a wheelchair... if

you ever get the chance to wake up at all.

Bracing myself, all I can do is straighten up and inhale a huge breath into my lungs, holding it high in my chest as I watch the first goon walk closer towards me. Then he's in front of me, his toes pushed against mine, his nose to mine and his old-fashioned aftershave scratching at my throat.

"I don't even know who you are," I say quietly.

"You're not supposed to," he slurs through an evil half smile, and then it starts.

The first hit is to the opposite side of my body, forcing me to try and bow that way as I fight to stay in control, but instantly the pain is fucking everywhere all at once. Only this time, the guy doesn't let up at all. There's no period of rest, no taking it slow. He goes all in and before I know it, my body, jaw and face feel like they've taken hit after hit after hit, left and right, straight in the gut, at the top of my thighs to dead leg me completely.

I'm not sure at what point my mind closes down on me.

I'm not sure at what point the pain proves too much.

But somewhere between one punch and the next, I'm out for the count, until my eyes flicker open sometime later, and all I can feel is the cold concrete against my cheek and the absolute agony of the beating as it rips through my body.

I've just been fucked up.

And I have no idea why.

Chapter Twenty-One

It doesn't take Darcie long to realise that something has happened. It feels like a lifetime, though. Through the blanket of pain, my only comfort is knowing that she's okay. I'm certain that they were here just for me, and they didn't get to her after they left me in a heap on the ground.

When I come to, I'm still in the alleyway, surrounded by darkness. A pain, ridiculously fierce and uncontrollable, shoots through every muscle I own, bringing me back down when I attempt to get up.

I'm not sure how, but Darcie eventually finds me and somehow manages to help me crawl my way over to the brick wall of the bar. No position I settle in once I'm sat down makes any difference. The pain is everywhere. Even my fingertips are swollen and bloodied. The inside of my mouth feels like it's been stung by a hundred bees, it's that swollen, and I can't see shit for shit.

I keep trying to replay the moment it all happened, but everything is blurred, confusing, like the adrenaline of the moment has wiped out the most important things I needed to remember. Gold teeth, though. I remember those. I also remember not being able to fight back.

The only thing I was able to do was tense my body, my fists and my legs whenever I knew another hit was coming my way. God, the fucking hits.

They were quick.

Or maybe I just wasn't prepared for the force that was waiting for me in the darkness – two ten tonne trucks on legs.

Not that any of that matters now. It's over, and there is only one question on my mind.

"Why?"

No matter how many times I replay it over and over, I'm none the wiser.

"Why'd they do this to you, Scott?" Darcie asks, and I flinch as a cold pack of ice is pressed against my ribs. "Sorry. I'm sorry."

I inhale a breath, which hurts like hell, and force a swollen grin onto my face. Coco the Clown hasn't got shit on me right now. "You said yourself this would happen one day, right?"

"Not like this. This kind of beating is not some petty feud over a woman."

"Maybe they just got the wrong guy. Maybe I'm too pretty for my own good." I try to laugh, but end up coughing so hard that I feel like I'm going to vomit up a lung.

"Scott, this… This is crazy. We have to call the police."

"No. Not happening," I force out through lungfuls of air while using my half decent arm to push myself up.

"No," she says, pointing a pink fingernail. "Do not even think about it. Lay back down."

"No police, Darce. I mean it. I don't want anyone knowing

about this. Not even D, do you hear me?"

"Well, too late for that," she mumbles, wiping a wet flannel across my left arm.

I shoot her a death glare.

"I had to tell him. What if they had shown up after we left? He's on his own."

She's right. What if they had got to him, too?

Sighing, I cautiously turn my torso into a position that feels even the slightest bit more comfortable. "You're right. But let's keep this between the three of us, okay?"

"You're hiding something from me, aren't you?"

"Trust me, Darce. This was random," I tell her, not quite believing it myself as I frown and try to remember what the big guy said to me before he used me as a punchbag. It's there, teasing me from a dark corner of my mind. I just can't see or hear it properly.

She nods, although she doesn't seem at all convinced.

"Thanks for this, love," I finally say, trying to change the subject.

"It's just a bag of frozen peas. No biggie."

"Not just the peas. This… Being here."

"Yeah, well I wish you'd let me call someone."

"I already told you. No one–"

"Can know about this," she interrupts. "You said that already. You might've broken a rib. Will you at least…"

"No. No hospitals, either. The peas are fine. They're helping," I lie.

"What about your face then?"

"What about my face?"

"It's already bruising nicely. How are you going to hide that, hey?"

"It's fine. I heal quickly."

"And you still don't know who or why someone would do this to you?"

"No idea."

"What about the two guys from the bar earlier?"

"We've gone over this already. I don't know. Maybe. It was dark."

"But they must have said something to you. They wouldn't just–"

That's when it hits me. All at once. Like a fucking bolt of lightning.

Make sure Walker sees this.

Ethan.

"Darce. Leave it!" I snap, no longer able to handle her questions mingling with all my own confused, messed up thoughts.

"But–"

"I said leave it the fuck alone already. Jesus," I force out through gritted teeth.

She pulls back, narrowing her eyes at me. "You do know something, don't you? What aren't you telling me?"

The truth is, I don't know shit, but until I do – until I have more facts, I'm not telling anyone about this. Especially not E.

"Babe, please. My head is killing. I can barely see or move. I don't know anything, so can you drop it? Please?"

"Okay. I'm sorry. Can I at least get you a drink? Yeah, you want a drink, right? Something strong maybe? To numb the pain? Hell, even I need something strong."

I nod. "Something strong would be great."

I don't go on to tell her that nothing, not even the biggest concoction of alcohol she could mix together, could numb the pain I'm feeling right now.

This is something else entirely. I can only hope that Ethan is safe and that whatever is going on his life, that little beating of mine has just bought him some time from someone or something. I'd take it all over again if it means he's going to be okay.

Chapter Twenty-Two

T he sun has stolen the night, the rays clawing and grasping at it so tightly that the dark is no longer around. At least to others, anyway. While mums, dads, grandmas and grandpas run circles around gardens, entertaining young children, I sit here alone in my apartment, surrounded by darkness with only the distant laughter of strangers to keep me company.

Everything is fucked up. It was only for a short while, but those weeks with Meli were possibly the best damn days of my life so far. They changed who I was, how I viewed life, what I wanted to become.

Then I pushed her away.

I let her walk away, and I couldn't even bring myself to stop her, even long after I realised how wrong I was to do so. I just want the guilt to go away. I want her to be mine without it feeling wrong in any way whatsoever. Instead, it's left me feeling angry and confused, wound up so tightly that I'm sure I'll snap at any second.

I push up from the recliner, stretching the taught muscles in my neck. The beating I took has taken its toll on me. Every muscle hurts, every breath feels like it could be my last, and the taste of copper in my mouth still lingers. I still can't get over the fact that it happened to me. Not because I slept with the wrong lass or gobbed off to the wrong guy. I took that beating because of my best friend.

Make sure Walker sees this. Fuck you, meathead. Fuck you and your sick warnings, hidden messages and lack of fucking morals. Ethan isn't seeing shit. I'll keep this from him, no matter what it takes.

The anger stays with me, refusing to go anywhere. I'm angry at them. I'm angry at Ethan; I'm angry at whichever God up there thought it was fair for me to take this punishment for a crime I haven't committed. I'm also angry at karma. I guess that bitch gets to you in one way or another no matter how much you try to avoid it. Was this punishment for betraying my brother? Is this how the circle of life goes? An eye for an eye, or in my case, a rib and a bust up leg for fuck all in return?

All this anger has to go somewhere.

There's only one thing left for me to do to deal with it.

I won't give myself time to think about what I'm about to do, though. If I did, I'd only have to admit what a bastard I am. I don't need that right now. I need a distraction, a release from the tight grip Amelia holds over me, to overcome the anger I feel at the hands of those men and not being able to fight back.

Amelia has quickly become everything I need and everything I shouldn't want, and I both hate and love it. I love the effect I have on her, the way her body responds to me with little effort. I love hearing her cry out my name when I tip her over the edge. I also hate how much I love all of those things.

I can never justify my intentions. I want her, and damn if she doesn't want me, too. I've never been a jealous man, but at this point in my life, I hate Liam. I despise him for being in her life, and I hate her for the claim she holds over both of us.

hate that I'm so out of fucking control.

She has chosen the better man. Liam wouldn't have stood there while two men beat the shit out of him. He would've fought back, no matter how many times he was knocked down. I can't protect her. I can't even protect myself. I'm the weaker brother.

Yet so many times I've had to stop myself from calling her or getting in the damn car to go and see her. I know the second I do that there will be no going back. I won't be strong enough to stop it again. I know how much she wants me. That much is obvious, but I can never be enough for her. I've known this from the start, and while my charm can melt the panties off most lasses, Amelia is in a class of her own. Her little lace briefs are bound so tightly that not even a blazing inferno can dissolve them. She might want me, but she doesn't need me. Not like I need her.

****

"Scott, please…"

I shake my head, dazed and confused. It's only when I drop my forehead and peer down that I realise where I am and what I'm in the middle of.

Big brown eyes gaze up at me pleadingly.

Shit!

I've zoned out again. Only this time, I'm not alone.

Amelia has not only stolen my heart, but my damn dick, too. I came here for one thing and one thing only: a distraction, and to prove to myself that I can survive without her. Letting her walk away was painful. I want to run after her, to tell her I'm sorry and that I never meant it. I want to lift her in my arms and tell her how much I want her, that nothing else matters as long as I have her. But I hold onto the memory of Liam almost catching us out. I hold it so tightly that it's become almost unbearable. I imagine his face if things had played out differently, his torn expression if he had to witness Amelia and I together. I cling to that painful imagine and it gets me through the nights, but my craving for Amelia is too much. It's why I've come here. Only I'm not doing so well.

I wonder if my dick will ever be the same. Will it ever respond to anyone but the girl that made it pulse with all kinds of sensations? Will any girl ever feel as good as she did? I fucking hope so.

I peer down, embarrassed and a little lost for words. I can't explain what just happened without earning myself a clout around the ear, and I figure the truth won't get me anywhere anyway.

So I do the only thing I can.

I imagine long, blonde locks splayed across the pillow, and bright blue eyes, darkened through lust and holding my own. I close my eyes and hold onto those memories. I do the worst thing imaginable.

I picture Amelia while I'm fucking Paige.

****

"Answer it, Scott."

"No. Whoever it is can fucking wait."

It has been ringing non-stop for the past twenty minutes. I've just managed to get into it with Paige. I'm not about to pull out to answer the damn thing, so I thrust deep, my frustration showing through every movement, but it's no good. My rhythm has flown out of the window along with my patience.

"Fuck's sake!" I curse, snatching the phone from the dresser. "What?" I growl out through clenched teeth, bringing the phone to my ear as I sink back on my heels.

Paige shuffles out from underneath me, wrapping the sheet around herself, and I give her an apologetic look. Pressing her lips to my forehead one last time, she heads out of the room.

My mouth goes dry as I listen to the voice on the other end of the line, my heart stopping for what feels like an eternity before the phone slips from my hand altogether, falling to the mattress.

"Scott?"

Nothing.

Just the thundering halt of my heart as it stops.

"Scott? What is it? What's wrong?" Paige asks from the doorway. I didn't even hear her come back in.

Still nothing.

All the oxygen has been sucked from my lungs and I struggle to push the words out.

"Scott. You're scaring me. Please... Say something," Paige pleads.

"I've gotta go."

"Why? Scott, you've gone so pale."

"I... Go..."

"Go where?" she asks me quietly.

"Ethan," I finally manage to say.

"Ethan? What about Ethan?"

Blinking slowly, my lips parting as a small shiver of dread runs down my spine, I finally manage to look up at her, showing her every ounce of fear I feel right down to my stone cold bones.

"He's in hospital."

****

I break every speed limit there is to get to the hospital. I'm not sure what I'm expecting to find when I eventually get there. All I know is that I need to be by his side.

I push through the glass doors to reception, panting heavily, not giving a shit about the funny looks I get from my own bust up face. "Walker. Ethan," is all I can manage as my palms slap against the counter. The petite brunette behind the desk widens her eyes and glances at her colleague, who only nods in response to the unspoken question.

"And you are?"

"His brother," I lie.

It only takes her a few seconds to find the information she needs, before she eventually stands and makes her way towards me.

"Right this way, Sir. His father and your other brother are here also. It's just down this corridor. I'll show you the way."

The walk seems to take forever, which is funny because it isn't all that far from where we started. My heart sinks as I will my feet to carry me to the unknown. All I can think is what if I'd answered the damn phone the first time. If I hadn't gone to see Paige, none of this would've happened. If I hadn't been too wrapped up in my own pity party, I could have been here sooner. What if I'm too late?

"It's just through here. The doctor will be along shortly."

"Thank you."

"Remember, it always looks worse than it is." She pats me on my shoulder and disappears while I just stare ahead of me like my world has come to an end when I see him hooked up to a million machines.

Time freezes as I listen to the doctor reel off fancy fucking words that I don't understand. I don't care what they mean or what they stand for. I just need to know that he's okay – that he's alive and is going to stay that way for a very long time. I can't remember acknowledging Dean or Ethan's dad, but before I know it, I've been standing in this room watching my best mate's chest rise and fall for an impossibly long time.

The exchange of words between Mr. Walker and the man in the white coat becomes distant after a while, and my anger towards Ethan, that has been dormant for so long, rises to the surface.

My hands ball into fists at my side and my knee jerks, colliding with the wall. Blow after blow, yet no pain or fight can erase the feeling that has settled deep inside of me. My knuckles scrape and crush against the cheap white paint, pound after pound. Nothing. I feel nothing. Not even pain from all the unhealed injuries to my own body.

Red smatterings of blood mingle against the dents almost in a pattern of fury. I'm not sure what's happening until two security guards have me pinned against the wall while I struggle to gasp for air.

A sharp pain in my hand has me recoiling, and the dull ache in my side reminds me of the injuries I sustained not that long ago, but I ignore them. Pain means I feel something and feeling something means I'm alive. I'm not sure I want to be alive, though. Not without my best friend.

"Get. The. Fuck. Off. Me," I spit out, tugging my arms to break free.

"Sir, you need to calm down or we'll have to ask you to leave," the bald one warns, showing no sympathy for what's going on at all.

I twist my head and snarl. "Calm down? Calm fucking down? Are you shitting me? My mate is lying in that fucking bed, I don't know if he's going to end up dead or alive, and you're telling me to calm the fuck down? Screw you!" I tug away again. "Let me the fuck go and I will go find someone who will tell us the truth."

Their hold on me loosens, and I push past the burly man with a shitty tattoo poking out from his veiny neck and glare down the hall, lost. Scrubbing my face with both hands, I drag them through my curly black hair, thin strands catching in the broken skin on my knuckles.

"Scott?" My head whips around at the sound of Dean's voice. "He's alive, mate."

"But for how long?"

"He's in the best place. You ain't helping."

"I know. I'm just…"

"Scared? Join the club, pal."

Looking up at Dean, I shake my head in defeat and sigh.

"What was it he overdosed on? Charlie? Crack? Both?" I spit out, pushing my cut hand into my pocket as I try to regain some control and hide what happened to me. Dean doesn't need to see or know about that. The kid's already seen enough to last a fucking lifetime.

"We're not sure. They're running tests now, but, Scott… We lost him a couple'a times. They managed to bring him back but he's in a bad way," he says through a strained voice, dropping into a nearby chair and burying his face in shaky hands. "He was taking something with Jessica Gregory."

"What?" My eyes widen as I watch him struggle to get his words out.

"And she… she didn't make it."

My shoulders sag instantly, and my face falls completely flat as I stare at Dean and wait for him to tell me he's kidding. Only he never does, and all the times I've wished Jessica Gregory dead come back to haunt me, singing in my ear how I finally got what I asked for.

"She's dead?" I ask quietly.

"She died quickly, apparently. Overdosed to fuck."

"Fuck. I can't even…"

"That could have been E. My E. My bro."

"But it isn't. It wasn't. He's here and he's not giving up."

"The bastard almost died."

I swallow down the lump that's lodged itself in my throat and slump down in the seat beside him. Guilt washes over me and I grip his shoulder for support. "I'm sorry, bud. Your big brother is a natural born fighter. He's gonna be fine."

"He better be."

"He will be."

"We'll see."

"Where did your dad go?" I ask, glancing around at the now empty corridor.

He shrugs. "I heard 'em say sommat about paperwork or some shit. I dunno. He told me to stay here."

I nod and flex the joints in my hand. Even though it's hidden, I can already tell it's swelling up.

"I can't lose him, Scott. Other than Dad, E's all I got."

I want to tell him that isn't true, that he has me, but I know what he means. His mum is impossible to replace. Ethan isn't a substitute parent, but he loves Dean and would do anything to protect him, and Dean knows that he won't be able to survive without Ethan. That worries me more than I can ever say out loud. "You ain't gonna lose him, bud. He's a fighter, like I said. Fucker doesn't know how to stay down unless it's on some hot chick." I smirk over at Dean, trying to lighten the mood and am relieved to see a small smile tugging at the corner of his mouth.

"I love him," Dean admits out loud.

"Me, too. He's my hero. He just needs to remember that."

"So, what happened to your face? Get caught banging some bird you shouldn't have been?"

"Something like that, kid. Something like that." The last thing Dean needs right now is me adding to his worry over Ethan. He has no need to know about the beating I took for his brother. Perhaps neither of us need to know why it happened. Perhaps some things should just be left a mystery and we should learn to appreciate the here and now moments – the moments that keep our loved ones alive.

"You'll never learn, will you, Jenkins?"

"I'm not sure I want to, mate." I smile, leaning back in to the chair and staring at the door to the room that holds my best friend's life in its hands.

Chapter Twenty-Three

Rehab?" I scoff. "He's never gonna go for it and you know it."

"He doesn't have to, Scott. It's all sorted. Once Ethan comes round and is given the all clear to leave, he's gone."

"And he doesn't get a choice?" I yell, pushing up from the uncomfortable plastic chair. "Fuck!" I curse, booting the hospital vending machine.

"I'm doing what's best for my son. I don't need to answer to you."

"What's best for him? You're fucking kidding, right? Where were you? Where the fuck were you when he lost Julia? Where were you when he needed his dad? He lost everything, goddammit. Where were you then, eh? At the fucking pub, drowning your sorrows like the selfish bastard that you are."

"Easy, Scott," Dean says, placing a hand on my arm.

I shake him off. "No. No, I won't go fucking easy. He kicked him out. He may as well have supplied the drugs for all the good that prick has done!" I yell, slapping my palm against the wall. I wince at the excruciating pain running from my fingertips to my knuckles, and whisper, "You don't know what's best for him." I shake my head, my lips set firmly in a hard line. "None of us do. That's why he's in this mess in the first place, because of us," I whisper, right before I walk out of that room and leave my words to register with the pair of them.

The bitter wind hits me as soon as I push through the glass doors and out into the hospital lay-by. Heavy drops of rain beat against my cheeks as I tip my head up to the sky. The dark storm clouds up ahead fly by, but they never break, and the sun never peeks through. A constant darkness surrounds me once again, and I drop to my knees, fisting my shirt as the pain from this evening takes over.

Why?

Why did you do this, E?

I can't live without you, mate. I don't want to.

Dropping my head into my hands, I make a promise to the big man upstairs that if Ethan pulls through this, I will do my absolute fucking best to be the friend I should've been this last year. I'll be there to guide him and look out for him when life gets too tough. I'll put myself and my feelings aside if God will just bring him back to us. To me. The old Ethan. I want him back, safe and sound.

An hour later and I'm finally calming, slowly but surely. I can't let what happened back there happen again. The only way I can be sure it won't is to take myself away from the situation altogether. Ethan will probably wake up again soon and I know he'll need fresh clothing and toiletries for when he does. So I make use of my idle hands before the devil does it for me. I go back to his apartment to collect some of his things. It isn't easy. The rooms haven't been touched. All the evidence is still scattered around in various places with little notes displaying numbers, and I can't control the sick feeling that washes over me as I take in the area where Jessica must have died. As much as I disliked her for everything she did, I can't help but feel sorry for her. I am human, after all. She might've been a bitch, but she was somebody's daughter. No one deserves to die, and especially not so young. She was stuck in a rut – a situation she felt she couldn't escape. The truth is, she had a whole life ahead of her, to find a mutual love and a home life. Hell, maybe even children. Whether Ethan realises it or not, he's lucky. We're lucky.

It takes almost thirty minutes to gather up his belongings. Every item has been noted and searched by the police before I'm able to place it inside the duffel bag I found under one of the beds. I guess it's standard procedure, but you would have to be completely stupid to not realise what happened here. The needles have remnants of brown liquid still sat at the tips. Add in the teaspoons and clear empty bags that sit forgotten on the ageing carpet and this is your basic set-up for a drug session gone wrong.

I'm still fighting back the bile that has risen in my throat when I force myself to stand and peer through the blinds into Ethan's hospital room again.

I wonder how I've ended up here. Not in the hospital waiting room surrounded by people I don't know from Adam, but here… at this point in my life.

Ethan has been in and out of consciousness for the past three hours. No words. No acknowledging where he is or the people around him. He's just floating in and out of himself. He freaked out and ended up being restrained, but he's stable. That's a good sign, but I can't help but feel like this is just the beginning.

"Mate, you can go in. That chick said one at a time, but I can't... I'm not ready yet," Dean says from behind me, his words trailing off to nothing but a whisper.

I'm not sure I'm ready, either. Witnessing the way he clawed at the tubes and equipment that kept him alive was too much to take. He panicked. I'd freak the fuck out, too, if I woke up in some random place with God knows what shoved down my throat. I'm pretty sure he was unaware that the equipment was what had kept him going all this time. I'm still not entirely sure he's aware of anything but the pain that's been enveloping him since he took that almost fatal hit.

He's my best mate, though, and he's currently all alone, with the exception of fleeting doctors and nurses as they go about their work.

With my back still to Dean, I nod once and curl my hand around the door handle, blowing out a shaky breath.

I'm not sure what I'm expecting to find as I push the door open to reveal him laid up in bed in nothing but a faded blue hospital gown. Maybe my best mate of nineteen years? The man that I've always seen as my hero? It definitely isn't this – a washed-up version of Ethan, with hair touching his chin and weeks, maybe months, of untouched facial hair. He looks old. His skin is darkened and blotchy with a scattering of spots from poor hygiene. Whoever this is, it isn't my Ethan.

"Mate, what have you done?"

Chapter Twenty-Four

I sit beside him for the best part of an hour. The rhythmic beeping of the machines is a constant reminder of how serious this is. They aren't just a reminder, though. They're hope. As long as the machines continue to blare out, Ethan's life remains intact.

I feel the bed dip all at once, pulling me out of my reverie. The cuffs that currently secure him in place begin to rattle against the metal frame of the bed and I lift my head, locking eyes with my best mate.

"Ethan?" I breathe, not meaning to sound so unsure.

"Sco…?" is all he manages before his eyes grow wide with panic, or fear. Maybe both.

He pulls at the restraints again, looking at me for answers to his unspoken question.

"You tried to pull the wires out, mate. It's just a safety precaution."

"Wh-what happened?" he asks, wincing.

Swallowing, I run my hands through my hair. "You don't remember?"

He shakes his head but the expression on his face says it

all. He doesn't remember anything. The drugs, Jess, freaking out when he came round the last time. He doesn't remember a damn thing. I'm not sure how to bring Jess up, but I know I have to. He deserves to know.

I shake my head and suck in a breath. "You and Jess... You... Mate, you had bad drugs. They saved you, barely, but Jess…" I pause briefly, unsure how to say the next few words without breaking. It could've been Ethan.

He continues to look at me as though this is all new to him. I guess in a way, it is. He might've been there when it happened, but he certainly doesn't remember. "She didn't make it. She was dead before the paramedics got there. If Paul hadn't come home sick from work, you'd be dead, too."

I lift my hand to place it on his arm in comfort, but let it fall to the bed. Ethan's eyes bug out of his face and I can almost hear his brain ticking, searching for answers. I can see the panic written all over him and I wince as he tugs at the restraints again.

His mouth opens as if to speak, but quickly closes as the door to the room opens, revealing the same doctor from before. His expression is less sympathetic this time. Disgust is written all over his face, and it's clear from Ethan's reaction that he's seen it, too.

"You got lucky, Mr. Walker. Your girlfriend wasn't so fortunate."

I want to smack him straight in the nose and make him do the job he's paid to do. He's judging Ethan by his medical chart and not for who he is.

"You're going to be tender for quite a while. You coded

in the ambulance and they had to perform CPR, also once in Accident and Emergency. Your body will inevitably start to crave the drugs as you're taken off the meds we're giving you. You should, hopefully, be in a rehabilitation centre by then."

I look cautiously to Ethan as he swallows down and croaks out, "Rehab?"

I'm stumped for words to say that will make any of this better. The dear doctor has already decided that Ethan is a waste of space junkie who needs a stint in rehab to sort him out, exactly the same way Mr. Walker has. I don't know. Maybe he's right. Maybe that's exactly what E needs to recover. All I know is that I want my best mate back, and if shipping him off to some rehab clinic is what it will take then maybe it isn't such a bad idea after all.

I only catch the tail end of the doctor's final words and they play over in my mind as I look to Ethan, horrified. "Next time your ride will be to the morgue."

Time stops as I watch the fear and hurt flash through Ethan's eyes. He starts to tug the restraints again, and this time, I feel thankful for their position. I'm scared for him.

"Ethan?" I say. "Mate, you know I'm not gonna judge you. I'm here, ain't I?"

For now, I'm here, but while he's in rehab, he'll have no one. He'll be spending the next month or so alone, exactly how he's spent the last year. I haven't been there for him. I've been so wrapped up in Amelia and screwing my brother over that I forgot about everything Ethan has done for me during our nineteen year friendship. But I will be there for him now, after rehab and every day beyond that.

"Mate?" I say, edging closer to the bed.

"I'm sorry, Scott," he breathes out, swallowing through the pain. "I... I fucked up, big time."

I want to tell him to stop speaking. I hate seeing the pain on his face as he pushes each word out as though it's the hardest thing to do. He needs reassurance that despite everything, I fucking love the bastard, and that will never change.

The tears begin to flow freely now, and Ethan makes no attempt to hide them. "You weren't yourself, E, and I... I never should have left you that night at the party."

The fucking party. The night that changed everything.

I feel my own tears welling in my eyes, but force them back. This isn't about me.

"Don't make excuses for me, Scott. I may not have had a choice that night, but I had one the next day and the one after that. I let you down. I let Dean down. I let my mum down."

"I hate seeing you like this." I do. He cries, and I let him. I let him because it's the exact thing I want to do, too, and screw it if that makes us anything less than human.

This all started because of grief. Maybe now he can grieve properly and regain some normalcy in his life that he hasn't had for the past year.

"Self-inflicted." He sniffs, his cheeks reddening even more. "I just can't believe my dad is making me stay in some hospital for a month."

"Maybe it's for the best?" I whisper. "Think about it," I continue, ignoring the incredulous look on his face. "What would you do if you got out and the cravings started? How long could you put that off?"

He doesn't say another word as he ponders what I've said. Although hearing it must feel like a kick in the teeth, I have a feeling he agrees with me. It's for the best. In a little over a month's time, we'll have Ethan back. My Ethan. My fucking hero. I'm not feeling great about the last year, and the past twenty-four hours have been the worst of my life, but finally, I can sit here in this damn waiting room and say, "I feel fucking hopeful."

Chapter Twenty-Five

August 2003

It's been three days since Ethan took the bad batch that saw him hospitalised and sent packing off to rehab. Knowing he's in safe hands has done nothing to ease the worry and guilt that I feel constantly. I carry it with me every second of every day. I know I messed up by not being there for him, and I decided right there in that hospital room that from then on, Ethan would be my only concern. That means I need to forget about Amelia, which is proving harder than I ever imagined it could be. The nights are dark, cold and so fucking lonely. Insomnia has taken hold of me, leaving me lost and broken throughout the day. I tell myself that if I can just hold her one last time, everything will be okay, but I know that one precious moment will never be enough. I need to face facts. She is no longer in my life, and it needs to stay that way. Despite the hole I've found myself in, I've forced myself to realise that there is far bigger stuff going on in the world than what I've lost. Though I haven't really lost her. She'll always be in my life as long as she's with Liam. Although that thought alone drives me crazy at times, I would rather have that than nothing at all. I almost lost Ethan, and I can't think of anything worse than that. That day has put my life into perspective. Losing him isn't an option. I'm ready to fight for him. With him.

Des has granted me what he is calling 'compassionate leave,' not that I need it. The truth is, I'm worse off than ever before now that I don't have rowdy customers to help take my mind off everything. I don't even have the torture of Darcie's bad jokes to keep me entertained.

Dodging calls from Liam and my mum hasn't been easy. While I know they're worried about Ethan, it's impossible for me to share the whole truth with them. I would have to admit that I've sat by and watched it happen for the best part of a year without saying a word or helping him. I can't witness the disappointment on their faces when they realise that, somewhere along the way, I have become that person. That selfish prick.

Paige showed up at the apartment the morning Ethan was sent to rehab, and I flipped out. Bat shit crazy doesn't even come close to how I behaved towards her that day. I was angry at the world, and I freaked out at her, blaming her for my not being there for Ethan when he was taken into hospital. Yet, it was my selfish feelings that had me rocking up to Paige's house with every intention of fucking Amelia out of my system. She isn't to blame. I am. And I hate the selfish bastard of a man I have become.

******

Two days later...

"Firstly, you look like you haven't washed in a month; you seriously could use a shave, and secondly, you should really sit down for this."

"That's three things."

"What?" she asks, clearly a little confused.

"I said that was three things. Wash, shave and sit down. That's three."

"Whatever, Scott," she huffs out in annoyance. "Just sit down."

"I am sat down," I hit back, narrowing my eyes and smirking.

"Yeah. Okay, good. Look..." she says, rubbing her temples with the palms of her hands before sinking down beside me.

I study her curiously, my brain ticking for answers as to why she flew through my front door like a madman on a mission. I've seen many sides to Paige recently, but this, whatever this is, isn't one of them.

Blowing out a breath, she chucks me a pained expression before parting her red-coated lips to speak. "I saw her today. Amelia whatever she's called. The girl from the club that night who ordered the fuk-me-up. She's who you've been seeing, isn't she? The one you failed to mention to me at any given chance, which, by the way, there were heaps of."

I close my eyes and inhale a breath. Just hearing her name mentioned causes my heart to constrict in pain.

Running a hand through my hair, I blow out a breath and

tilt my head to face her. "Look, about that–" I begin, only to be cut off mid-sentence with a waft of her hand.

"Don't. It's none of my business who you date, Scott. Admittedly, it would have been nice to know, you know? Considering we're friends and all. Anyway, look, I really don't know how to tell you this, but I think... Well, I know..."

I flinch as she drops her head into her lap and curses under her breath. "What do you know?"

"God, this sucks. For the record, I haven't come here to rub your nose in it, although I can't say that thought hasn't crossed my mind. Truth is, you're an arse, Scott Jenkins. But no one, not even you, deserves that."

"Deserves what? I'm really fucking lost here, sweetheart."

She lets out a groan before blurting out, "I saw Amelia kissing Liam. Amelia? She's the girl from the club, right? And your brother? As in Liam, Liam. Liam Jenkins, Liam. Your big brother, Liam."

Yeah, yeah, I get it. Liam.

Even though this shouldn't surprise me, it does. I've seen them kiss a million times before but I can't help the stabbing sensation that I feel in my gut. The thought of anyone, even my brother, touching her, tasting her, well, it's enough to send me over the edge, digging and twisting the knife in that little bit further.

"Paige, I was never dating Amelia. She's Liam's girlfriend. Has been for as long as I can remember."

"But you... I saw you. The way you were around each other... I'm not blind, Scott. It was obvious that there was something between you both. I saw the way she looked at you and that wasn't just friendly."

"You've got it wrong. She's Liam's."

A look of horror flashes across her face, causing her cheeks to pale and I struggle to find the words to put this right.

"No. No. No," she chants, shaking her head. "You... You wouldn't. Not you."

"I wouldn't what?"

"Oh, God."

"Paige?"

"No. Tell me you didn't. Your brother, Scott? How could... Why? Why would you do that?"

"What? How do you? I mean… where did you?" I pause, staring at her, unable to hide the truth any longer. "Shit, Paige."

"Holy. Shit." Her eyes are wide, her face displaying all her shock. "Why?"

My stomach churns as I push up from the couch and begin to pace the room. "I don't know. I never meant for it to happen. Neither of us did. It just happened."

And it did.

"It just happened? Like that makes this whole big fucking mess okay?"

"No. No, it fucking doesn't. None of this is okay, Paige. Don't you get that? I feel sick to my stomach. Guilty as fuck and–"

"So you should!" she yells, forcing me to wince. "You can't just waltz in and take what doesn't belong to you, Scott. She. Wasn't. Yours. To. Take."

"Don't you think I fucking know that? Every day I wake up hating myself for what I did, for the way I felt about her.

Feel, about her," I correct. "I love her and there is nothing I can do about it. I tried! I tried so fucking hard to resist her. I told myself every day that she wasn't mine. But when it came down to it, I couldn't. I couldn't leave her alone because I wanted her. And no, at the time I didn't care about hurting anyone else. I didn't give a fuck about Liam. No one else mattered but her."

I grip the window ledge and push my forehead against the glass, welcoming the coldness. Did I just say that I love Amelia? Do I love her? I'm not sure. What the fuck do I know about love?

I'm not sure how long I stay like that. Seconds, minutes, hours could pass me by as I watch the outside world continue to live. Unbeknownst to them, there is someone not far away dying inside, with nobody to blame but himself.

A small touch is placed upon my shoulder and I tilt my head and glance down.

"You love her?"

I'm not sure if it's a question or a statement. I'd say statement, considering I just told her so. I meet her big brown eyes and nod. "Yeah. I mean, I think so."

I don't have a chance to digest my own admission because a harsh sting blazes across my cheek. I don't move. I don't try and soothe it. I just stare, my expression remaining blank, and no words are needed because for the first time in my whole fucking existence, I deserve to be bitch slapped by a girl.

"I knew I disliked you when I came here!" she cries out. "But now I really fucking despise you. I have no idea who you are anymore and I'm not sure I want to know. Goodbye, Scott. Enjoy your lonely, miserable existence, screwing up everyone else's lives."

I'm not even surprised by this shit anymore.

Twice now I've been walked out on by a lass. The first one cut so deeply that I'm not sure I'll ever recover from it. This time, however, I know for a fact that I will never get over it. Relationships end. That's how the world works. But friendships should be for keeps. Friends battle through the ups and downs, holding onto each other, never letting them fall and being there to pick them up when they do. I lost Amelia, but she was never mine to lose. Now I've lost Paige, and that hurts far worse than any fallen relationship ever could. I've taken her for granted and used her as a pawn in my sick little game. She thought she knew me before, only now she's had a glimpse of the real me, the one who never deserved her friendship in the first place.

It feels like there's not much left for me to lose at this point.

Everything I thought I stood for is now beneath my own feet, my self-destruction practically visible for me to see as I look out on the streets below me and let my eyes follow Paige as she storms out of my life.

Sucking in a huge, tired breath, I place both hands on the window and lean forward. Compared to a lot of people out there, my life shouldn't feel as bad as it does. I hate this feeling sorry for myself. I hate not knowing what to do, and no matter how much it hurts, I know that there's only one place for me to go from here.

Up.

And only I can be the one to take myself to higher places.

Chapter Twenty-Six

June 2004

What a difference a bit of time makes.

It's been ten months since Ethan got out of rehab, and after a brief stint at my place, the lad has finally moved into an apartment of his own. It hasn't been an easy ten months by any means, but with every month that passes us by, the future becomes that little bit brighter and more hopeful.

I don't want to smother Ethan, and I have tried to give him enough space to think about his own life and where he wants to be, especially while he was crashing at my place. At first, he seemed lost. Rehab wasn't easy for the kid but he saw it through until the end and for that reason alone, I'm proud of him.

He was surprised to see Dean and I waiting for him the day he walked out of the rehab centre. It was almost like he'd expected to leave the joint alone. Maybe I hadn't made it clear enough that I was in it with him for the long haul, but he soon realised that he was wrong about that. I meant what I said that day in the hospital room. He was my only concern. I stuck by that. Even to this day, he's all that matters. I know I can't carry the guilt around with me forever, and slowly but surely, I have started to indulge in the things that make me happy. Mainly booze and birds.

I've learned that I need to take a step back and let Ethan live the life he deserves.

Soon after leaving rehab, he enrolled in evening classes at the local school. I'm talking late-night studying, coursework, diplomas, the lot. Dude was freaking me out with all this college shit, always sat on the sofa with a book in his lap or notebook by his side where he scribbled all his ideas down. But he needed the distraction, to feel like he finally had a purpose in life, and whatever kept him off the hard stuff was fucking perfect by me. I, for one, knew exactly what it felt like to have something drawing you in, something that was wrong. I had been there one too many times. Watching him leave every evening wasn't easy, though. The urge to follow him was always in the back of my mind. I was proud of who he was becoming and what he had left behind, so I learned, in a not-so-easy way, to let him go. I needed to trust him to make his own choices, and that is exactly what I did. Drugs will likely always play a part in his life. An addict will always be just that: an addict. He's learnt to deal with the cravings and focus on a life that will better his chances of survival. He now has a business studies qualification under his belt and a place of his own, along with a business plan that he has every intention of sticking to.

Fuck me, the guy has done good.

Better than I could ever have dreamed he would.

I guess that's partly why I have never brought up the night I was attacked outside the club. He didn't need to know, and I couldn't risk him slipping away again. One wrong move and it could all go to pan. No. Him knowing benefitted no one but the fuckers who did what they did.

Every day I find myself smiling more and more. A future that once seemed bleak and void soon becomes more positive. I see light instead of the darkness that has been a constant in my life for so long. My past mistakes become just that: mistakes. I'm learning to grow from them and to encourage myself to be a better person. Sometimes it proves harder than I thought, though.

I haven't had any contact with Paige since she walked out on me ten months ago. It isn't through lack of trying. I have tried endless times to contact her and beg for her forgiveness, but each time she hangs up on me it feels like another slap to the face. I continue to check up on her through mutual friends, who assure me she's doing well. Last I heard, she's met someone and they're planning to move in together. Although I no longer have her in my life, I take comfort in knowing that she's found someone who can make her happy in ways that I can't. I haven't given up on her. I have become a strong believer in second chances, and I hope that one day soon, mine will come and surprise me, too.

Amelia and Liam moved in together not long after Ethan moved in with me. It took me by surprise, but I managed to throw on a brave face because seeing Amelia happy was all I had ever wanted. Do I love her? Yes. Do I wish I were in

Liam's position? Hell yes. But everything in life happens for a reason. I like to tell myself that it just isn't our time. Maybe in a different life I can be everything she wants me to be. But this life belongs to them.

****

My relationship with Beth is very different to the one I have with Liam. Don't get me wrong, we still annoy the hell out of one another and hold some sibling rivalry, but when it comes down to it, we're more like friends. She deems it acceptable to share her relationship status and sexual encounters with me, while I find it more acceptable to push away any lad that comes within a ten mile radius of her. So far, she hasn't cottoned on to my brotherly ways, which means that my messages have always registered loud and clear with whoever it is I've warned off. Ethan and I have been doing it for years.

When she called this morning and asked to meet up, I figured why not? It's been months since we've had the chance to catch up properly and honestly, I miss the kid, even if her stories freak me the fuck out, and her choice of men, even more so. Not to mention it'll give me the chance to grill her about Paige. I know they have mutual friends and Beth has always been forthcoming with her knowledge.

"Jesus, Scott! I see you haven't fixed this yet?" Beth says, stating the obvious while tugging one of my curly strands between her fingers.

"Nope. And I ain't going to either."

"Ugh." She groans, stirring the sugar into her coffee.

"So, whats new?" I ask, bringing the cup to my lips before studying her curiously.

She shrugs. "Not much. Swamped with coursework. Lost my job at Rivers. Oh, and dad flipped out when he received a fine in the post. Damn bus lanes," she grumbles.

Chuckling, I shake my head. "Dad went through a bus lane?"

"Noooooo. Dont be silly," she says flippantly. "I did! Completely by accident, might I add? How was I meant to know they had damn cameras? Still, you know what he's like. He didn't appreciate the fact that it would have cost him more if I'd scuffed his alloys trying to go through the bollards."

Folding my arms over my chest, I sink back in the chair. "Ain't it about time you bought your own damn car?"

"My thoughts exactly, brother. So, you gonna lend me the money then?"

"What the hell? I'm younger than you. Shouldn't that shit be the other way around?"

"Please, Scott. I promise I'll pay you back."

I grin. "You don't even have a job."

"Maybe not yet, but I will."

"I should've known there was more to this meet than just a brother-sister catch up."

"Don't be like that." She pouts. "I really did want to see you."

"Sure you did," I say, rolling my eyes. "So let me guess... Dad won't let you use his car anymore?"

"How did you know?"

"Mum called this morning."

"Dammit!"

Ignoring her childish mumbling, I pull out an envelope from my inside pocket and slide it across the table. "Don't blow it on clothes, and when you find a car, let me know. I'll get Ethan and Dean to take a look at it first."

Squealing, she throws herself across the table and dives on me. "Oh my God. Oh my God. Oh my God. I love you, I love you, I love you."

"Only when you want a new car, Beth." I chuckle.

"That's not entirely true."

I quirk a brow.

"Okay, it is, but whatever." She shrugs. "Speaking of... How is my brother from another mother? Still off the crack?" she asks nonchalantly.

I stare at her, dumbfounded. "He's doing good. Better than you are, anyway," I point out.

"It was just a question, Scott. I didn't mean anything by it."

"I know you didn't. Anyway," I say, changing the subject. "Have you heard anything from Paige?"

Beth eyes me skeptically and frowns. "Look, I've tried talking to her. She's not interested. Won't even tell me what you did wrong."

"It was a misunderstanding."

"Some misunderstanding that was. You've really done a number on her, Scott."

"I know," I agree, blowing out a breath.

"Just give her time. She'll come round eventually."

I can give her time. It isn't like I don't have enough of it.

"If you say so," I whisper before clearing my throat and

going back to my drink. "As long as she's happy."

"She's happy." Beth pauses, and I can tell what she's about to ask before she even spits it out. "What about you? No major loves in your life that I need to know about?"

"Beth?"

"Yeah?"

"Let's assume that the money I've just handed over has also bought your silence regarding my love life for, say, the next twelve months."

"Gotcha."

"Good girl." I grin.

Chapter Twenty-Seven

One week and two days later

I was all set to have a lad's day today. I'd even managed to rope Ethan into coming, which wasn't easy. The fucker is up to something. I have no idea what, but I'm determined to find out, one way or another. I'd hoped today would be the right time to push him for a little info, but with luck clearly not on my side, I've had to cancel the whole damn day.

Liam called at the crack of dawn, practically begging me to pop round to my parents' house this afternoon. I'm not sure what's gone down but whatever it is seems important to him. Being around Amelia the last few months, I've learned to maintain a façade that appears somewhat normal to others.

I've convinced my family that I still hate Amelia, which hasn't been all that difficult. I toss shit her way at any given chance, tease her on her day's clothing choice, take the piss out of her new hairstyle and pretty much anything else I can think of at the time. No one really bats an eyelid because it's standard procedure. However, it is hard to miss the sadness in her eyes each time I crack a joke and pretend that I don't care. I wonder if I'm pushing it too far sometimes, but I don't know what else I can do. I'm so desperate to convince everyone that things are still the same way they've always been, that I worry I'm beginning to hurt her feelings. I can't just stop, though. That would arouse suspicion. There are only two ways I can act around Amelia. I can carry on hating her and allow life to continue how it's always been. Or I can love her. The second choice isn't an option. My heart is still recovering from its own admission. I definitely don't want to feel that kind of pain again so it's easier to not feel at all. The trouble is, that's easier said than done.

I pull into the driveway, late as usual, and push open the front door, which isn't locked, before calling out my arrival.

Something is off. I can feel it instantly as my eyes scan the empty living room.

"In here, love," my mum calls out from the kitchen.

I sidle up behind her and plant a kiss on her cheek. "Hey, Ma," I say with a genuine smile.

Greeting her with a kiss is something I've done since I almost lost Ethan. I realised that day that not only had I been a crappy friend, but I'd also been a shitty son and brother, too. Since then, I've tried not to take them for granted, and every chance I have, I show them how much they mean to me. I won't be planting any smackaroonies on Liam's cheek anytime soon, but I have slowly started to make an effort with him, even if it is just inviting him for a few bevvies down the local now and again.

"I've missed you, darling," Mum admits, squeezing my

cheeks with both hands.

"I only saw you yesterday," I say with a chuckle as I bat her hands away.

"So? A mother is allowed to miss her baby boy, you know?"

"Mum, I'm all man." I groan, puffing out my chest and adding a wink so she doesn't slap me on the shoulder.

"You'll always be my baby boy, Scotty. You just remember that."

"Alright, Mum," I agree, shaking my head. I can't help but smile as her warm eyes gaze at me in admiration.

"Oh, and just to warn you, Dad isn't happy that you gave your sister money for that car."

"When is he ever happy, Ma?" Some things never change.

"He's under a lot of stress at the moment. I'm sure it'll all be fine. Anyway, take a seat at the dining table. Everyone else is already in there."

"What's this all about anyway? Liam was in a right flap on the phone," I ask, remembering his weirdness on the phone this morning.

"Who knows with Liam?" she says, unfazed. "I guess we're about to find out."

"I guess so," I reply, ushering her through first.

As Mum said, everyone is already seated at the table. Dad's head is in the newspaper, and Liam's eyes are on Amelia, who appears to be unaware of anyone else in the room but me as I round the table and take the seat across from her.

"Nice of you to join us," Liam chimes in, briefly turning his attention from Amelia to toss me a look that says he isn't at all happy about my late arrival.

"Sorry, bud. I'm here now, though." This whole scene feels too weird. It's been a long time since we've all sat around this table as a family.

An awkward silence fills the room as all eyes, including mine, are on the smiling pair of lovebirds in front of us.

"Well?" Beth blurts out, seemingly bored.

I would laugh if it wasn't for the sparkling glint of something shiny on Amelia's ring finger that catches my attention.

"Hang the fuck on," Liam curses. "I'm getting there." He flashes a smile at Amelia before rising to a stand.

A bead of sweat has begun to appear on his brow. He seems anxious, agitated, even. He looks exactly how I feel.

"Firstly, I just want to thank you all for being here. I know you had plans for today, Scott, and I appreciate you coming here at short notice, but I wanted you to be here to hear this. So, you know how we've been living together for a while now, and it's going great. Better than great, actually," he adds, gazing down at the blonde beside him. "So much so that I decided that it was time to make an honest woman out of the love of my life. I've asked Amelia to marry me... and she said yes."

The gasp that leaves my lungs thankfully goes unnoticed as squeals and cheers of happiness begin to bellow out around me. Beth kicks my ankle under the table to get my attention. I glance at her, shocked, and she rolls her eyes. She isn't happy, either, although she has no idea why I feel like I've just been punched in the stomach.

I fight for every breath that I'm given, but the feeling of suffocation won't leave me.

For months I've tried to move on, to be a better person, yet I can't seem to form a single word. Everything I've worked so hard for is slowly crumbling to nothing as the world around me dissolves, leaving me with nothing but those final three words racing around my head. *She said yes.*

"Well? You gonna congratulate me or what, bro?"

"Scott, congratulate your brother and Amelia," Mum says, eyeing me curiously, and then she continues to beam up at her son. Unlike myself and Beth, she *is* happy.

"Eh... Yeah, sure." Pushing my back against the chair, I stand and offer a shaky hand to my brother. "Congrats, bud. Chuffed for you... Both." I let my eyes fall on Meli, but only long enough to catch the silent apology sprawled across her face. *She said yes. Fuck.*

"Cheers, Scotty. It was about time we took our relationship to the next level. Shit," he says, placing his hands on her shoulders and gently squeezing. "I can't wait to get you up the duff."

"Liam," Mum squeals, trying hard to hide her amusement behind her own hand.

"Eww! I think I just puked a little in my mouth," Beth adds in disgust.

"Liam," Amelia whispers from beside him, clearly embarrassed.

"It's true, babe," he tells her. "All that practicing is going to be..."

"Don't you swear, Liam Jenkins! Not on such a splendid

occasion," My mother warns him.

"Yes. There's plenty of time for all that, baby," Amelia adds with a nervous laugh. "Let's just take it one step at a time for now, though, hey? No baby talk."

"Yeah, look..." My eyes dart around the room, taking in every single smile and the genuine happiness all around me. Marriage, babies, I can't...

The walls slowly begin to close in on me, and I'm fighting for breath again as the invisible choker grips me like a vice.

Breathe, Scotty. Just. Breathe.

"I've gotta go," I say sharply.

"Go?" Several voices chime out all at once. "You only just got here," Mum says sadly.

"I need to open up the bar," I lie, needing to get away.

"Thought you were off today?" Liam chirps up. Fucker. Stole my girl and now he's trying to make a mug out of me.

"Des called on my way over. He needs me."

"Oh, okay. Well, cheers for coming. We'll have to celebrate properly soon, yeah?"

"Sure. Congratulations to you both. I'm... really happy for you."

I nod weakly and eventually make my way around the table, but my knees are too weak to function properly and the ground becomes unsteady beneath my feet. I stumble forward, catching the sideboard just in time to save myself from falling. I don't even look back to see if anyone witnessed me almost making a tit of myself. I just need to get out in one piece.

Fishing my keys out of my back pocket, I pull open the door and leave the laughter and cheers behind me as I pull it shut.

She's marrying him.

It really is all over.

What the fuck do I have to do to get over her?

****

Time seems to pass by at a slow, torturous speed. I swing by E's apartment to pick him up and we make our way to the local boozer in silence. One word is all it takes for him to shove on a pair of jeans and a shirt and close the door behind him. I shrug off his look that clearly says, *what's the deal, Scotty?* There are only two things I need and a row with Ethan isn't one of them.

I've never confided in Ethan about Amelia. Even after he got out of rehab and was able to hold a conversation, I still couldn't bring myself to do it. But fuck if I don't want to right now. The only thing that stops me from opening up my heart to him is the inevitable backlash I'd receive in return. After all the shit I've preached to him about – the drugs, the birds, letting his mum and Dean down – how the fuck can I just blurt out that I've been shagging my brother's soon-to-be missus? Not just once. Not even twice. But several times, in fact. I may not have been ruining my own life like Ethan was, but I was risking ruining my brother's, even if he didn't realise it was happening.

Only three words continue to play through my mind as we drive the short distance to the pub. Three fucking words that hit me like a freight train.

Sister-in-law.

The beer flows easily through my veins, and it isn't long before Amelia is semi-forgotten, but not completely. I convince myself that every blonde who walks through the bar is her. Somehow, I come up with this crazy thought that she will come and find me and tell me this whole engagement bullshit is a fucking joke.

Only she doesn't come, and this... This is real.

I feel a strong arm gripping my waist, followed by bubbling laughter. "Easy, bud. You'll do yourself some damage there," Ethan states, pulling at my shoe, which clearly doesn't want to budge, once he gets me home. Good job I let the lad keep his key for my place. I laugh back as if he's just said the funniest shit in the world, and I'm met with a disapproving frown from my best mate.

"Dude, whatever it is that's going on, you don't need to deal with it on your own. Remember what you said to me? A problem shared is a problem halved. You're better than this. The drink – It's not you, mate."

"Yeah, well," I slur, "You're one to talk."

"Low blow."

"Would you rather I kick you in the balls?"

"No, I'd rather you stop being a tosser." He laughs. "Like I said, all this, it ain't you."

I fumble my way over to the bed and let my dead weight fall. With my arms above my head, I let out a yawn and cast my eyes to the side. "Maybe it is. Maybe this is exactly who I am – a waste of space piece of shit with no morals what so fucking ever!"

The bed dips beside me, making my stomach churn, and that feeling of motion sickness washes over me in waves. Curling my arm over my face, I groan my disapproval at the insensitive bastard beside me.

I take a deep breath and slowly release it.

And then I repeat.

In... Out...

In… Out...

Not that it does any damn good.

"Scott, that's bullshit and you know it. You seem to forget that I know you better than anyone else, and that... This… It's not you, no matter what you think of yourself. I've been there, remember? So I qualify to tell you when you're fucking up. Whatever's going on, you can tell me. I'm not exactly in a position to judge now, am I?"

A shower of guilt lashes at me, pelting and hitting me full force in the chest.

"I lo..." I manage to stop myself mid-sentence and turn my cheek, burying my face in the pillow with a groan. "I'm wasted, E. Well. And. Truly. Fucked!"

"I know, bud." He chuckles. "Get some sleep and I'll be here bright and early with a bit of grease. That'll sort you out."

"Where are you going?"

"Wouldn't you like to know?" he sings, no doubt sporting that cocky fucking grin of his.

I mumble something unintelligible and bury myself with images of blonde hair and those eyes, newborn babies and vows exchanged by me and her, with all our family there to see.

Chapter Twenty-Eight

I wake, hazy and sleep deprived. I want nothing more than to forget about yesterday's events and throw them to the back of my mind where they belong. Yet, even through my half-sleep, half-awake stage, I find myself tossing and turning, never quite getting in the right position and reeling over everything that's happened this past year or so. It doesn't matter how much time has passed; she's still all I can think about.

I want to rid her from my life altogether, but it will never be possible now. Not just because she's my brother's fiancée and soon to be a Jenkins, but because I'm in love with her, and I know that will never, ever go away. For the first time in my life, I'm in love. And I fucking hate it!

The buzzer to the apartment has been going off for ten minutes straight, but I can't even force myself to move a single inch.

Use the fucking key, E. I silently plead, hoping he pissed off early to go and pick me up some grub.

I groan and bury my face and ears into the pillow, but the noise continues and the sound appears to grow louder by the second.

"Use your key, dick!" I manage to yell through cotton mouth and chapped lips.

I've had my fair share of piss-ups and dodgy hangovers, but never in my whole life have I felt this crap. If it wasn't for the fact that I'm actually in my own room and not in some lousy hospital bed, I would swear I've been hit by an HGV. Twice over!

The buzzer continues to taunt me, and I find myself wincing and gripping my head to ease the pain as I roll over cautiously, my legs dangling off the edge of the bed.

I glance down at my feet and stifle a laugh, which is a bad move on my part. The tiny lemmings that have taken up residence in my head continue to chip away, bit by bit, and each move I make has those very fucking same lemmings doing some kind of happy dance just to top me off.

Raking my fingers through the tangled mess of hair on my head, I glance briefly at the clock on the wall, noting it's almost 5 p.m.

Shit. How long have I been out?

I pull the door open and make some sort of animalistic growl that wouldn't even scare a damn kitty cat. "I swear to fucking god, E, if there ain't a bacon wrap in that hand of yours, I'm gonna..." My sentence drifts off, just as my mouth falls open.

"I'm sorry. I didn't mean to... Uh... What the hell happened to you, Scott? And why the hell are you only wearing one shoe?" I can see the amusement dance across her face, those bright blue eyes twinkling even though she's trying to hide her humour.

Fuck you and your damn eyes, Amelia, I curse inwardly.

"Cheers for that, sweetheart! Can't all be pretty… like your fiancé."

I realise the second I say the words that I sound bitter and twisted, but right now, I couldn't give a rat's arse.

Dropping my head with a sigh, I use the foot encased with a shoe to kick the door shut. Her reflexes are far more alert than mine this afternoon, though, and she easily catches it before it shuts in her face, moving quickly inside as she shuffles through.

"Hello to you, too," she mumbles under her breath.

"I wasn't the one to start with the insults, Meli."

"That's not… I'm sorry. I didn't… It's just…"

Tossing my head back on a groan, I pause. "Just what?" I ask with exasperation.

"I shouldn't have let you find out that way. It was cruel. Yesterday, I mean. I shouldn't have let it happen. It was wrong, and I'm sorry."

My shoulders slump, and I drop my head. I don't need to hear this. I need to be left alone to wallow in self-pity. Not be reminded of the fact that I've just lost the only girl I've ever loved to my own damn brother.

"You came all this way to apologise?"

"Yes."

"Bullshit. What are you really doing here, Meli? If it's to rub salt in the wounds then save it. Nothing you can say or do will make me feel any worse than I already do."

"I didn't come here to make you feel bad, Scott. Please, just let me explain."

"No need. I get it all. Now go."

"Ten minutes, Scott. Give me ten minutes to explain and then you can leave."

"Leave?" I snort. "Sorry, peaches, but the last time I checked, this was my apartment. If anyone's leaving, it'll be you, which is exactly what I want you to do. Now, if you don't mind," I plead, pulling the door open and ushering her out.

"Not here, Scott. Meet me at Groves field at nine."

"And why would I do that?"

"Because…" she starts.

If she says *because you love me,* I swear…

"Just give me ten minutes, please."

"Groves Field?" I ask in confusion, sighing as I shake my head and groan. "Look, whatever game you're playing, I don't want any part of it. Go of your own free will, before I remove you."

"Fine, I'm going, but I'll be waiting for you, Scott."

"Wait all night if you want. I ain't gonna be there."

"If that's what it takes, that's what I will do," she says, before closing the door behind her, taking all the air from the room along with her.

And all I'm left to wonder is… why the fuck can't she leave me alone?

******

Pulling into the car park at Groves field, I blow out a breath and cut the engine. The blackened sky sends a shiver through me as I glance up through the windscreen at nothing in particular.

The park is deserted. There's no life beyond the car except for the shadow of a figure a few feet in front, propped against a car.

Headlights from passing vehicles cast a faint glow over the slender woman – not enough to see her face, though. Not that I need to see her to know who she is. I have her build and features perfectly memorised. It's hard not to know who is in front of me, when she's all I can ever think about.

I'm not entirely sure why I've come here after saying I wouldn't. Hope and closure spring to mind, but, as with most things, nothing is set in stone.

I finally open the door, making it obvious that I don't want to stay by leaving it half open. "You've got ten minutes," I say, climbing out and resting my back against my own car like I'm already bored.

"Do you remember this place?" she asks quietly.

I fold my arms across my chest. "Yeah, we used to come out here every summer, when school let out. Meli, why are we here? I'm fucking confused and cold."

Pushing up from the hood of her sleek *Mercedes*, she takes a few steps forward, the ground crunching beneath her. Then she stops.

She stays there.

Completely still.

Her eyes appear to be transfixed up ahead, staring into the open field.

"It was the day of our final exam," she begins, only pausing for a fraction of a second to look up into the star-filled sky. "We were on such a high that day. It was hot. I remember it so clearly, like it was yesterday."

I remember that day, too. How could I not? I lost my virginity that night, in a dirty, overgrown field, surrounded by bracken and rotten apples. But back then, it was fucking perfect. Funny how things change when you finally realise what truly matters.

"I spent hours getting ready that afternoon," she continues. "Hair, make-up, my mum's awful red lipstick that she kept under lock and key." Her shoulders rise and fall as she laughs quietly to herself. "I was so fucking nervous that I was sick three times that day, but I had never been more determined in my whole life than I was in that moment. It took ages for the sun to set, for the darkness to fall upon us. But when it did, all the waiting and nervous trips to the bathroom no longer mattered. You looked so beautiful in your ripped jeans and white t-shirt. And your hair was all messy and dark. It had just started to grow after Ethan shaved it off for a dare. Do you remember that? I hated him for that. Despised him, even. Anyway," she quickly adds, shaking her head, "you were beautiful, and I wanted to tell you that. For years I tried to get you to notice me, Scott. So many years I spent following you around, making awkward eye contact in the corridor in the hopes that you would finally notice me. Then I realised that probably wasn't ever going to happen. I knew you were too good for me. I hated myself when I finally came to the realisation that you would never truly see me. Not for me, anyway. But I gave you another chance. That night."

I watch her as she speaks, her body here but her mind elsewhere. She is stunning, but I am still confused, even more so with every word she speaks, so I remain silent, no doubt appearing more indifferent than I feel.

"I sat on the memorial bench a few yards away and watched you. You were smiling and laughing like you didn't have a care in the world. You were so happy, Scott. It was infectious. When you smiled, the whole world around you smiled, too. Including me."

Uncrossing my arms, I can't take the distance anymore, so I stalk across the deep grass towards her, stopping just inches away to give her time to finish. Her breaths come quick, and I can almost feel the slight trembling of her hands, yet, she tries to remain stiff, and it takes all the strength in me to not wrap my arms around her and run my hands over her bare skin. Instead, I push my hands into my pockets and shrink inside my jacket.

"You eventually started the fire, and everyone clapped, cheered and passed drinks around, but you just stood there, staring into the fire like it held the answers to your future. Your shirt was dirty and black soot was smeared across your face, but you were still beautiful. If not even more beautiful in your imperfection. Back then, no one could compare to you. You were the boy – the one every teenage girl spent her nights dreaming about. You were my one. I took the deepest breath I had ever taken and told myself to move. By this time, the nausea had started to creep in again. I didn't let it get to me, though. I had made my mind up. I needed you to know."

My mouth opens to say something, all her revelations

taking me by surprise, but I quickly close it again, too lost and too desperate to hear how she saw me back then.

"It didn't take me long to get to you, but I remember it felt like an eternity. Every step felt like a lifetime, and every breath felt like it was my last, but I focused on your face, the way the light from the fire crackled in your eyes as the flames danced in bright reds and oranges. I knew your hands would be warm, and I wanted so much to feel them, to look up into those soft green eyes of yours and watch the glow from the fire as you held me close. I can still picture your face now, even after all these years."

Stunned.

"You didn't look at me, Scott. You didn't even know I was there. It wasn't until Liam called you from behind me that you noticed me. I will never forget the look on your face as you frowned down on me. Disgust, anger, hell, none of it was remotely pleasurable. So I took a few paces back. I didn't want you to see me cry. I never wanted that. But somehow you always knew how to get to me. I hated that about you, but I loved you anyway. I held onto the hope that one day you would see me as someone that could mean something to you. But none of that mattered because Carly found you that night. I saw the way you gazed at her, that appreciative smile and cocky smirk. But mostly, I saw just how much you hated me and would never look at me that way, and so I walked away."

"I didn't hate you," I finally manage to croak out, feeling sick having seen that night from her point of view. I never wanted anyone to see me as such an arsehole, but I deserved every bad thought Amelia had ever had about me. I know that now.

"You taunted me at any given chance. You put me down and made my life hell. Sure, you didn't hate me," she whispers with a sad smirk on her face.

You were meant to be my angel, I want to tell her.

"I didn't hate you, Meli. I just disliked the way you looked down your nose at me. Like I was a piece of shit that you'd just stepped on."

"That's not true. I wanted to speak to you, but every time I tried, I got nervous. It's hard to be around someone you have feelings for and not show an ounce of emotion. I didn't want you to know how crazy in love with you I was. If I had, you and Ethan would've spent the rest of your days making fun of me."

"Was? As in past tense? So... not anymore?" I ask, a hint of desperation lacing my words.

"See, that's the thing. That's why I brought you here. You didn't just break my heart out on this field. You made me stronger. I vowed to never let anyone treat me that way again. I wouldn't give my heart away so easily for it to only be broken somewhere along the way. That's why I got with Liam. I knew from the beginning that he never really cared about me or my feelings, at least not back then. And that was fine by me. Like I said, I never really wanted to feel that kind of attraction again. I figured that as long as I had Liam, I had every chance at getting closer to you. By getting closer to you, I could make you notice me and then I could hurt you like you hurt me. Only it didn't end up that way."

"What the fuck? You got with Liam to get closer to me and

then what? You break my heart and the score is even? That's just bullshit! We were just kids. You hated me that much that you used my brother to get at me?"

"No. Yes. I don't know. Maybe. I was confused. You hurt me, Scott. I wanted to get you back and..."

I can feel the anger bubbling to the surface, and no matter how hard I fight to push it back, it's no use. She used me. None of what we had was real.

I ball my hands into fists and raise them to my temples. "You wanted revenge? Is that what this was? This thing between us? It was about revenge?"

"No, not all of it. Liam was fun, and for a while I had forgotten what it felt like to be hurt by you. He helped me forget, and somewhere along the way, I fell in love with him. That doesn't mean I didn't feel anything for you, too, Scott. This thing between us wasn't about revenge."

"If it wasn't about revenge then what the hell was it? Because you're making about as much sense as a baby not shitting."

"I know. I know. I'm sorry. This is really fucking hard, Scott. It boils down to the fact that I am still in love with you. I always have been and probably always will be. But it's because I love you that I can't do this. I can't let you hurt me again. Those feelings and emotions don't just go away. They haunt you and stay with you. I would always be wondering how you really felt about me. Is it the challenge he thrives off? The danger of not knowing if someone is going to walk in on us? You pushed me away before, Scott. How do I know you won't do it again?"

She loves me. She might've used me, but she loves me. That thought alone is enough to push the anger down just a tiny bit. Just enough for me to think straight and talk calmly.

"I dunno, Amelia. Maybe…Because I love you. Because I can promise you that no matter what life throws at us, I will always, always love you." I stalk over, tip her chin with my finger and gaze into her beautiful blue eyes before swallowing down. "I was a kid back then, too full of myself to care what others thought about me. Including you. Not anymore. I don't care about anything but you, and I promise, hand on heart, that I will spend the rest of my days proving to you how much I love you. You can't stay with Liam, not when you love me. Please, Meli. I can't sit back and watch you ruin what we could have." I pull back, not even attempting to wipe the wetness from my cheeks. "I love you," I say, before pressing my lips to hers.

"You love me?"

"I do."

"Then find a way to prove it to me," she whispers, her face completely straight. "Find a way, no matter how long it takes, to show me that I can trust you."

Then she turns her cheek and walks away, like I haven't just handed my heart to her on a plate, leaving me standing there broken, wide-eyed and more confused than ever before.

Chapter Twenty-Nine

April 2005

It has been ten months' since Amelia left me in Groves Field with only two words lingering in the air that night. Two words that have haunted me ever since. *Prove it.*

She made it clear that I had hurt her. Broke her, even, but she hurt me, too, and I still to this day have no idea how to process any of that. As much as I want her in my life, I know the only way that either of us stands a chance at happiness is if I push each memory I have of her and our time together to the back of my mind. Loving her hasn't been good for either of us, and while I know I will never get over her, the months that pass do become easier. I try not to think about her, but sometimes that proves easier said than done, and mostly I just distract myself in other ways that don't allow me to think about her.

Family events aren't nearly as tough as I expect them to be, and slowly but surely, life has started to ease back into normality. But every morning, I awake to those two words in my mind: *Prove it.*

Everyone is busy preparing for the wedding, which has been set for November next year, I believe. I try to help as much as my heart will allow me to, but *that* has proved harder than I anticipated. Luckily, I've been given a free pass when it comes to the wedding plans, apparently being labeled as 'useless' and 'way too sarcastic' for any of my suggestions to be taken seriously. The only thing I have been trusted with is the stag party. Yeah, Liam called around one night, completely out of the blue, and asked if I'd be his best man. It shouldn't have, but it took me by surprise, and it wasn't like I could say no. Agreeing was the biggest blow to my gut to date. Shouldn't a best man be happy for the bride and groom? Either way, I will do it. I like to think that I've changed in the last few years, but the truth is, if things were different and we were given a second chance, I wouldn't hesitate in taking it again. Months down the line and I still miss the fuck out of her. I'm starting to believe that missing her will always be a part of me now.

The only thing I can do now is find a way to live around it... or with it... starting with a new distraction.

It was another typically normal day to everyone else, but to Ethan, Dean and I, the day we signed those papers, it was the start of something new. A derelict warehouse that needed a complete redo soon becomes everything we had ever dreamed of as kids. It's our business venture. *Club Crystal* isn't going to be just another high-end strip club on the outskirts of Manchester. It's going to be the building that is going to change our worlds entirely. With Ethan's business know-how, my previous bar experience, and Dean's appreciation and knowledge of a fine pair of boobs, we're convinced we're onto a solid gold winner, here.

This is now our life. And fuck, if we aren't determined to make this work. It's what we all need – a focus, a new kind of family. Brothers creating better futures for each other.

But it doesn't come easy, yet we all relish in the hard work, especially me and Ethan. For months and months, we pour our blood, sweat and tears into making a bona fide business for ourselves, and while Ethan is unequivocally the owner of our new lap dancing place, it having been his secret master plan all along, and him having poured the majority of the funds into making this happen, he has no qualms about letting everyone and anyone know that I am his right-hand-man.

The doors officially open in March 2005, and the launch of our new baby was more successful than we could have hoped for it to be. I can still picture Ethan's face the second he locked the doors and breathed a sigh of relief that our first night went down a storm. Although exhausted, we were both buzzing off our man titties. Despite the odds that were stacked against us, we are finally getting ahead and getting closer to that life we have always dreamed of.

Ethan is pretty much back to his old self. My best mate. Sometimes he goes quiet and I know exactly what is playing on his mind. The drugs are still very much a part of him, but not in the way that could see him hospitalised again. He doesn't touch the stuff; I have no doubts about that. But it doesn't stop him from wanting to, and that's when I step in, playing mother hen, reminding him how much me and his little brother need him in our lives. It annoys the shit out of him, but his protesting is never going to stop me. I like having Ethan back. That other side of him? Well, it fucking sucked, but it was what it was. When it comes to hiring the dancers now, or any staff for that matter, I make damn sure they know we work on a zero-tolerance rule when it comes to drugs. They can use all they want in their own time, kill themselves for all I care, but the second they bring that shit into the club, they're gone. Ethan might be a sucker for a sob story and call me a heartless cunt every now and again, but I'm not gonna go through that again. It's one thing to crave the shit and not act on it, but when the temptation is staring you point blank in the face, you're not gonna be able to resist. Ethan might be a tough little shit, but when it comes to drugs, he's weak. Even he understands why I put that policy in place, and he has never once fought me on it.

The power trips and sharp as shit suits we wear aren't the only perks that come with running our own business. The girls fucking love us, and we are never short of a quick screw or two. If we wanted, we could each have a different chick every night. It's like taking candy from a baby, only they beg us to take it. They probably see pound signs or something, but it doesn't stop us from bending them over the desk and putting a smile on their face for free, though. We like to keep our girls happy, after all.

As the weeks roll on by, turning the months over, I find a new woman to distract me from my thoughts of Amelia, most days

I grin up at the beauty above me now actually, and I run the pads of my thumbs down the insides of silky smooth thighs. Leaning back on my desk, legs wide open, she is leaving nothing to the imagination.

"What can I do for you today, Sir," she purrs.

The rapping of knuckles against my office door has Leo-whatever-she's-called flinching. Catching this chick's name wasn't high on my list of priorities, unless she was capable of reminding me of it while her lips were wrapped around my cock.

The loud tapping rings out once again, and soon has the hot brunette leaping off the desk and scurrying across the floor to retrieve all her garments.

"Shit," she mutters, causing me to huff out a laugh.

"Why don't you go out there and show me what you can do?" I ask with raised brows, as a hint of a smirk tugs at the corner of my mouth. Doing the gentlemanly thing, I offer a hand to help the poor damsel knelt on my floor.

"Yeah. Sure."

I grin and usher her towards the door. "Good girl. I'll see you out there."

Pulling the door open, I give the lass, who I'm pretty certain is called Tina, a gentle nudge, ignoring Sapphire's judgey little eyes.

"You alright, love?"

"There's a reporter here. Says she's booked in to interview Mr. Walker."

"He's in his office, Olivia. Just tell him I sent you up."

"Yes, boss," she says on a shy, yet sexy little smile.

"Nice one, and, Liv? Make sure you knock first, sweetheart. There's shit that goes on up there that would ruin you for life."

Her eyes go wide and I let out a laugh, shaking my head. As her clicky heels strut down the hall, I close the door and zip up my trousers before I turn and sink back into my chair, letting out a sigh.

The more I think about it, the less convinced I am that this interview with the local journalist is a good idea. The exposure could get club *Club Crystal* out there... really out there. And that's great and all, only there is a chance that the punters won't be the only rich, seedy bastards walking through those damn doors. One flick through the local paper could end Ethan's life in a second. It could bring all those old trouble causers he used to knock about with flooding through the doors, looking for a place to trade all their shit. It could bring other people knocking on his door that I don't want to have to beat the fuck out of his life. I know I'm probably worrying too much, but that's what happens when your best mate is an addict: you think of everything. And this interview? It's a risk I wouldn't have chosen to take.

Turns out I don't have long to let my thoughts carry on down that road, though. Olivia soon comes back down the stairs, asking me to meet Ethan in the changing rooms. The bastard. I know instantly what he wants me for, but I'll be damned if I don't drag this out a bit, so I stand propped up against a locker and wait for him to arrive. Another one of the dancers, a petite blonde, chooses this exact moment to whip her clothes off right here in front of me, and for just a minute, I'm lost in the flawless curves of her body and her smooth skin. Oh, the skin. Her tight little arse wiggles as she pulls on a pair of lace knickers. The thin scrap of material barely covers her arse and I swallow down a groan and remind myself why I am here.

I love my job.

Ethan chooses that moment to push through the door, his eyes only falling on the lass' rear for a second before they find me.

With a lazy smile, I push up from my leaning position. "You want me to do the interview?" There's no point in dragging it out any longer than needed. I have an itch that needs scratching just as soon as the interview is done.

"It's a lot to ask," he says, feigning concern over his request. "But you have such a pretty face and all that charm."

After a bit of our usual banter, going back and forth, I eventually agree, promising to tell all the club's secrets to the press on his behalf, including the naughty ones. Rolling his eyes, he gives me a small shove onto the club floor without another word.

When it comes to Ethan, I push my damn luck. A lot. But like the good mate he is, he takes it on the chin. Anyone else and they probably would've knocked me out already.

I clock the blonde reporter immediately, sitting at the far end, and I quickly shrug Ethan off. I don't need a fucking chauffeur. The prick!

Making my way around the bar, I toss Leoooo… Tina a wink and pull out the chair in front of the journalist. She doesn't seem to notice me approach at first, and if it wasn't for the annoying scrape of the chair, she would probably have her head still stuck in her notepad. Finally registering my presence, she fumbles with a loose strand of her golden hair, tucking it behind her ear before she holds out a firm hand.

"Mr. Umm… Walters, I presume?" she stutters, and I almost laugh out loud, but instead choose to hide it under my breath. Mr. Walters. I'll be calling him that from now on. Some reporter this chick is. Can't even do her damn homework before showing up here to ask her questions.

Taking her hand in mine, I smirk. "You presume wrong, love," I correct her before sliding onto the chair opposite. "Scott Jenkins. Partner."

"In life or business?" she questions, pulling her hand away, leaving me shocked and quite frankly, a little bewildered.

Who the fuck is this woman and where the hell can I get one?

I have no words and I stare in astonishment. From some unknown place, I manage to gain some form of composure. "Just business. You are?"

"Miss Moffit. No jokes, please. I've probably heard them all before." Tucking that damn hair behind her ear again, a frustrated – or is it embarrassed? – blush explodes over her skin.

Whatever the cause, it leaves a pink trail, starting at her exposed neck and ending at the apple of her cheeks, a pretty shade of pink, marring her otherwise flawless skin. I wonder if every inch of her is as perfect.

No point in going there, Scotty. She's probably into the fanny. She's definitely not giving off the penis loving vibes, that's for sure.

"Sorry," she continues. "This isn't my normal gig. I'm doing a favour for a friend."

Well, that explains it, I think to myself. "So, what is it you do, then? I'm guessing it doesn't involve writing up a report on the new local businesses?" I say pointedly. "Especially when half the staff are pretty much naked and gyrating against cold metal poles."

"Huh?" she asks, tearing her eyes away from the notepad.

"I saw you looking. You don't approve?"

"Approve? It's your life, Mr…"

"Jenkins. Or Scott. Whatever you wanna call me, sweetheart."

"Like I was about to say, Mr… Eh… Jenkins. It's your life. I'm just here to interview you."

Hiding a grin, I lean back in the chair and roll my neck. "Fire away, peaches."

"Moffit. It's Miss Moffit," she interjects, her annoyance and sarcasm not going unnoticed.

The interview continues, and I somehow manage to dodge any questions that could lead the bad boys of Ethan's old circle to the club, especially one fucked up beast who I believe is called Daggs. Ethan doesn't talk about him much, but I see the unspoken fear in his eyes when Daggs' name accidentally falls from his mouth.

I'm not sure how I manage it when, for some bizarre reason, I feel like I could easily tell this girl anything and it would somehow stay private, despite her being a part of the press. I can feel Ethan's eyes boring into the back of my head, and I wonder if he is just as enchanted as I am. Her easy charm and shy demeanour make her all the more likeable, and when I say something that she doesn't like or agree with, her frustrated anger only makes my dick twitch in my pants. *Who the hell is she?*

Maybe she just reminds you of Amelia.

Fuck off, I say to myself in my mind, not wanting to even think about that name.

Towards the end of the interview, she says something that makes me sit back and really look at her. It isn't even something remotely important, but the unimportance doesn't matter. I know this girl. I'm sure I have seen her before, not underneath me, or in passing, but I'm damn certain I know her. If not, I certainly feel like I do. Maybe she is good at what she does, after all.

A commotion behind me quickly has the two of us turning our heads to see what has just caused all the noise. Delilah, one of our dancers, stalks across the room, her face a picture of fury as she looks between me and the blonde. Lucky for me, Ethan guides her off the floor and out the back, leaving me to work out how the hell I know this woman.

By the end of the interview, I'm still none the wiser. Maybe it's just wishful thinking on my part, and it's probably for the best that the penny isn't dropping, or that she isn't biting at any of my attempts to flirt. I'd only ruin the lass. She's entirely too innocent for me. Too pure, too… vulnerable behind all that façade.

Still, one last effort can't hurt.

Miss Moffit shoves her notepad back in her bag and I find myself gripping the edge of the table with both hands. "That went well, yeah?" I ask, flexing my biceps for added affect.

"As well as can be expected. Thank you, Mr. Jenkins."

"Call me Scott, love," I tell her as I smirk, pulling my card from my pocket and sliding it across to her. "I'd love to take you out for a drink sometime."

Oh, jeez.

Shit.

Bollocks.

Wank, wank, wank.

What the fuck am I saying? *"I would love to take you out for a drink sometime."* How desperate do I sound? If I wouldn't look like a fucking pansy, I'd run the hell away.

I drop my eyes and watch her delicate, yet authoritative fingers slide the card away from her like it's carrying a damn STD before she confirms my suspicions about being a lesbo. "Never going to happen, *Scott*."

And with that, she picks up her shit and turns to leave.

Shaking my head, I round the bar and backhand Ethan on the shoulder as I watch the hot little blonde march across the floor, away from us.

"Fabulous, tight arse, mate, but she's a hundred percent carpet muncher," I say, flicking my tongue and smirking. "Might have to see about turning her straight."

"She's off limits."

"The fuck you talking about?"

"Off. Limits. Scott."

What does he mean...? Why would she be...?

I begin to protest but he cuts me off with a warning glare. Snapping my jaw shut, I narrow my eyes in confusion before suspicion takes its place.

Folding my arms across my chest, I cock a brow. "So, who is she, mate?"

"Remember the night we followed Liam?" he asks as the door slams shut.

Just as my brows begin to crease into a frown, recognition hits me. *"Foos girl?"* I laugh and throw my hands up.

His irrational behaviour makes sense now. He couldn't take his eyes off of her back then, either. It also explains the huge eye shaped holes I felt in the back of my jacket the whole way through that interview, and why he sent me to do it in the first place.

I'm not sure why the fuck he had me interviewed by her, but I don't argue with him when he refuses to answer me. Truth is, I'm still going over the whole thing in my head. That doesn't stop me hoping the two of them get a chance to meet somewhere down the line. If there's anything I want in life, it's for E to be happy. I just hope we'll both find our forevers one day. We've been through enough hell to deserve a little bit of heaven, right?

Chapter Thirty

The following year

We soon learn that owning a club isn't all fun and games. Although we make sure the fun still happens frequently, as soon as it's over, we get back into work mode. We wouldn't have believed it all those years ago, but here we are, learning to be professional when it comes to the club, and it's starting to pay off considerably. We're never short of members and the club is now an elite business. The status means takings are stupidly high and we are, as Ethan would say, "raking in the dosh."

So we deserve a holiday, right?

Damn right.

The trip to Italy was a memorable moment for us. Some uptight twat in a posh suit tried to convince us that bringing wine to the club would increase our profits. We didn't need the extra money but we could hardly turn down a free trip to Italy. So we packed up our shit and jumped on a plane. The three amigos taking on Italy. They didn't know what was about to hit them. Turns out we spent half the time rat-arsed or searching for a willing bird to lay. Although we had the time of our lives, I vowed to never return. The women weren't nearly as eager as I would've hoped and one memory that hasn't been washed away by the booze consists of Dean quoting Shakespeare off Juliet's balcony. Suffice to say we got kicked out and banned from ever returning. The rest of the trip went pretty much the same way, although we did bring something back from our little jolly boy's outing: A twelve month supply of wine that we hadn't even tasted. But surprisingly, it turns out we did good. It's gone down a treat with the ladies and I have grown a secret love for the red stuff. Not that I'll ever let on to Ethan. He'd be questioning its disappearance as soon as the confession left my mouth. So when he's around, which is most of the time, I stick to my trusty *Budweiser*.

Don't get me wrong, though – working with your best mate isn't always going to be smooth sailing. As much as we try to remain as professional as possible when it comes to business, sometimes we struggle to set our friendship aside when it comes to the running of the place. That proves hard on occasion, especially when Ethan makes calls that I don't agree with in any fucking way whatsoever. One being the hiring of a girl named Paris.

A girl who he met on the drug scene, and a girl who doesn't even try to hide the fact that she is knee-deep in drug shit.

Why can't he see the warning signs?

It's not like I don't like the girl. To be fair, I really hardly know her, but I know she's bad for the business. It's written all over her grey, gaunt face. Her eyes are hollow and empty, telling me enough to know that in that space where the darkness lives, all her clarity and good judgment calls have disappeared.

Ethan doesn't seem to agree with me, though. Since rehab, he's become a firm believer in second chances, but with Paris, those chances are already quickly becoming tedious. I'm all for helping the needy, but Paris is nothing more than a lost cause with a crazy arsed boyfriend, who is apparently, capable of pretty much anything.

Ethan played a risky game when offering her a job at the club. Despite being high, she knew that, too. But I trust Ethan, and when he said he could change her, I believed him.

But it doesn't work. Some leopards don't want to change their spots, and not everyone has Ethan's strength to bring change into their lives so easily.

After a random locker check, my suspicions about Paris and her lack of respect for the club are confirmed.

Not only does Paris shown up for work high as a damn kite, she has also been stashing her shit in the locker for Sapphire to find. Rather Sapphire than the fucking cops. It's a no-brainer. Paris needs to go. It's time for me to put my foot down, but Ethan, being Ethan, isn't having any of it. Even after all Paris has done, he still believes in her. Or maybe he believes that every drug addict was a kid once and they just need a little help from the right person?

All I do know is that I'm tired of arguing with the kid when it comes to Paris. If he's that invested in her then he can deal with her from now on.

Luckily, that doesn't last long. We got a call yesterday to say that Paris won't be working at the club anymore. When I find out, I breathe a sigh of relief. I'm not a harsh bastard, no matter what Ethan thinks. To me, she was gone the second she brought that shit into the club for Ethan to see. He might be sober, but he's still an addict. He's my main concern. Not some chick I barely even know.

I have my head stuck in figures when Sapphire's head pops round the door one night. "Hey, boss. There's someone out front to see you."

"We're not open yet, Saph," I remind her.

"That's what I told her, but she insisted on seeing you. I think you may want to see this one. She's really hot," she adds in a whisper, her eyebrows wiggling suggestively.

I still need to get the figures done before Ethan chases my arse. "Fine. Send her in, would you?" I'll just have to shun him until I get it done.

"Sure thing, boss," she says, swinging her ponytail to the side before bouncing off.

I glance over at the monitor, scrunching my eyes to get a better look, only it's no use. All I see is the back of her head and long dark hair. Realistically, it could be anyone.

Seconds later, I hear a soft tap on the door, causing me to look up. "Come in," I call, pushing the bullshit papers to one side.

"Hey, Scott," a soft voice greets smoothly.

It's not the way she says my name that has me lifting my eyes from the papers, nor is it the way she addresses me as Scott and not Mr. Jenkins like most acquaintances do. It's the sound of her voice, the recognition of the softly spoken words that has me dropping my pen and my jaw practically dropping to rest on the desk.

"Wow. Not exactly the greeting I was expecting." She cringes, tucking her hair behind her ear.

"Paige?" I gasp. Although I make it sound like a question, it's not really a question at all. Or is it? I'm not exactly sure. All I know is Paige is here and she looks... Well, she looks good. Great, even. Happier than the last time I saw her.

She quirks a brow and grins in amusement. "The one and only. How are you Scott? I can still call you Scott, right? I mean, you're wearing a damn suit and you're sat at a desk – I feel like I should call you Sir, or something of importance, like... judge."

Chuckling, I spread my arms out wide, before gripping the edge of the desk. "I know. It's crazy, right?"

"No. No, it's not crazy at all," she says, shaking her head. "It's perfect. It's... Well, it's just you, I guess. Wow, I always knew you'd make something of yourself, and now this." Her eyes widen as she takes everything in. Eventually, they settle back on me again before she adds, "I'm really proud of you."

"Thanks, Paige. It's all on Ethan really. He fronted the cash and found the place. I was just... there. Right time, right place, kinda guy."

"I'm sure he doesn't see it that way. He loves you and wants you to succeed, too. I bet having you by his side means the world to him."

I let her words register before I shake my head and push my back against the leather chair. "Sorry, I must've left my manners at home this morning. Sit. Please," I quickly add, gesturing to the chair opposite.

She smiles a warm smile and slides into the chair, crossing her legs.

"It's good to see you," I tell her, and I mean it, too.

"I wasn't sure I should stop by."

"You should. Always."

"So, other than being busy running an empire, how have you been?"

I shrug. "Same old, same old. Just trying to keep myself out of trouble. You know how it goes."

"And Ethan?" she asks, raising both her brows. "How is he doing?"

"He's... He's Ethan. Pretty much back to normal now. We got lucky there."

"That's great. You must be relieved, right? I remember how much you were worried about him. I hated that."

"I'll never stop worrying about him, Paige. It's what friends do. They worry. They stalk. They check your *Friends Reunited* page to make sure you're still alive."

"Are we still talking about Ethan, or me?"

"You. Both. Although, I don't actually stalk Ethan's internet shit." I chuckle.

"That's good to know," she says as she joins in with the laughing. "I'd be worried."

"I still can't believe you're here," I say, shaking my head.

"Me either," she confesses.

"You've been speaking to Beth, haven't you?"

"She might've mentioned that you asked after me once or twice."

"I should've known. Is that why you're here? Because of

my sister? 'Cause you have to know that I never intended for her to–"

"That's not why I came. Although, I'd be lying if I said that her persistence hadn't had an impact on my decision."

"Thanks for the honesty."

"Yeah, well dishonesty gets us nowhere. You of all people should know that."

And there it is – the slap in the face I guess I've been expecting since she walked through the door. An actual slap would've hurt less, but I guess I deserved that.

"Anyway," she continues. "You're not the only one to have grown lately, Scott. I have, too. I'm not the weak, love-struck girl you once knew."

"I never would have said you were weak, Paige."

"Maybe not, but I was. When it came to you, I was weak and pathetic."

I drop my chin to my chest, my eyes closing involuntarily as her words cut through me like a jagged knife. I know I hurt her back then, but the severity of that hurt hits me like a freight train. What's worse is that I know exactly how she is feeling because I felt that, too... With Amelia. For Paige to expose herself and her pain to me, guts me. I never wanted her to feel that way about herself, and the strength she carries was what attracted me to her in the first place.

It all hits home.

"I didn't come here to make you feel bad, Scott. I'm sure you've been through the ringer enough over the years and I'm not here to add to that misery."

Pushing up from her seated position, she plants her hands

firmly on the desk and continues.

"Look, all I'm trying to say is that I've had a long time to think things over, and I now realise that you're not the only one to blame for this. I am, too. I think I knew it back then, deep down. I was just too stubborn to admit it. Scott... I've realised recently that life is too short to hold grudges. I spent a long time resenting you, maybe even hating you, but I... I miss you. I miss you, Scott. I miss our friendship. I miss your terrible, floppy hair and your cheesy grin. I miss your laugh and your hand to hold when I need a good friend by my side."

I peer up, a small grin tugging at the corners of my mouth. "So, you haven't come here to slap me again? Or suck my dick?" She shoots me a warning glare, one that I haven't seen for a long time, but fuck if I haven't missed it. "Too soon?" I add.

"At least two years too soon."

"God loves a trier."

"You're an idot." She laughs.

I nod weakly and tip my chin. "For the record, I miss you, too. I took you for granted, Paige. Something I never thought I was capable of, and I regret it every day, but what's more is that I used you and broke you. I won't ever get over the way I treated you, but for what it's worth, I am sorry."

"You're forgiven, Scott. I forgave you a long time ago but you need to know that as much as I do forgive you and miss the friendship we had, I can't just switch off the pain and hurt you caused me. Yes, I forgive you and yes, I was partly to blame, too, but it doesn't change the fact that you hurt me more than I ever dreamed you could. I'm not sure if we can ever get back what we had, but I do want to at least try. Just at my own pace. I'm sure you can appreciate how hard it was for me to come here after all this time. Can you at least give me that?"

"Of course. Anything. We'll go as slow or as fast–"

"Slow. Slow is good," she interjects. "Baby steps."

"Baby steps," I repeat.

She nods, almost pleased with herself for having stood her ground. "And they'll be no sexual encounters of any kind, even if we're both horny and uptight as hell. No sex. And none of those sexual innuendos either," she adds in, wafting her hand. "Oh, and no flirting. Flirting leads to forking and forking leads to unfriending. Well, you get my drift."

She inhales a much needed breath and blows out, causing me to chuckle at her aggravation.

"Yes, ma'am. Understood. No sex. No innuendos. No flirting. Anything else you want me to add to the list of not to do's?" I ask, reaching for my ball pen.

"This isn't a joke," she says sternly and I almost cower in the corner like a goddamn baby. When did she get so fucking feisty? "I want to leave here with a mutual understanding."

"No joke. I'm not laughing," I force out through strained breaths, trying my best to hold back the laughter that's bubbling inside of me.

"Scott..." she warns.

"What? Okay, I get it. Jeez... You really haven't changed, have you?" I mumble, repeating her words back to her.

"Touché, pretty boy. Touché," she says, flashing me a wink.

A wink? A damn wink? In my mind, I'm crossing out the "no flirting" rule because to me, that was flirting.

I open my mouth to speak but she cuts through my thoughts.

"Anyway, I should get going. Wouldn't want your empire to crumble now, would we? I'm sure you have tons of important work to get back to so I won't keep you. I'll call you. Maybe," she adds, not hiding her shrug of indifference.

I roll my eyes. "Okay, sure. I'll look forward to maybe hearing from you then." I grin as she turns her back on me, and pulls the door open to leave, but not before throwing out a few last words.

"Take care, Scott."

"You too, Paige." I say to the door she's now slammed on me.

And just like that, on another ordinary day at work, one of my biggest regrets in life is finally laid to rest.

I wonder what other unexpected curveballs life has waiting just around the corner for me?

I have a feeling that this is just the beginning of a new chapter in my life, and I've no desire to take the grin off my face as I realise that for every shit time I've had in my past, there's probably something waiting out there for me to counter it.

I just have to make sure I'm not late for any of those very important dates.

Chapter Thirty-One

November 2006

Before I even have the chance to process everything that has happened these past few years, November has already drawn upon us. It's the big day. The one I have been dreading since Amelia walked away from me on that night.

A thin layer of frost covers the pavements, and the tree branches glisten in the light morning breeze. It is fucking freezing. Why anyone would want their wedding in the middle of winter is beyond me. Something about the anniversary of something or other, apparently. Fucked if I care. I just know it was a crazy idea.

I let the cigarette hang loosely between my lips, inhaling and exhaling slowly.

From the moment I opened my eyes this morning, I've regretted it. The house is like a fucking warzone. Aunts and uncles flit in and out of the rooms. Cousins who I've never met before have spoken to me like I ought to know exactly who they are and what their second wife's youngest son's shoe size is. It's like a scene from some warped horror film. I've tried to escape the crazy, but no matter where I go, someone always seems to follow.

I draw in a large amount of nicotine and release a far from contented sigh.

"Since when do you smoke?" Beth asks as she stops beside me and pulls the little piece of heaven out from my mouth.

Blowing out a cloud of smoke, I shrug and push my hands into my trouser pockets. "I don't. Not often anyway."

"You looking forward to today?" she asks, taking a toke.

Nodding, I nudge her shoulder with mine and smirk. "Nice dress, by the way."

"It's fucking hideous, right? I can't believe she's making me wear a damn dress."

Chuckling, I toss my arm around her shoulder and squeeze. "For what it's worth, I think you look beautiful."

"N'aw, thanks, little brother. You don't look too bad your–"

"What on earth are you doing, Beth?" Mum whisper yells, pulling the cancer stick from her mouth and tossing it straight into the nearest bush. "Eleanor will throw a fit if she so much as catches a whiff of smoke on that dress."

"Jeez, Ma. Why is everyone so damn touchy today? Aren't weddings meant to be happy occasions? Newsflash! I don't see one happy face in that house."

"No, I know. The nerves are getting to everyone this morning," Mum agrees, glancing up at the bathroom window with concern etched all over her face. "Scott, will you please go and help your brother out. I've already had Eleanor on the phone twice this morning."

"What the hell am I meant to do? Hold his hand while he takes a crap?"

"Can you at least ask him how long he's going to be? The car will be here in twenty minutes and I still need to sort out the flowers and buttonholes, and…"

"Fine! I'll go and check on him. Just stop stressing. It's just nerves."

"Oh, I hope he isn't having second thoughts. That happened in a movie I saw once. He did a runner seconds before the wedding. How on earth would I begin to tell Eleanor?"

"Mum. Chill. He hasn't changed his mind. The wedding is going ahead. Look, why don't you finish getting ready and leave Liam to me, yeah?"

"Yes, okay. Please, Scott. I just want everything to be perfect."

"And it will be," I assure her. Leaning in, I press a kiss to her cheek and grin.

"I love you, Scott. I love you all," she adds, dabbing the corners of her eyes.

I shake my head and shoot Beth a warning glare. The ceremony hasn't even started and the women are already crying.

As I take the steps two at a time, I hear the toilet flush, closely followed by the hand basin taps turning on. I wonder if whatever has gotten into Liam – nerves or whatever else – has been flushed away along with the contents of his stomach.

I feel bad for the kid. I'm not a fucking monster, but I'm not alone in thinking that we don't have time for this. Eleanor has been on the blower more times than I care to remember and she isn't the only one with her knickers in a twist. Mum is beginning to flap, too.

Blowing out a breath, I call out while tapping my knuckles against the bathroom door. "Liam? Mum's having kittens down there. You gonna come out anytime soon?"

"I don't think I can," The voice behind the door responds weakly. It really doesn't sound like my brother at all.

"What do you mean you don't think you can? Open the damn door, Liam, before I kick the fucker in."

There's more shuffling and flushing of the toilet before the door eventually opens.

"Mate, you look like shit," I say, stating the obvious.

His face is dishevelled and pale, dripping with what I can only assume is sweat. His hair clings to his forehead, covering his right eye, which is red and swollen. He really does look like death.

"What's going on?" I ask, easing myself through the small gap he's left for me, shielding my nose from the toxic fumes.

"I can't stop shitting. Just when I think that's bad enough, I've got my arse on the loo and my head in the sink. I think I'm dying," he says, clutching his stomach.

I do feel really bad for him but I can't hold back the laughter as it bubbles from deep within.

Still shielding my nose, I use my free hand to dig in the inside pocket of my jacket. "Here," I say, chucking the pink bottle to him. "That'll sort your gut out."

"Cheers, mate. Is this normal?" he asks, unscrewing the cap and taking a swig.

"Is what normal?" I reply, although I already think I know

what he means.

"This. The nerves. I honestly don't think I can do this. I feel like... like I'm on death row or sommat."

I chuckle and toss a fresh towel at him, which he easily catches. "Of course you can, you big baby."

"No. I really don't think I can."

"Look, mate. You've got a beautiful fiancée waiting for you, and I can guarantee you she's feeling exactly the same way. I've not been in your position, thank God, but I have seen enough movies to know that what you are feeling is a million and one percent normal."

"You're probably right."

I smirk over at him. "I'm always right."

"But what if you're wrong? What if I'm not ready for this? What if she's not the one?"

"Do you honestly think that?" I ask, my tone turning serious as I try to ignore any thoughts of Amelia at all.

"Yeah. No. I dunno. My head's a mess. I couldn't sleep last night wondering if I was making a huge mistake. I don't wanna just get married, Scott. When I get married, I want it to be for keeps. I just don't know if Meli is the one, that's all."

"Are you serious?"

"I don't know," he whispers.

"I can't make that decision for you, Liam, but I can tell you this. That girl loves you more than she's ever loved anyone. Including herself. And you might not feel it now but I know you love her, too. Don't let the nerves get the better of you. Don't break her heart. She doesn't deserve that."

"Careful brother, you're starting to sound like you actually give a stuff about her."

I shrug. "Things change. She's a good girl, Liam. She'll treat you well, and you will look after her. If you don't, and if there is a single doubt in your mind that you will treat her anything less than the best she deserves, then walk away now. Don't ruin her with broken promises and shattered dreams."

"Fuck me."

"What?"

"Broken promises and shattered dreams? You been reading one of Mum's dirty books?"

"There's all kinds of levels to my smoothness, dickhead. Don't hate what I got."

"You're right. I can do this. It's just nerves."

"Good lad," I say, slapping my hand to his shoulder and squeezing. "Now, scrub your face and brush your damn teeth. I want to see you down those stairs in ten minutes, tops."

"Okay, ten minutes. Got it. Shit! The rings?" he blurts out, his face paling even more.

"I've got 'em." I chuckle, patting my jacket pocket.

Chapter Thirty-Two

Later that day...

A few hours later, Liam and Amelia are man and wife.

The deal is done.

The girl has gone.

Everything I ever felt gets swallowed and locked up tight in a box in my heart the very moment I see them kiss after they've been pronounced man and wife. A strange feeling makes a wave-like motion in my stomach. Regret, perhaps? Wishes that it could have been me? Lust? Fantasy? The end of something that could have been good had we been different people at different times.

I'm not the same person anymore, though, and neither is she. For a moment, we connected. For a moment, I felt like I couldn't breathe without her, and here I am... breathing without her, watching my brother claim her as his for eternity.

I'm breathing, but it isn't easy.

As the day draws to an end, the tension around the table grows thicker and thicker. Despite hoping to maintain a cheery disposition for the entirety of the night, I find myself all worn out, done with small talk and even more done with this fake arse smile I've been carrying around all damn day. I kept up my end of the bargain all morning, all through the ceremony and all through the night. I've played nice, engaged in idle chit chat, and never once looked like a man scorned. But now my batteries have run out.

Glancing at my watch, I stifle a yawn and press my back against the chair as I prepare to leave this day behind me. I've survived until this point, which is more than I thought was going to be possible.

"Hey, you ain't leaving already, are you?" Liam slurs, dropping into the seat next to his new wife.

He's pissed already, which doesn't really surprise me. If Liam isn't working, and I use the term 'working' loosely, he is usually off somewhere getting drunk. I'm not sure why he drinks so much. He doesn't have complications – none that he knows about anyway – or parents breathing down his neck, telling him how to live his life. He has the most beautiful woman in the world on his arm forever now. The fucker has it easy. Too easy.

I yawn again, hoping to pull off the "I'm absolutely fucking shattered" look, and then I rise to a stand. "Yeah, bud. Long arse day. It's worn me out."

"Don't talk shit! I ain't even had the chance to thank you for today yet. Even got us a bottle to celebrate." He grins, a bottle of *Jack* hanging loosely between his fingers, mid-air.

"But…"

"Sit down, Scott."

I sigh inwardly and sink back into the seat. "Sure, just a couple, though. Some of us have work tomorrow," I reply, adding in an eye roll while reaching for the bottle.

"Nice one," he slurs again, pressing his face into the crook of Amelia's neck, slobbering all over her like a lovesick puppy.

She giggles beside him, probably just wanting to appease him. Everyone knows what Liam is like when he's had a skinfull. He's a loose cannon. No one really ever knows when he'll blow or which way it will go.

It makes me cringe just watching him. I can't take it. His drunken hands grab and pull at Amelia while she laughs like she doesn't really want him to stop, even though she bats his hands away playfully. But me? I know her too well. I see the subtle flinch in her shoulders and the slight narrowing of her eyes as she tries not to watch me watching her. I see how uncomfortable she is. Her cheeks have reddened with prolonged embarrassment.

Not that I care how she feels – at least that's what I keep telling myself in order to survive this shit. She made the choice to spend the rest of her life with him. Now she has no one to blame but herself.

Pouring the caramel liquid into an empty glass, I lift it to my lips and knock it back, welcoming the burn as the alcohol glides down my throat, barely touching the sides before landing in the pit of my stomach with a hollow thud.

"Here. I wanted to thank you for today. You held it together and I wouldn't have gotten through the service without you," Liam starts to tell me, reaching for the bottle and pouring himself another one.

My thoughts drift back to this morning and the small glimmer of hope I felt when Liam freaked out. A part of me wanted him to bolt, to say he'd made a mistake, that she wasn't meant for him. I knew it was only nerves. I've seen enough weddings to know that he wouldn't have ditched her. Still, I held on to that small piece of hope for as long as I could, which wasn't long enough. I put his happiness before my own. I didn't even know I had that kind of brotherly love in me.

I swallow and force down the painful lump in my throat. "No problems, mate. It's what brothers do, right?"

"Right," he agrees, lifting his glass in the air to toast. I glance down at my empty one and shrug before clinking mine to his. "Besides. I'll be doing the same for you someday." He gives me a knowing grin, his eyes searching the room before landing on Paige.

I scoff. "Not a chance, mate."

"Never?"

"Nope. In case you hadn't realised, I don't date and she's taken."

"Please. You hang out with the chick all the damn time. You bring her as your "date" to our wedding. And it's obvious you've banged her. Maybe the wedding isn't on the cards just yet, but soon. I guarantee it." Nodding, he tips his chin and waggles his brows.

Ignoring his statement, I roll my eyes. Liam talks shit when he's drunk anyway.

"Leave him alone, Liam," Amelia grumbles beside him, not hiding her sudden frown.

"What? He knows I'm messing with him. Anyway, if he

ain't serious about the girl then he should tell her. Something tells me she ain't aware of his true intentions."

"She knows," I snap back, earning all eyes on me.

"Sure about that?"

I risk a glance at Paige. She looks happy. Her long brown locks sway along with her head to the music as she moves around the dance floor with Beth. "She knows," I whisper.

"But what I really wanna know... And this is serious shit now. Have you, Scott Jenkins... Ever. Been. In love? With someone other than yourself, of course."

I snap my eyes to meet his, my face heating with anger. It's a simple question, but for some reason it irritates me. Almost like he knows, and he's trying to goad me. Fuel my fire. Try my damn patience.

"What?"

"Come on, little bro. It's a simple question. Have you ever been in love?"

Before I can even consider lying to him, I find myself blurting out words I had no intention of saying. "Yes." And if that wasn't enough, my mouth continues to open and close without thinking. "Once upon a time, yes."

An uncomfortable silence fills the table. All four eyes are firmly on me. Even my parents seem to have put a halt on their private conversation and are now watching me intently as if waiting for me to elaborate.

"Serious?" Liam asks, clearly surprised.

"Yup," I push out again, clearing my throat quickly and looking up through cautious eyes.

"Wow! I don't know what to say to that," Liam pipes up.

"I've got nothing either," Dad says, twisting in his seat to face us.

Way to go, Scotty!

"Well, I do," Mum says, a twinkle of interest sparking in her emerald green eyes. "What happened?"

"Yeah, bro. What happened? Your charm not work on this one?" Liam smirks.

"Stop winding him up, Liam," Mum warns him, swatting the back of his head in annoyance.

"Nothing major, just didn't work out. I wasn't enough for her. She didn't love me back," I admit, wondering what the hell is going on with me tonight.

"No shit! How is that even possible?" Liam shouts, rubbing the back of his head. "I mean, you're not me, obviously, but still... You've never had trouble winning a lass over before."

My eyes involuntarily close, and I grit my teeth to hold back the burning rage. If only the fucker knew what he was talking about. That would wipe the smug grin off his pretty face.

Sighing, I lean forward, both hands clutching the edge of the table. "I dunno. Maybe she prefers drunken bastards who use her for nothing more than a piece of arse, rather than someone that could actually make her happy. Who the fuck knows?" I avert my eyes towards Amelia briefly before turning them back to my brother. "Her loss is someone else's gain, right?"

Ignoring the stares and the look of horror from Amelia, I scrape the chair back and decide that now is as good a time as any to leave. "Congratulations on your happily ever after, though. Good luck to the two of you."

Rounding the table, I go in search of Paige and spot her near the bar at the far end. My pulse is in a frenzy as I take long, purposeful strides towards her.

Why the fuck did I say that? Why don't I have any control? This is my brother's fucking wedding, for Christ's sake. I have got to get a grip.

"Because Liam has a way of getting to you," my inner voice taunts.

You're not wrong there, but still... Wrong time and definitely the wrong place.

Part of me wants to go back and wipe that smug fucking grin off his face, but all I really want to do now is get Paige and take her home.

My heart sinks all over again as she clocks me coming, a beautiful smile spreading widely across her face.

"Hey you," she coos, throwing her arms around my neck.

I laugh, placing my hands on her hips.

"You ready to go?" I ask, pressing a kiss to her cheek.

"Hmm... I am so ready. Who knew weddings could be this tiring? Remind me never to get married. EVER!" She blows a loose curl from her face and I chuckle.

"Only if you do the same for me."

"Deal."

"Hey, Scott. Can I have a word?" Liam calls out, causing me to turn my head and stop in my tracks.

"We were just leaving."

"It won't take long."

I turn to Paige apologetically. "Do you mind?"

"No, go ahead. I'll wait at the bar for you."

"Okay. It won't take a sec, I promise."

"Take your time," she says, waving me off.

As soon as she's out of earshot, I turn to Liam and frown. "What's up?"

He drapes an arm around my shoulder and gives it a squeeze. "I'm sorry about before. I shouldn't have pushed you. It was a dick move."

"Don't worry about it. It's already forgotten," I lie, shrugging him off.

"Yeah, okay, cool. Hey, look. I need a favour on behalf of the new Mrs."

"A favour?"

"Yeah. Meli wants a dance."

"A dance?"

"With you."

"What?"

"I'm sorry. I told her about this morning and how I freaked out."

"You did?" I ask, raising both brows.

"Yeah. Not all of it, though. I guess she wants to thank you or something. I dunno. You know how persuasive she can be."

Yeah, I did know, but since when did Liam do anything Meli wanted?

"Ah, I'm not sure, mate. Just tell her it's cool, yeah? I should get back to–"

"Humour her, please?" he pleads.

I shake my head no, unsure how to tell him I can't do it. I just can't.

"Five minutes. Paige won't mind."

I turn to Paige who nods silently, a reassuring smile falling from her lips.

Turning back to Liam, I let out a sigh. "Two minutes."

"Yeah, fine. Whatever," he says, not hiding his smile before walking off. "She's over there waiting for you."

I rock back and forth on my feet, looking over the crowded room until I finally spot the blonde head on the opposite side. Inhaling and exhaling slowly, I cross the dance floor and make my way over. Every fucking step has my heart beating out of my chest.

I gaze up as the lights dim, fading to white.

"Scott?"

"What the fuck are you doing to me?" I whisper, unable to look her in the eye.

"I want a dance with my brother-in-law. Is that too much to ask?"

"You know it is."

"Please, Scott."

Glancing down, I narrow my eyes. "One dance, Meli."

She smiles a knowing smile which is still there when I look back up, and she nods in agreement. "That's all I need."

"Good," I say, holding out a hand.

She shakes her head and grins before slipping her hand in mine.

We walk in silence, hand in hand as we maneuver through the couples scattered on the dance floor. As the previous song ends, it intertwines with the next and I curse under my breath as the words flow through the speakers.

I frown. "Is this a joke?"

Smiling up at me, she shrugs. "It's just a song, Scott."

I inhale a breath and push her towards an open gap in the middle of the floor. It isn't just a song. It's our song. The lyrics always play through my mind on a constant repeat whenever she's around.

This whole scenario feels wrong, like I'm cheating on my family right in front of their faces. I shouldn't be the one standing here about to take her other hand in mine. It should be Liam. It's in that moment that I find myself glancing around the room, wondering what everyone must be thinking. Can they see something more? Can they see what I feel around this woman?

Amelia leans towards me, her lips dangerously close to touching my neck. "Relax, Scott. No one is watching," she whispers. "It's just us."

And she's right. No one is paying us an ounce of attention. They're all too busy gazing into their partner's eyes, or sharing a private joke, clinking glasses or trying to remember where they left their kids.

I swallow down and curl my fingers around her wrist, placing my other hand in hers. "For the record, sweetheart, this is awkward as fuck."

"You're the one making it awkward, Scott. I'm just dancing with my brother-in-law."

"You know what I mean, Meli. Don't play games."

"Who's playing games?"

"Don't act coy with me, either."

"Oh, lighten up, will you? It's just a dance. If I'd have

known you would behave like this, I would never have asked you."

"Why did you?"

"Because I needed to."

I'm not sure when we started moving, or when I let my eyes fall shut, but when I open them, we are alone.

I glance around, my brows furrowing in confusion as I wonder what the hell just happened.

"You can come closer, Scott. I don't bite."

My eyes shift to the bar where Paige is sat, alone, watching. I would have half expected her to get up and walk out by now, but the reassuring smile she gives me tells me all I need to know. She wants me to do this.

I shake my head and glance down at Amelia with a grin. "I disagree, sweetheart."

A slight blush creeps up on her and I tug her closer, just how she wanted me to be.

"You and Paige look happy. I take it things are going well between you both?"

"We're friends. She agreed to come tonight. That's a start."

"You didn't think she would?"

"It took a lot of persuading."

"Is there any chance of you two ever…"

"Just friends."

"Would you think differently of me if I said that makes me happy?"

"Since when do you care what I think of you?"

She stares up at me for the longest moment. An expression that not even I can grasp settles across her face.

When her head falls to rest against my chest, I inhale and breathe her in. Everything about her, including the way she smells, has a sudden sense of warmth and comfort flowing through me. I'm unable to stop the next words that leave my mouth, and even if I could, I wouldn't want to.

"You look beautiful, by the way."

She nuzzles into my neck and I feel her smile against me. "Thank you. You look really good, too."

I pull back, raising a brow. "Just good?"

She smiles shyly and lowers her eyes slightly before lifting them again. "Great. You look great. And handsome. Actually, you look really fucking hot."

"Good to know you still find me irresistible."

"Always have, always will."

I pause, my eyes narrowing down at her as I search hers to try and read what's going on in that head of hers. "You feel it, don't you?" I ask quietly. "You feel this…"

"Always have, always will," she repeats through a sad smile, a sheen of water coating her eyes as she tries to look brighter than she feels.

Now would be a good time for me to turn around and walk away. Now would be a fucking good chance to take those words, lock them away in this manly heart of mine and throw away the key. Now would be a good time to let her live in peace, forever, with the man she has just married.

But I've never been good at being good.

"You know I'll always wait," I tell her, my head lowering down to hers.

"You know I will, too."

"For what? What are you waiting for, Meli?"

"For you to prove to me…"

"I have proved it to you. Today. This morning. The last God knows how many years. I sacrifice all of me for you. Your happiness. It's all that matters."

She blinks slowly, her head tilting to one side as she looks up and sighs. "Thank you."

"I mean it. Always."

"I know you do. Now shut up and dance with me, Scott Jenkins."

I laugh, even though I don't feel any kind of happiness at all. "Yes, ma'am."

Her hands curl around my waist before resting on my back, and with a final look around, I drop my forehead to hers and sigh contentedly.

Although the words 'I love you' haven't been said out loud, they are still here – in the way she holds me closely, through the lyrics of the song and through the final breath she takes as she gazes at me for the last time and walks away.

This is our final goodbye.

Now all I have to do is find a way to live without her forever.

Or at the very least, until she decides that she can't live without me at all.

EPILOGUE

Seven Years Later...

I've never seen Ethan quite like this before, and despite me being over the fucking moon excited for him, I can't help but wind him up even more.

"A fucking flannel shirt?" I smirk.

"What about it?"

"Mr. Suit and Tie, and you're wearing a fucking flannel shirt to take the girl of your dreams out?"

"Shut up, Scott. I'm gonna fuck it up without your help, mate."

I flip the top off the bottle of *Bud* and tilt the head towards Ethan. "So you're going to sabotage yourself?"

"Stop psychoanalysing me and suck my dick, you bellend," he snaps, before flexing his pecs in the damn mirror.

I wasn't kidding about the shirt. He really does look like a bit of a dick. You'd think that today of all days, the biggest day of this guy's dating life, he would want to go all out and blow this lass off her feet. Or at least get blown himself.

"You're being an arsehole about this, lad. Eleven years, E.

Eleven, and you've never thought you were good enough to even talk to her. It's completely natural to feel nervous."

Who am I kidding? I've never seen anyone look more nervous than Ethan does right now. Yet, I can't help but feel proud of him. Finally he's getting *the* girl. *The* blondie that he saw all those years ago when we followed Liam. That chick that was a total walking, talking contradiction, who interviewed me at *Club Crystal*. He's finally getting his shot with her... So long as the flannel shirt doesn't let him down, that is.

"Mate, I ain't good enough for her. No amount of suits and ties or fine restaurants and fancy cars will ever change that."

Swallowing, I press my lips against the rim of the bottle and grin.

"Don't look at me like that."

"Like what? I ain't looking at you like anything. I just wish Dean was here to see you like this. It's funny, mate."

He shoots me a warning glare before leaping over the couch and forcing me into a headlock. I'd laugh if I could breathe.

"Not a fucking word."

He pushes against me, a grin finally breaking free until I force my way out of his grasp, jabbing him in the side. Ethan laughs and shakes his head. I've made the fucker relax. My work here is done. Only with Ethan, I always like to push him just that little bit further. Probably because I always get away with it. "Jesus! I thought you'd forgotten how to laugh for a minute there. I'm seriously gonna have to take another look at Little Miss Journalist if this keeps up."

"You're a barrel of laughs today, ain't you? Don't think I

haven't noticed your good mood lately, Mr. I'm going for a drive, see you in eight fucking hours, and come back smiling like I got my dick sucked."

My eyes widen in horror and all the air seems to have left my lungs in one swift motion.

Does he know? How can he?

No way. He's bluffing He's been too busy with the journalist, finding ways to get to her like a lovesick puppy, his tongue dropping to the floor every time she is even mentioned. He's just messing with my head now.

I shrug it off and try to act indifferent. "Don't know what you're talking about."

"Right," he snorts before pulling out his phone and engaging in whatever conversation he is having with whoever the hell is on the phone.

Digging out my own phone, I swipe away at the screen and groan impatiently.

Still nothing.

It has been a day of waiting. Not just for E, but for myself.

It has been a lifetime of waiting, actually. Days working my arse off at the club, trying to create a life away from what I once knew, constant streams of chicks to distract me until I finally got hold of what was truly meant to be mine.

It's still early days and telling Ethan is the last thing on my mind, along with rushing things. Besides, I want to keep this feeling to myself as long as possible. The butterflies? Yeah, I have them, too, but unlike, E, this isn't my first encounter with them. I've been here before, only now I'm a little bit older, a little bit wiser, and a lot more aware of just how quickly time flies by. The last decade has slipped through my hands in the blink of an eye. Now I know that it's important to make each moment count, no matter how much of a selfish prick that makes me.

While Ethan swears a bucketload of curses down the line, I let my mind drift to a memory. Not just any memory, but probably the only memory I have of my father that wasn't through raised voices or disapproving glares. It's one of those distant memories that stays with you forever. I couldn't have been any more than six, maybe seven years old. It was snowing that day and we'd just had dinner. Jam sandwiches and tea. It was a tradition in our house for a long time, until Liam and I spoiled the routine by growing up.

I looked at my dad and said;

"Dad, what does it feel like to be in love? I love my family, and my mum and stuff, but when you say it to Mum, what does it mean?" I asked, bringing my legs up to my chest and dropping my chin to my knees.

He glanced at my mum from the corner of his eye and a knowing smile played on lips. "Son, one day you'll meet someone who will change your life. You won't see them coming, and you sure as hell won't be prepared for it, but it'll happen and there isn't a damn thing you can do about it. But when it does, it'll be like everything you ever thought you knew was wrong. Everything you thought mattered, no longer will. Except that one girl. She'll strut into your life, whipping the air right out of your lungs until you can't think straight. You'll be blinded. Fixated on this one woman. You'll forgive her mistakes, and you'll argue until the sun comes up but you'll love her for all her faults and inhibitions. She'll turn you into a man, and you'll buckle under the pressure. Ain't no man strong enough to resist that kind of strength, and one day, son, that'll be you."

"But how will I know she's the one? If she takes my air, how will I survive?"

"That's the funny thing about love, Son. Once you find that love, you never give up on it. You'll suffocate because of her and you'll find yourself thanking her for it. You live to love. We all do."

Smiling to myself at the memory, I look up to find Ethan grinning back at me. I know what he wants, and I know exactly what that freakish smile of his is for.

"Beth has my car, mate. Her clunker bit the dust last week." His car is currently on its arse, and he was relying on Dean to fix it up for him, but by the look on his face, his brother hasn't been able to pull through and save the day for him.

"I'm going to cancel."

"The fuck you are." No way am I letting him cancel this. This is all his Christmases come at once. This is his chance for a happy ever after and if anyone deserves it, it's Ethan Walker.

"I can't show up on the fucking bus."

"If she likes you on a bus, you'll know she ain't after your money."

"What money?"

"Fuck off, E," I say, rolling my eyes. "I ain't blind, mate." The guy has more cash than he ever lets on.

"I wonder sometimes," he quips back, shoving his keys in his pocket. "But if I'm going to get the fucking bus and make it on time, I'd best be leaving. Don't drink all my beer, and lock the door before you leave."

I can't be arsed to argue that the beer is mine, so instead, I nod my head and play along. "Yes, Mum."

"Fuckhead."

"Tosser," I call out just as the door slams shut, the smile on my face ridiculous as I silently mouth a good luck to my best mate. *God, let this be his time for happiness now.*

I dig my phone out of my pocket again and noting the blank screen, I toss it over the other side of the couch. A groan falls from my lips when I realise I've been stood up again. Dammit. I'm about to sink into the sofa and wallow in my own pity, when the door flies open, forcing me to grip the fancy cushion off the couch, turn and launch it at Ethan's head for being such a pussy and giving up too easily.

"Get the fuck ou–"

But it isn't Ethan.

"I'm so sorry," she says, blowing a strand of hair from her face. "How late am I?"

She's here. Thank fuck, she's finally here.

I leap off the couch like a sixteen-year-old kid about to get his first blowy and charge towards her, unable to hide my grin. "About twenty-nine years too late, peaches."

"Oh. I should probably go then," she says, turning on the spot. "What with being a constant let down and all."

"Not a fucking chance, Meli," I warn, catching her arm and tugging her against my chest. "What are you even doing here? You said you'd call before…"

"I wanted to surprise you, so I waited outside for Ethan to

leave. Is he on a date or something?"

"The biggest date of his life."

"He looked nervous, which is weird. I always thought he was so... cocksure."

"He's in love. We're talking marriage, babies, the whole damn works. He sees stars and hearts in his eyes when he thinks of this chick."

"Shit. Is it that serious already?"

"Yeah, they just don't know it yet," I hit back, winking.

"What do you mean?"

"This is their first date."

"So how do you know it's serious?"

"Because..." I say, pulling her impossibly closer. "He's waited his whole life to get her. He's watched her from a distance, never thinking he was good enough for her. He's spent years dreaming of making her his, and now he's got the chance to make it happen, I know he won't let her go."

"Oh, it's like that, is it?" she sings, slipping her hands around my neck, pulling me down.

"Yep, exactly like that."

"You sound like you know what that feels like first hand?"

I flash her a knowing grin before pulling her flush against me. My lips fall to hers and I breathe her in. Breathe the moment in. Commit it to memory because it's one I will keep and cherish forever, and I never know which kiss is going to be my last.

"Scott?"

"Hmm...?"

"How long have we got?"

I pull back and smile. I told her all those years ago that I would wait for her, and even though it took longer than I thought it would for her to turn up on my doorstep, the moment she did and begged me to hold her, I knew there was no going back. What we have is wrong. We both know that. What we do is even worse. We dream of a future we can't possibly have. We betray those we love and we do it without much regret. No one can take this from us now. We can't live without each other.

Blue eyes gaze into mine and a smile that matches my own promises a future, even if it is an unconventional one. Our future will be one of love, passion and enough drama to fill the dull days and turn them into something bright.

We're like Tweedle Dum and Tweedle Dee, both clueless and lost, just going with the flow until we end up on the road we're meant to be on. I know we'll find a place together soon. I know we'll find some kind of heaven on earth that will make all our struggles worthwhile, but for now, I take what I can when I can.

I cling on to moments like this.

Another memory for me to store away.

Everything I have ever wanted in life, I now have in my hands.

I drop my forehead to hers and lift my head just enough to brush my lips across her soft skin and say, "We have all the time in world, peaches. All the time in the world."

"You promise?"

"Cross my heart…"

TO BE CONTINUED…

Scott Jenkins' Road to Wonderland

Scott Jenkins' road to wonderland playlist

I couldn't go a day without writing and listening to some inspiration along the way. There were so many that contributed to my story, and here are a few of those little treasures.

Kodaline – All I Want

Tom O'dell – Can't Pretend

Sigma – Nobody To Love

Freddo Starr – Shining Through

Rudimental – Waiting All Night

Disclosure – Latch

Tom O'dell – Another Love

Tove Lo – Stay High

Ron Pope – A Drop In The Ocean

I hope you guys enjoy these as much as I did.

Charlie M.

xoxo

Scott Jenkins' Road to Wonderland

Made in the USA
Charleston, SC
05 May 2016